THE MERMAID MYSTERY

Also by Tamar Myers

The Pennsylvania Dutch mysteries

THOU SHALT NOT GRILL
ASSAULT AND PEPPER
GRAPE EXPECTATIONS
HELL HATH NO CURRY
AS THE WORLD CHURNS
BATTER OFF DEAD
BUTTER SAFE THAN SORRY
THE DEATH OF PIE *
TEA WITH JAM AND DREAD *
PUDDIN' ON THE BLITZ *
DEATH BY TART ATTACK*
MEAT THY MAKER *

* *available from Severn House*

THE MERMAID MYSTERY

Tamar Myers

SEVERN
HOUSE

First world edition published in Great Britain and the USA in 2024
by Severn House, an imprint of Canongate Books Ltd,
14 High Street, Edinburgh EH1 1TE.

Trade paperback edition first published in Great Britain and the USA in 2025
by Severn House, an imprint of Canongate Books Ltd.

severnhouse.com

Copyright © Tamar Myers, 2024

All rights reserved including the right of
reproduction in whole or in part in any form.
The right of Tamar Myers to be identified
as the author of this work has been asserted
in accordance with the Copyright,
Designs & Patents Act 1988.

British Library Cataloguing-in-Publication Data
A CIP catalogue record for this title is available from the British Library.

ISBN-13: 978-1-4483-1319-8 (cased)
ISBN-13: 978-1-4483-1663-2 (trade paper)
ISBN-13: 978-1-4483-1489-8 (e-book)

This is a work of fiction. Names, characters, places and incidents are either the product of the author's imagination or are used fictitiously. Except where actual historical events and characters are being described for the storyline of this novel, all situations in this publication are fictitious and any resemblance to actual persons, living or dead, business establishments, events or locales is purely coincidental.

No part of this book may be used or reproduced in any manner for the purpose of training artificial intelligence technologies or systems. This work is reserved from text and data mining (Article 4(3) Directive (EU) 2019/790).

Typeset by Palimpsest Book Production Ltd.,
Falkirk, Stirlingshire, Scotland.
Printed and bound in Great Britain by CPI Group (UK) Ltd, Croydon CR0 4YY

The manufacturer's authorised representative in the EU for product safety is
Authorised Rep Compliance Ltd, 71 Lower Baggot Street, Dublin D02 P593
Ireland (arccompliance.com).

Praise for Tamar Myers

"Plenty of humor and twists"
Booklist on *Mean and Shellfish*

"Of all Magdalena's rollicking adventures,
this one contains the best mystery"
Kirkus Reviews on *Death by Tart Attack*

"Fans of wackier culinary cozies will have fun"
Publishers Weekly on *Mean and Shellfish*

"This offbeat cozy, filled with laugh-out-loud humor, is
distinguished by its numerous quirky characters"
Booklist on *Puddin' on the Blitz*

"Quirky characters abound . . . the acerbic, opinionated
Magdalena's first-person account drives this at times
laugh-out-loud cozy"
Booklist on *Tea with Jam and Dread*

About the author

Tamar Myers was born in what was then the Belgian Congo in 1948, where her parents were American-Mennonite missionaries to a tribe of headhunters. She moved to the USA at the age of fifteen. On her mother's side, Tamar is descended from one of the first Amish families to settle in America in 1738. She is the author of more than forty mysteries and many short stories.

www.tamarmyers.com

'The least initial deviation from the truth is multiplied later a thousandfold'
—Aristotle

ACKNOWLEDGEMENTS

This year I have a new assistant. Her name is Laila. When I'm on my way to my office, she'll leap out from behind a chair and tackle one of my ankles with her slender black arms. Then she'll leap away and hide somewhere else, with the intention that I should pass by her again and be the victim of her very gentle attacks. Sometimes I will hide and lie in wait for her. When I leap out, she zooms around the house, pretending to leap up the doorsills, and bounces off the furniture until she reckons that it's her turn to hide again. Other times we will play peek-a-boo, as when I raise the newspaper up and down in front of my face for various lengths of time, to gauge her reaction. After we have played a good long while, and she has helped me make the bed, by depositing her toys on top of the blanket, we finally make it to my office. Here she jumps up on my desk and plops down on a mat next to my computer and takes a well-earned nap.

Laila is a black and white (mostly black) American domestic shorthair cat that is approximately fifteen months old. She is a rescue cat from our local shelter and was dropped off as a stray. Here in the States, black cats have a low rate of adoption. I felt sorry for her on that account, but what really touched my heart was something that happened the day before I met Laila. My husband went to scope out the available cats at the shelter (we were hoping for a tabby), and he said that when he walked up to her cage, she slipped a slim little arm through the bars, as if to say: 'Here I am. You came to get me, didn't you?' Well, I couldn't get that image out of my mind, so the next day I went with him to the shelter and when we returned home, Miss Laila was with us.

PART ONE
THE MERMAID

ONE

The mermaid was as ugly as homemade sin. Even a sailor who'd been shipwrecked for a dozen years wouldn't find her attractive. Miss Lucy, as she was destined to be called, was never intended to be beautiful – just plausible as a creature that was supposed to be half human and half fish. Since these two animals diverged on to different evolutionary paths at least three hundred million years ago, and the former is warm-blooded, while the latter is cold-blooded, a real mermaid was a physiological impossibility. However, a mermaid assembled by a committee of ten was quite another matter.

'She looks a sight better than the woman that you're dating now,' Sheriff Ryker Saunders said to Gunner Jones.

Most of the Big Ten members laughed, including Gunner Jones. It was common knowledge that Gunner didn't date local women. Just whom this rugged outdoorsman dated was anyone's guess. He lived alone, behind his taxidermist shop. Although he was frequently seen driving to and from the small seacoast town of Tidal Shores, South Carolina, he always returned by himself. As far as anyone knew, Gunner Jones was a solitary man.

Adelaide Saunders, the town's mayor, forced a smile. 'In any case, we have Gunner here to thank for this – uh – remarkable – creation.'

'You mean abomination,' Reverend William Robert Henderson growled. 'As I said from the beginning, you won't find them things mentioned in the Bible.' Of the Big Ten, the Reverend (known only to his close friends and relations as Reverend Billy-Bob) had been the lone dissenter in this particular plan to rescue the community of Tidal Shores from its dire financial straits. Except for those parts of the Bible that he felt conflicted with his self-interest, Reverend Billy-Bob Henderson believed in a strict, literal interpretation of the New King James Version.

'Reverend Billy-Bob,' said Ewell Saunders, 'kangaroos and koalas aren't mentioned in the Bible, either, but they exist. And speaking of kangaroos, which kind was able to hop all the way to Noah's Ark? The red species, or the larger grey ones?'

'Don't make me mad, Ewell,' Reverend Billy-Bob Henderson said. 'Just because I'm a man of God, that doesn't mean I have to put up with the crap you're always throwing my way. So, what if you're a high-school principal? That doesn't mean you know everything there is to know about science, and you certainly don't know your Bible. I bet your copy of the Good Book is gathering a thick coat of dust.'

'For your information, Reverend, my undergraduate degree was in science education. And not that it is any of your damn business, but my wife and I read our Bibles every morning before we start our day.' It was a lie, but lies came easily to Ewell Saunders when he was challenged by the pompous likes of Reverend Billy-Bob. Besides, what high-school principal had time to read *anything* in the morning?

'Lay off each other for a while,' Sheriff Ryker Saunders said. Sheriff Ryker Saunders was Ewell Saunders' fraternal twin brother, older by twelve minutes, but the two were as different from each other as salt is from pepper. Ewell Saunders was slender and fair, whereas Sheriff Ryker Saunders was stocky and swarthy. The gossips of Tidal Shores floated the theory that Isadora Kitchens Saunders, their mother, uncovered her nakedness twice the night the boys were conceived. It was even whispered that Sheriff Ryker Saunders' fraternal family tree contained distant ancestors who were enslaved persons.

'Just saying, Ryker,' Reverend Billy-Bob said. 'I don't think the Lord's going to be too pleased with this monstrosity that is not of his creation.'

'Then the Lord can kiss my butt.'

All eyes turned to the speaker, Miss Georgina Legare, who was the last of the Big Ten to arrive. No one in Tidal Shores knew how old she was, but some said that Miss Georgina Legare (pronounced Luh-gree) played with God as a child. The fact that she looked as if she could have been childhood chums with the Almighty was not Miss Georgina Legare's fault. She couldn't help that she was born with hair the colour of tangerines, and skin so pale it brought to mind low-fat milk with its hints of blue. Back in the days when Miss Georgina Legare was growing up, there were no protective sunscreens available, just oils, the purpose of which was to baste one to a deep golden brown like Sunday's roast. Poor Miss Georgina Legare never tanned, but she did manage to freckle – albeit unevenly – and eventually her mottled skin wrinkled to where it resembled tissue paper that had been crumpled many times, and then pressed with a cool iron. Her orange hair retained a semblance of its original colour, thanks to the application of chemicals four times a year.

Although there were many gasps in the room, no one dared to chide Miss Georgina Legare for her blasphemy. Folks in the South respect their elders too much to correct them, although Reverend Billy-Bob did turn his head completely away so that he could roll his eyes in protest.

'Welcome, Miss Legare,' Emmeline Davis chirped. 'I'm so glad you're here. I want your opinion on the makeup job that I did on her. It's not actual makeup, of course, but acrylic paint. Just a hint of it on her lips, and the teensiest bit of blush on her cheeks, for that lifelike look.'

'Emmeline!' Reverend Billy-Bob snapped. 'Would you stop saying *her*? She's an *it*, not a *her*, dang it. I mean, *it's* a her. An *it*!'

'Well, Emmeline, I think that you did a fine job,' Miss Legare said. 'Why, I believe that she could run for Miss South Carolina, if Gunner had given her a bigger bosom.'

Sheriff Ryker Saunders snickered. 'Bosom. I haven't heard that word since Grandma—'

'Miss Legare,' Gunner Jones cut in, 'I expanded her bosom as much as I could. But considering that she's been dead for at least seventy years, I was lucky to get this much.'

Miss Georgina Legare nodded agreeably. Then again, given her advanced age, perhaps she was dozing off, or even having a mild stroke.

'Until I saw this one, I didn't even know that monkeys had breasts,' Adelaide Saunders said. In her capacity as mayor, Adelaide Saunders' ignorance could be forgiven, but as a former biology teacher, and wife of high-school principal Ewell Saunders, she should have known that all mammals have mammary glands – hence the first four letters of the word mammal.

'Miss Lucy was not a monkey,' Gunner Jones said through clenched teeth. 'You, of all people, should know that.'

Adelaide Saunders put her hands up in mock defence. It was an uncalled-for gesture, because everyone knew that Gunner Jones was a true Southern gentleman. With the exception of Miss Georgina Legare, all the members of the Big Ten had known each other since nursery school, or before.

'Excuse me,' Adelaide Saunders said, 'your monkey was an ape. Is that better?'

Gunner Jones shook his head. He almost wished that he hadn't sacrificed Miss Lucy to save the town of Tidal Shores, South Carolina. On that fateful day when he'd opened his big fat yap, he could just as easily have not shown up for the monthly town council meeting. Being unattached like he was, he could have easily rented a truck from up in Georgetown, or down in Charleston, and moved anywhere in the contiguous forty-eight states. A first-rate taxidermist, which Gunner Jones was, need not be a prisoner of geography.

There had been just one hitch, one problem that would have kept Gunner Jones from leaving town that day under any circumstances. That month's meeting of the Big Ten was scheduled to meet at Gunner Jones' house.

That's where the plan to save Tidal Shores had been hatched. What's more, the impetus for the plan came from Gunner Jones himself. At any rate, it was an ingenious, if somewhat bizarre plan that was bound to succeed – if no one veered from the script.

TWO

In the old days, pre-pandemic (known locally as P.P.), Tidal Shores was South Carolina's best kept secret. This tight-knit community was a miniature version of Myrtle Beach. It had all the amenities that a wholesome, God-fearing, middle-class family could possibly want. Tidal Shores had a miniature golf course with a pirates theme; three restaurants, two full-service, one just for breakfast (Tanya's Pancake House); four fabulous antique shops; a white sandy beach with three lifeguards during daylight hours – however, one-piece bathing suits were strongly encouraged; a five-hundred-foot wooden pier from which tourists could line fish; a deep-sea fishing company from which boats could be chartered six days a week to take them out into the Gulf Stream for serious fishing; and a community church that had a full-time pastor who believed that the Holy Bible was the inerrant word of God.

It's conceivable that the Big Ten preferred that the folks who enjoyed themselves at Tidal Shores were of predominately northern European extraction. Of course, legally there was nothing that they could do to enforce this unwritten policy. However, they could, and did, erect a large billboard at the main entrance to the town that pictured identical seagulls standing along the edges, facing the centre of the board. In the middle of the billboard was the message: *Birds of a feather flock together.*

This is not to say that members of the Big Ten themselves were racist. Adam Patel, owner of the Abide Awhile Motel, was one-eighth Gujarati from India. Except for his surname, which he proudly refused to shed upon attaining majority, Adam displayed no hint of his rich Asian heritage. Adam, who looked white, had grown up as a classmate of everyone else on the city council, with the exception of Miss Legare. When Adam married a lily-white girl by the name of Caroline Crawford, who was also a local, he effectively washed the Gujarati right out of his family line. When Adam and Caroline's son James turned twenty-one, he legally changed his surname to Crawford.

Besides, for quite some time, anyone was more than welcome to spend their precious few vacation days at Tidal Shores. But since this wasn't Europe, with its gallingly generous holiday lengths, who in their right mind would voluntarily spend their limited time and hard-earned money only to be constantly subjected to 'that look,' the one that says, 'I'm not prejudiced, but I can't speak for everyone here. Wouldn't you be more comfortable driving up the road another thirty miles? I'm sure that you'd feel much more relaxed up there.'

Now back to those people who did find the billboard a relief and were delighted to spend half of their miserly two-week vacations at Tidal Shores. Virtually every one of the adults, even many of the children, spent a great deal of their time shagging. The Shag is, after all, the official state dance. Based on the rhythm and blues of the 1920s, the Shag involves fancy footwork but no opportunity for groping, hence it had Reverend Billy-Bob Henderson's seal of approval.

But then one day a guest informed the good reverend that the word 'shag' had an altogether different meaning in the United Kingdom. At first Reverend Billy-Bob Henderson was appalled. Then he became outraged – so much so, in fact, that he wrote a letter to Her Majesty, Queen Elizabeth II (who was reigning at the time) and demanded that she do something about her subjects' egregious appropriation of an innocent term for an enjoyable form of exercise. When after a year had passed, and Her Majesty failed to even acknowledge Reverend Billy-Bob Henderson's complaint, the distraught clergyman sent an email to his parishioners urging them to boycott English muffins, English breakfast tea, Scottish shortbread, marmalade, and of course Irish whiskey, which they shouldn't be drinking anyway (although a nip of American bourbon might be excused on special occasions).

But then the pandemic hit, and Reverend Billy-Bob Henderson's protest lost its traction – not that it ever had much. Suddenly the members of Tidal Shores' Tabernacle of Truth found themselves fighting over the last roll of toilet tissue, or driving to racially diverse communities in search of antibiotic counter cleaners. Who cared how the Brits defined 'shag,' now that the dance floors had all been enclosed? Even when enough townspeople had been vaccinated, and the rate of infection had slowed enough to warrant reopening business, only a trickle of tourists found their way back to Tidal Shores.

By then, two of the restaurants, along with the pancake house, had folded. The third restaurant survived only because it had come to rely on the locals eating there to mark special occasions. Two of the three motels had closed, and so had all the antique shops (however, Miss Legare declared that her Den of Antiquity could open at a moment's notice when tourists returned). Hoyt Hunter's deep-sea charter business was virtually shut down, and along with it, so was Gunner Jones' taxidermy business. Eighty percent of Gunner Jones' business consisted of mounting game fish that Hoyt Hunter's customers had caught. As for Emmeline Davis's beauty salon, Turning Heads, only two of the six chairs were staffed by certified beauticians, and Emmeline was one of those beauticians. Also closed were the gift shops, swimwear shops, fast-food vendors, even a tattoo parlour that specialized in 'wholesome' images, like flowers, unicorns and crosses.

Of course, not everyone in Tidal Shores worked in the tourist industry, but the majority of the populace was connected to it in some way or the other. They relied upon their town council, which even they called the Big Ten, and with whom they had been satisfied for some years already (why rock the boat, was the mantra at election time). Therefore, when the Big Ten decided to repaint the billboard at the town entrance, to have it depict a variety of local birds, with no slogan, there were very few complaints. 'Welcome to Tidal Shores!' Seriously, who, except the most disgruntled and bigoted amongst the citizenry, could object to that message when a state of emergency existed?

Well, almost no one complained except for Reverend Billy-Bob Henderson, who cautioned that the new wording might invite practitioners of voodoo or, worse yet, atheists. After all, it was widely known that atheists were incapable of behaving morally. The United States of America had Roman Catholics as presidents twice! That in itself was shocking, and a slap in God's face, since God was a Protestant. Heaven forfend that this country would elect a Muslim, or a Jew, as president to the nation's highest office. If that happened, then the next step would be the election of an atheist, and Reverend Billy-Bob would be forced to emigrate.

Unfortunately, changing the sign made no discernible difference in the amount of tourist trade Tidal Shores received in the first few weeks after health-related restrictions were lifted. To the contrary, word of the new policy might have leaked out to some of the town's former 'white bread' clientele, because some of the long-standing bookings that Abide Awhile Motel had were soon cancelled. If the

Big Ten didn't come up with a fix pronto, then come the next election, they were going to be out on their expensively clad butts (to a person, they were guilty of skimming from the town's revenues).

Then that fateful town council meeting took place at Gunner Jones' house that had the potential to turn everything around.

THREE

Reverend Billy-Bob Henderson was the last of the Big Ten to arrive at Gunner Jones' house, which was behind his taxidermist business. The preacher had been counselling one of his parishioners, a very attractive young woman who was contemplating leaving her husband because she was deeply attracted to another man. A married man. Reverend Billy-Bob Henderson had been both shocked and flattered to learn that Dolly, the married woman, was fixated on him. As a seminary-trained professional, Reverend Billy-Bob knew that he should have insisted that Dolly seek counselling elsewhere, but he hadn't. Reverend Billy-Bob Henderson chose to interpret Dolly as a gift, sent from God to test his faithfulness – both to his wife, Margaret, and to God.

For the first time in years, Reverend Billy-Bob Henderson found himself whistling as he walked across town to Gunner Jones' place. Even though he'd packed on a good eighty pounds since speaking his vows to Margaret, there was a lightness in his step that afternoon. His hearing seemed to have improved as well. Reverend Billy-Bob Henderson did not remember Tidal Shores having such a goodly number of songbirds, and never had the ocean sounded so close, when the water was calm. Before turning the corner to Gunner Jones' house, Reverend Billy-Bob Henderson glanced around and, seeing no one about, he skipped for several steps.

But when at last Reverend Billy-Bob Henderson crossed Gunner Jones' threshold, for the first time in many years, his jowls, and both his chins, began to quiver. Even though his choice of dress was optional, Reverend Billy-Bob Henderson had worn a clerical collar to his counselling session that afternoon, and it was a darn good thing. Without the starch, and the support that this tight garment gave him, the intense jiggling of his corpulent head might have resulted in a detached retina – or two.

'What the hell ya doing with an idol in your bookcase?' Reverend Billy-Bob demanded.

'It's not an idol,' Emmeline Davis said quickly. 'It's a statue of the Laughing Buddha, and I gave it to Gunner. See his big round belly? It symbolizes good luck and prosperity. People rub his belly to bring them good fortune.'

'Take note of that, Reverend Billy-Bob,' said Miss Legare. 'It may be that all you'd have to do is smile to get rich. You know, smile, and rub your own belly.'

Only a woman as old Miss Legare could get away with a comment like that. Well at least the crone thought that she could. One of these days the old bat was going to go too far, and then she'd get her comeuppance. There were other members of the Big Ten who'd been victims of Miss Legare's sharp tongue. Hell, anyone who knew her – and that was half the town of Tidal Shores – had undoubtedly been sliced and diced by her hurtful comments. Some blamed Miss Georgina Legare's abrasive manner on the fact that her parents had been Yankees – that is to say, Northerners. However, since Georgina had been born in Tidal Shores, South Carolina, and at home no less, she considered herself to be a true Southerner. This was not a sentiment that everyone shared. As the saying goes: 'Just because a cat has kittens in an oven, that don't make them biscuits.'

Reverend Billy-Bob Henderson, who'd been on Cloud Nine just a minute ago, was not about to take Miss Legare's bait. 'Get that idol out of here,' he said to Gunner Jones. 'It has no place in a Christian house.'

'I'm not a Christian,' Gunner Jones said.

Emmeline Davis gasped softly. Gunner Jones was her best friend, and she was well aware of his beliefs, but she certainly had not intended for her birthday gift to him, of the Laughing Buddha, as it was called, to cause him any trouble. When she'd spotted the rosewood carving in a New York City gift shop the year before, she was immediately charmed. It occurred to her then that her friend would enjoy looking at *Hotei*.

'You most certainly *are* a Christian,' Reverend Billy-Bob hissed. 'Your great-grandparents were missionaries to Africa, your grandfather was once the minister of the Tabernacle of Truth right here in Tidal Shores, where I preach, and your parents still attend services every Sunday. In fact, nine of us in this room attended the same catechism class, and we were all baptized together at the end of seventh grade, and by proper full immersion, having by then reached an age of understanding. Only one person in this room was not baptized along with us, and we all know who that was, and why.'

Miss Legare waved a withered and blotched arm gamely. 'That

was me, and the reason I wasn't baptized alongside y'all was because John the Baptist had already given me a good dunking in the Jordan River back in the day.'

Gunner Jones was one of the people who laughed at that sacrilegious attempt at humour. This behaviour caused Reverend Billy-Bob to dislike the taxidermist even more. Gunner Jones was one of those men that God had seen fit to bless with a tall, lean physique that included a broad chest and shoulders, and narrow hips. Gunner also possessed regular features, with a strong jaw and chin. His brow was straight, not sloped like that of an ape, or a Neanderthal. He had a full head of sandy hair and eyes the colour of Delft china – well, that's what Reverend Billy-Bob Henderson's wife claimed. In the most secret chamber of his heart, where it was difficult for even Jesus to take a peek, and He was a permanent resident, Reverend Billy-Bob sometimes had to squash down shameful memories of Gunner Jones showering after gym class. There were times back then when young Billy-Bob Henderson's adolescent body did not obey its owner's commands, and he'd had to skip out on the shower altogether.

'You can joke all you want, Miss Legare,' Reverend Billy-Bob Henderson said, 'but don't think for a minute that the Good Lord finds Gunner's salvation a humorous matter.'

Adelaide Saunders stood and clapped her hands to get everyone's attention. As mayor of Tidal Shores, she was the de facto leader of the Big Ten. Mayor Adelaide Saunders came from 'good people' and had been raised with a sense of *noblesse oblige*. She was always attired like a proper lady, in a dress that covered her knees. She applied just the right amount of makeup, skilfully, and visited Emmeline Davis's beauty shop, Turning Heads, every Saturday morning to get her hair professionally rolled and combed. Despite her wavering personal beliefs, Adelaide Saunders saw it as her mayoral duty to attend Reverend Billy-Bob's church every Sunday, and to at the very least present the image of a pious person.

'Attention, please,' Mayor Adelaide Saunders said, and everyone listened. Momentarily, at least. 'I'm calling this meeting to order. Our agenda this morning is – well, I'm sorry to say it's the same thing it's been for the last six months. Our beloved community depends on the tourist trade, but now people continue to move out of town because tourists no longer come here, and what few businesses remain – all of which are represented here – are getting fewer and fewer customers. If this keeps up, we're going to have to close the schools, and then there won't be any more Tidal Shores.

'At our last meeting I asked every one of you to put on your thinking caps and come up with an idea or two – no matter how outlandish it might seem to you – that might be an inducement to tourists. Anything. Anything at all. So, I'm going to go around the room, and ask each of you to tell me what your big idea is. And please, don't hold back.'

Miss Legare cackled. 'When has this bunch of yo-yos ever held back?'

'In that case, Miss Legare,' Adelaide said, 'you're up to bat first. What's your big idea?'

'With pleasure,' Miss Legare said. 'I think that we should capitalize on our state's pirate history. In 1718, in nearby Charleston, forty-nine pirates were hanged in two mass executions.'

Sheriff Ryker Saunders, the mayor's brother-in-law, laughed. 'Are you suggesting that we recreate public hangings? Have actors dress up like pirates?'

'No, you nincompoop,' Miss Legare said. 'But with so many pirates who plied up and down our coastline, including the infamous Captain Blackbeard, we could host some sort of treasure hunt. We could spread the rumour that pirates buried their treasure – perhaps a great chest full of gold doubloons, or precious jewels – somewhere on our beach. I guarantee you that news of buried treasure somewhere along the beaches of Tidal Shores will bring in visitors faster than a piece of jam bread does cockroaches.'

'With all due respect,' said Tanya Kitchens, owner of Tanya's Pancake House, 'if we went with your buried treasure idea, after just one week, our beach will resemble a battlefield. One that's been bombed repeatedly by Russian aircraft.'

'Why Russian?' Miss Legare said. 'And why are you so quick to shoot down my idea?'

'Because it was nuts,' Sheriff Ryker Saunders said. 'Adelaide – I mean, Madam Mayor – may I go next?'

Mayor Adelaide Saunders nodded.

'Well,' Sheriff Ryker Saunders said, before he stretched and yawned, 'I've got me a plan. It's like this. We let folks arrest each other, and make them bail – well, buy – themselves out of jail. Half of the money goes to charity, and the rest goes to us.'

'Brother,' Ewell Saunders said to his brother, 'you swore off the grape when Mama died.'

Sheriff Ryker Saunders scowled at his sibling, and then quickly smiled at the group. 'No, really, I have thought this through. People will love this idea. You see, the way it will work is that *anyone* can arrest *anyone* else. Let's say that Miss Legare thinks that Emmeline here wears too much makeup, well then, she can arrest her on suspicion of being a trollop.'

Emmeline laughed. 'A trollop? *Moi?* Ryker, is that because I wouldn't go out with you in high school?'

Sheriff Ryker Saunders' dark complexion grew even darker. 'Maybe that was a bad example. Let's say that a tourist feels that Reverend Billy-Bob's sermons are too long—'

'That's ridiculous,' Reverend Billy-Bob said. He paused to push his wire-rimmed glasses back into place. It was a never-ending task. Despite having a long, aquiline nose, Reverend Billy-Bob had an equally long, sloping forehead, with no indentation on which his spectacles could perch.

'Perhaps you have a better idea that you'd be willing to share, Reverend,' Sheriff Ryker Saunders's sister-in-law, Mayor Adelaide, said.

'Yes, ma'am, you bet I do. I think that we should bring God back to Tidal Shores. I mean in a big way. We should start holding old-timey revivals, with all-day preaching, and gospel choirs brought in from all over. America is a Christian country, and South Carolina is a Christian state. There is no reason that Tidal Shores couldn't be the Mecca for Christianity in this country.'

Her Honour, Adelaide Saunders, who had a law degree from Emory University, politely covered her mouth as she snickered. 'America has no official religion, Reverend Billy-Bob, so how can you say it's a Christian country?'

'Well, it ought to be,' Reverend Billy-Bob said. 'Since Christianity was good enough for Jesus, then it is good enough to be our national religion – the Constitution be damned.'

No one even twittered. It was the group consensus that Reverend Billy-Bob was not the brightest of the Big Ten. However, even in supposedly secular America, but especially in the South, clergymen enjoyed a special status in society. As Tidal Shores' only man of the cloth, Reverend Billy-Bob was automatically on the town council. The clergy had always been on the town council, and they always would be. God bless America.

Adelaide Saunders cleared her throat a couple of times and faced her husband. 'Ewell, what idea have you managed to come up with to save our beloved town?'

'Books,' said Principal Ewell Saunders.

'Well, then you're even more stupid than you look,' Miss Legare said. 'I'd have thought a high-school principal could come up with a better idea than cooking the town books. Sure, your darling wife might be able to skim a few dollars off our budget here and there – I did it when I was mayor – but lining your own pockets isn't going to help the town out.'

'Aha!' Sheriff Ryker Saunders pumped a fist above his head. 'I always knew that you were a crook.'

'Hush your mouth, boy,' Miss Georgina Legare said.

'Nobody calls me "boy,"' Sheriff Ryker Saunders said, who'd taken the word as a racial slur, although it probably wasn't meant that way. Miss Georgina Legare could be mean as a bag of cut snakes, but she had a reputation as a social liberal.

Ewell jumped to his feet. 'Listen everyone, I meant books, as in a book fair. Actually, many book fairs. We invite famous authors here to give seminars – and they'll come because of our lovely weather – and their fans will come in by the droves. And we can have arts and crafts fairs. Juried art shows, even. We can become the cultural hub of the South.'

'With the books and artists will come the Devil,' Reverend Billy-Bob said. 'Mark my words.'

'Oh, give it a rest, Reverend Billy-Bob, will you?' Adam Patel had not planned to speak until called upon, but today the preacher was getting on his nerves. A quiet, thoughtful man, Adam had spent a lifetime honing the ability to remain silent while others made fools of themselves.

Reverend Billy-Bob would not publicly admit to being a racist, but in his mind Adam Patel, despite his diluted Gujarati ancestry, and white skin, was not quite one hundred percent American, and therefore always a little suspect. An honest to goodness American is of Scotch-Irish, English, or even German ancestry. French as well – if they are of Huguenot origin, but no one from southern France, and definitely no one from the Mediterranean region. Ironically, going by Reverend Billy-Bob Henderson's standards, neither Jesus nor his parents would have been eligible to immigrate to America.

'OK then, Adam,' Reverend Billy-Bob Henderson said, 'let's hear your brilliant proposal.'

Adam Patel was a handsome man who brought to mind a younger George Clooney. Although he was a man of few words, his smile conveyed a wealth of emotion.

'For the record,' he said, 'I don't have any big ideas. I'd like to hear what the lovely Tanya Kitchens has to say.'

Few men ever called Tanya Kitchens lovely. Nature had not been kind to her from the start. Poor Tanya never did have much baby fat, and by the time she began high school she was already looking hollow-eyed and haggard. The captain of the football team was even heard to remark that Tanya looked as if she'd 'been rode hard and put away wet.' Tanya forgave him. Despite being decidedly unattractive, Tanya Kitchens had a kind and generous soul, and gave virtually everyone the benefit of the doubt. At least once.

'Have any of you watched *The Great British Baking Show*?' Tanya asked.

'What of it?' Miss Legare snapped.

As Tanya smiled, she made eye contact with everyone in the room. 'Well,' she said, and swallowed hard, 'I was thinking that we could hold a contest similar to the one on that show. That's a very popular show. One can tell because it has been on TV for several seasons—'

'Behold another nincompoop,' Miss Legare said. 'I watch that show, and I know for a fact that there are only twelve contestants on that show. How much business would that bring in?'

Tanya blushed which, bless her heart, made her look even less becoming. 'But I read online that as many as twelve thousand people apply to be on that show. We could host the try-outs here as well. Twelve thousand people here, even for just a short while, would be a sight better than what we have now.'

'Pass,' said Miss Legare. 'Next!'

'Ahem,' Mayor Adelaide Saunders said. 'I'm still the mayor, and as such, *I'm* the head of this council. I'm running this meeting, Miss Legare, not you.'

'Good for you,' Principal Ewell Saunders whispered to his wife.

'Therefore,' Adelaide said, 'I am handing the metaphorical mic over to Miss Emmeline Davis.'

The owner of Turning Heads blushed. The extra pink brushed across the apples of her cheeks was attractive on her. Although everyone in the room had been born in the same year, except for Miss Legare, plastic surgery plus Botox and collagen injections kept

Emmeline Davis looking much younger than her contemporaries. In fact, Emmeline Davis could have passed for Tanya Kitchens' daughter – except for being ten times more attractive. Tanya forgave Emmeline Davis for that too.

Anyway, when Emmeline Davis smiled, she made a point of showing her perfect white teeth to everyone assembled. 'I thought we might hold a beauty pageant. As y'all know, I was a fifth runner-up to Miss America, and before that Miss South Carolina, of course. Y'all may also remember that I was also Miss South Carolina Plough Mud, Miss Sewee Grass and, it goes, without saying, Miss Tidal Shores.'

'Then why did you say it?' Miss Legare said.

'I beg your pardon?'

'Never mind her,' Mayor Adelaide Saunders said. 'It's not a bad suggestion, Emmeline, but in order to have even one sizable beauty pageant, we would need an auditorium in which to hold it. Our high-school gymnasium is just too small. The only other option that I can think of is Reverend Billy-Bob's church.'

Nine pairs of eyes focused on the preacher.

'Over my dead body,' Reverend Billy-Bob Henderson said.

FOUR

'We think that we might have an answer,' Hoyt Hunter said.

'Who is *we*?' Miss Legare demanded.

Hoyt was sitting next to Miss Georgina Legare, and he reached over and patted her arm affectionately. The rugged, bearded captain of the charter boat *The Reel Life* was one of the few people in Tidal Shores who was genuinely fond of the old lady. Then again, Hoyt Hunter liked most people. The only person in Tidal Shores who rubbed him the wrong way was Reverend Billy-Bob Henderson.

'We,' Hoyt Hunter said, 'is Gunner Jones and me.'

'Aha,' Reverend Billy-Bob Henderson said.

'Aha, *what*?' Hoyt Hunter said. He guessed that Reverend Billy-Bob Henderson was jumping to conclusions about Gunner Jones' sexual preference, and that's one of the things that irked him. Hoyt Hunter didn't give one hoot if Reverend Billy-Bob Henderson thought that *he*, Hoyt Hunter, was gay. Hoyt Hunter wasn't gay; he'd been happily married to Jolene Hunter (née Adams) for twenty-six years. Although, if Hoyt Hunter *were* gay, maybe he would be attracted to Gunner Jones – but not because Gunner Jones was such a handsome man. Gunner Jones was an altogether decent human being.

Reverend Billy-Bob Henderson pushed his wire-rimmed glasses back up his bridgeless nose. '"Aha," as in that it's no surprise that the two of you would work together, knowing that you're such good friends.'

'Tell us your solution, Hoyt,' Adelaide said. 'Please. We're all ears.'

'Actually, Gunner gets the credit, not me. It was all his idea.'

Gunner Jones stood to address the room. At six feet two inches, he was a commanding presence.

'Have any of you heard of bonobos?'

'Aren't they a kind of French pastry?' Tanya asked.

Gunner Jones smiled politely. 'No. Bonobos are a species of ape from the Democratic Republic of the Congo. That's the only place that they are found. At first glance bonobos look like a young chimpanzee, except that their foreheads are less sloped, and they have smaller ears. Also, the females, when lactating, have larger breasts than chimpanzees. Oh, and they spend more time walking upright than chimpanzees do.

'The two species behave quite differently as well. Chimpanzees can be quite aggressive. They settle their grievances with violence at times, whereas bonobos prefer to make love, not war. For them, conflicts can be worked out by having sex with any member of their group, the one exception being sex between mothers and sons. Bonobos would appear to have a taboo against that.'

'With all due respect,' Adam Patel said, 'why are you telling us this? Are you suggesting that we build a zoo? If so, please bear in mind that we'd be competing with Riverbanks Zoo up in Columbia, and that would be a hard act to follow.'

'No. No zoo,' Hoyt Hunter said. 'Gunner was just giving you a thumbnail sketch of these special apes. You see, his great-grandparents were missionaries to the Belgian Congo – that's what the country was called then – back in the 1920s. They heard about an albino bonobo, with an albino baby, living in the forest near their mission station.'

'I'll take it from there,' Gunner Jones said. He shook his handsome head. 'In addition to being a missionary, Great-granddaddy was also a taxidermist. The plethora of wildlife there was one of the reasons he felt drawn to Africa – besides saving souls, of course. Sadly, he put a bounty on this rare, white, female bonobo. She was killed with a poisoned arrow, and delivered to him shortly after being felled, along with the baby. The infant died a few weeks later, possibly from grief.

'At any rate, Great-granddaddy preserved the albino female and shipped her back to his parents in the States – to right here in Tidal Shores. The stuffed and mounted specimen has been passed down from father to son, until me. But she has never been put on display, because – well, certain formalities were not followed.'

Miss Legare snorted. 'Do you mean to say that your grand-pappy smuggled the beast out of the Congo illegally?'

'Reverend Thaddeus Jones was my *great*-grandfather, and Miss Lucy was not a *beast*. Bonobos and humans are both descended from a common ancestor. As a result, we share ninety-eight percent of our DNA with them.'

'Maybe you do,' Reverend Billy-Bob Henderson said. 'I know that I didn't descend from any pre-human ancestor; God made my ancestors from dirt. It says so in the second chapter of Genesis.'

'You definitely come from dirt, Reverend Billy-Bob,' Miss Legare said.

'Amen to that, sister,' Reverend Billy-Bob Henderson said, although frankly, he was a mite confused why Miss Georgina Legare was suddenly being so nice to him as to agree with something that he'd said.

Her Honour, Mayor Adelaide Saunders, glanced at her watch. 'Please move it along, Gunner.'

'Yes, ma'am. Well, like I said before, Great-granddaddy was interested in the variety of African wildlife, and that included fish. So, when the local natives caught a one-hundred-and-forty-three-pound *Hydrocynus goliath*, otherwise known as the goliath tigerfish, Great-granddaddy bought it from them. He and Great-granny ate the flesh, but he preserved and mounted the skin, and had it sent back to America.

'Hoyt Hunter is the only one of you who has ever seen my storeroom. I showed it to him because he sends me a lot of business. He sends me his customers' trophy fish.'

'Gunner Jones does the mounting for me,' Hoyt Hunter said. Then he turned to Reverend Billy-Bob. 'I saw you just roll your eyes.'

'No, I didn't,' Reverend Billy-Bob Henderson said.

'Just leave it,' said Gunner Jones. 'Reverend Billy-Bob's always had a juvenile sense of humour.'

'I have not!

Gunner Jones shrugged. 'Anyway, now for the big disclosure, and great reveal. Hoyt, I want you to have the honour of taking it from here. After all, it was your idea.'

'*Me?*' Hoyt Hunter said, sounding quite alarmed. 'But you did all the work!'

'With your encouragement, Hoyt,' Gunner Jones said softly. He stepped closer to his friend and whispered a few words into his ear.

'Sweet nothings?' Reverend Billy-Bob Henderson said.

'Put a sock in it,' Miss Legare said. 'Out with the big surprise, boys, or I'm going home. At my age, every minute is precious.'

'The surprise,' Hoyt Hunter said, 'is that we have created a mermaid.'

'A mermaid!' Emmeline Davis was on the edge of her chair.

'Adelaide,' Sheriff Ryker Saunders said to his sister-in-law, the mayor, 'do we have time for this nonsense? After all, Miss Legare is about to topple over dead at any minute.'

'You can put a sock in it, too, boy,' Miss Georgina Legare snapped.

Mayor Adelaide Saunders held up two fingers. 'You gentlemen have exactly two minutes to finish presenting your case, and then I'm calling an end to this meeting.'

'Yes, a mermaid, Emmeline,' Hoyt Hunters said. 'Gunner took the top half of that albino bonobo that his great-grandfather sent back from the Congo – remember, it's the most human-looking of the great apes – and he did a bang-up job of sewing it to the bottom half of that large goliath tigerfish that he also had in his storeroom. I took the liberty of shaving off all the hair that wasn't on top of her head, and Gunner plumped up her breasts as much as he could with silicone inserts.'

'Bear in mind,' Gunner Jones said, 'that flexibility is a problem that presents itself in seventy-year-old skin that's become dry and somewhat brittle.'

'Tell me about it,' Miss Legare said.

'I left her eyebrows on,' Hoyt said, 'but they'll need to be tweezed and shaped. Emmeline, I'm counting on you to do that. Also, she needs a proper head of hair – like a long wig. Something long enough to meet the public's perception of a mermaid. Maybe light brown, with strings of dried seaweed tangled in it.'

'So, where's this all headed?' asked Principal Ewell Saunders.

'Yes,' Mayor Adelaide Saunders said. 'What is your end game?'

Both Gunner Jones and Hoyt Hunter smiled broadly.

'Miss Lucy,' Hoyt Hunter said, 'as we have named our creation, is going to make us all very wealthy – not just our town, but us as individuals. The plan is to exhibit her in front of Gunner's shop in a weather-proof booth. We'll say that he discovered her in an old trunk that his missionary great-grandparents brought back from the Congo. The only way that they could get there in those days was to cross the Atlantic Ocean on freighter, which made lots of stops along the coast of West Africa before reaching the mouth of the Congo River. After a particularly nasty storm, the corpse of Miss Lucy was found floating in the water off the Cape Verde islands, which was the ship's first stop. Fortunately, the missionary taxidermist had all the supplies he needed on board with him, and the captain was willing to let him do his work aboard ship. Of course, the captain and all the crew returned home with the amazing story of what they had seen, but they were never taken seriously. After all, for centuries sailors have reported seeing mermaids, and the black and white photos that the captain did manage to take could easily have been faked.'

Miss Legare snorted. 'So now this *thing* is called *Miss* Lucy, and we haven't even had a chance to see it.'

'Then come this way,' Gunner said, and led the way through his dining room and into his workshop.

Although there were several mounted specimens hanging on the walls of this room, or sitting on tables – a buck's head, a pheasant mounted as if in flight, even a coyote – Miss Lucy the mermaid took centre stage on a grey Styrofoam rock. One hand was placed palm down on the rock beside her, and the other hand reached up as if to extract a string of seaweed that had gotten caught in her hair.

'Oh, my Lord,' Miss Legare exclaimed, 'she looks just like my grand-niece in Columbia. Except for the tail. Patricia – or Patty, as we call her – was born with a tail, you know, but it didn't have fins on the end.'

'Or scales either, I reckon,' Sheriff Ryker Saunders said.

'Look how blue her eyes are,' Tanya Kitchens said. 'I didn't know that mermaids have blue eyes.'

'Those are glass eyes,' Hoyt Hunter said, 'and this mermaid is Gunner Jones' creation, so he got to choose the colour. Bear in mind, Tanya, that mermaids aren't real.'

'Never mind her blue eyes,' Mayor Adelaide Saunders said. 'Look at her hands! Gunner, did that ape have naturally webbed fingers, or did you do that?'

'I did that, ma'am. I thought that if I – we – were creating a mermaid from scratch, then she should have a feature that would enable her to be as good a swimmer as possible. Remember she needs to outswim sharks.'

'Does she have gills?' Principal Ewell Saunders asked. 'Do you mind if I check?'

'She doesn't,' Hoyt Hunter said quickly. 'Contrary to popular mythology, mermaids don't live under the sea. Can you imagine what your skin would look like if you lived under water the whole time?'

Mermaids live on rocks along the coast of islets – little uninhabited islands that dot the tropical latitudes, but that lie off the shipping lanes. If a storm washes them too far north, or too far south, they die of exposure, because, as you see, they wear no clothes.'

'Also,' Hoyt Hunter said, 'due to global warming, and the rise of ocean levels, the low-lying rocks that they call home will all be covered within the next one hundred years. That means that these awesome beings will either have to make themselves definitively known to the outside world, or else drown.'

'Ha!' said Reverend Billy-Bob Henderson. 'How do you explain their survival during the time of Noah's Ark, when the earth was completely covered with water for one hundred and fifty days?'

'They clung to the sides of the ark,' Gunner Jones said. 'But a lot of them did drown, especially the merchildren. It has been said that Noah and his family were deeply troubled by the mournful cries of the merfolk, as their little ones slipped from their weakened arms. As the story goes, one day Noah peaked out at the merfolk through a portal and found himself face to face with a voluptuous red-haired mermaid – bare-breasted, of course – who was nursing her child, while barely managing to hang on to the side of the ark. The sight filled the old man with lust instead of pity, so he nailed the portal shut.'

'Blasphemer,' Reverend Billy-Bob Henderson shouted. 'There is not a word of that in the Bible.'

'Reverend,' Hoyt Hunter said. 'Miss Lucy is a way for your church – and you – to double your income. Maybe even triple it. Think of all the good you could do with a budget that large.'

'And think about the largest TV screen imaginable in each room of your house,' Miss Legare said, and snickered.

'OK,' Reverend Billy-Bob Henderson said, 'I'm willing to listen. But only because a bigger operating budget for my church will allow me to do more outreach in the community.'

Miss Legare snorted. 'Now that Billy-Bob's finally sold his soul to the Devil, can we go back to your living room, Gunner, and sit down? My dogs are killing me.'

FIVE

After they'd all been seated, Gunner Jones hastily served refreshments: sweet tea and cheese straws for everyone, and two fingers of Scotch for Miss Legare. Sweet tea, the preferred beverage of card-carrying Southerners, is simply iced tea with enough sugar added to make a body instantly happy and not really give a damn that they'll be plunking their chubby self into a dentist's chair three months down the road. This was a strategic move on Gunner Jones' part; he waited a couple of minutes until everyone, except Miss Legare, was on a sugar high before making his sales pitch. As for the old crone, she was headed down her own familiar path.

'This is how it will work,' Gunner Jones said as Hoyt Hunter nodded enthusiastically. 'Tidal Shores is going to become famous for the town where Miss Lucy the mermaid was washed up on shore after a particularly ferocious storm. Then *you*, Reverend Billy-Bob, who just happens to be a nationally famous preacher—'

'I *am*?' Reverend Billy-Bob said. 'Nationally famous, I mean. I know that I'm a reverend; after all, I was ordained at the Tabernacle of Truth Theological Seminary in Grassy Flats, Alabama, along with all six members of my class, even though I failed my course in Biblical Hebrew and barely passed Greek. Frankly, I don't see the point in making us study them foreign languages when everybody knows that the Bible was written in English. If you don't believe me, then just pick up your Bibles and peek inside, and see if you can read a page. Because if you can, then either you can read Hebrew, or else your nationally famous preacher here is lying.'

Gunner smiled warmly. 'Reverend Billy-Bob, you are indeed our local celebrity. I reckon that you've shaken more hands, and kissed more babies, than even Her Honour Mayor Adelaide Saunders has. Anyway, Reverend Billy-Bob, you were the one who found Miss Lucy lying on the beach. Then you immediately called Sheriff Ryker Saunders.

'Sheriff Ryker, you called your sister-in-law, Her Honour the Mayor, and then *you*, Adelaide, called your husband, who was a biology teacher, before he became a principal. That's when you, Ewell, realized that Miss Lucy was a biological phenomenon, and that she needed to be preserved before decay set in.'

Hoyt Hunter pushed Gunner Jones gently aside. 'We'll put Miss Lucy on display – inside the community centre. We'll publicize the heck out of our so-called discovery. We'll call the Charleston, Charlotte, and Atlanta newspapers, and invite all of them to send reporters down to do a feature story on this incredible find. You know what? We'll call all the TV stations as well. Before you know it, everyone and their fifth cousin is going to want to drive down and see Miss Lucy.

'We'll charge a premium for folks who want to get in the door to see her – much more if they want to photograph her. We'll create merchandise: Miss Lucy T-shirts, Miss Lucy mugs, we'll put her name on posters, dolls, figurines, refrigerator magnets, placemats, pens, teaspoons – y'all can help us think of even more things.'

Now Gunner Jones nudged Hoyt Hunter aside. 'Everyone and their fifth cousin, as Hoyt so colourfully put it, is going to want to spend their vacation at a beach where a genuine mermaid – no matter how unattractive she is – was discovered. Instead of deep-sea fishing customers, Hoyt will be taking tourists on mermaid-spotting tours. And you, Tanya, might think about decorating your restaurant in a mermaid theme. The same thing goes for you, Emmeline, with your beauty salon.'

'Hold your horses,' Sheriff Ryker Henderson said. 'How many mermaid-spotting tours do you think there could be, Hoyt, with no mermaids spotted, before someone cries foul?'

SIX

'Oh, I would see to it that one was spotted,' Hoyt Hunter said. 'My boat is almost always followed by dolphins. I just need to say that I see a mermaid swimming with them. Believe me, because people see what they want to see, some gullible tourist is going to fall for the power of suggestion, and at least get a glimpse of my imaginary mermaid. By the time that she – and it will be a she – gets back to shore and has lunch, or dinner, that mere glimpse of a mermaid – pun intended – will turn into a full-fledged sighting.'

'Horse pucky,' Miss Legare said. 'I know that people can be gullible, but—'

'With all due respect, Miss Legare, it's already happened. I took my niece, Audrey, out with a group of her classmates to celebrate Audrey's eighteenth birthday. I was just joshing them when I told them that I spotted a mermaid, but by the time we docked, eight of the ten girls aboard *The Reel Life* were believers.'

'Empty-headed teenagers,' Miss Legare said. 'Had you gotten them liquored up? And speaking of which, I need a refill.' She held up the empty Scotch glass.

'You better not have gotten them drunk,' Sheriff Ryker Saunders said. 'My *daughter* was on that trip!'

Reverend Billy-Bob Henderson sighed. 'I baptized your niece, Hoyt. She always seemed so level-headed.'

'Relax, gentlemen,' Hoyt Hunter said. 'I did not serve alcohol. I was just trying to prove my point about the power of suggestion.'

'Hoyt is right,' Emmeline Davis said. 'When my customers ask for styling advice, I find that I sell them a whole host of products and services if I tell them there is a good chance that they will look ten years younger when they have completed my treatment plan. I mention the names of various celebrities, and it works every time.'

'Emmeline,' Miss Legare croaked, 'did *I* look any younger after I suffered through your torturous regime of toxic fumes and flesh-eating potions?'

Emmeline neither flinched nor blinked. 'I sold you hope, didn't I?'

'I get it now,' Reverend Billy-Bob Henderson said. 'You want us to sell the public lies. Well, the Bible says: "Thou shalt not lie."'

'No, it does *not*,' Gunner Jones said emphatically. 'It states: "Thou shalt not bear false witness against thy neighbour." Madam Mayor, you're a lawyer – tell them what it means.'

Adelaide looked decidedly unhappy about being called upon to spontaneously testify without having a chance to prepare a brief. Although she attended Reverend Billy-Bob's church regularly (as mayor, it was expected of her), it had been thirty years since she'd cracked open a Bible of her own. For all she knew, her copy *was* printed in Hebrew. One thing was for certain, she'd never once listened to Reverend Billy-Bob's sermons. Instead, she listened to racy romances on e-books from the iPhone in her purse. The earbuds she used, besides being incredibly small, were well hidden under her wavy, shoulder-length, chestnut-coloured hair. The previous Sunday morning, while Reverend Billy-Bob Henderson railed against the sins of the flesh, Mayor Adelaide Saunders spent a happy hour pretending to be Harriet, in *Harriet Humps Houston*.

'The Bible verse, if quoted correctly, refers to making false claims against your neighbour – just like it reads. Don't claim that your neighbour stole your goat, or blinded your camel, if these claims aren't true.'

'Goats and camels are not allowed in Tidal Shores,' Reverend Billy-Bob Henderson said. 'Says so in the covenants.'

'Reverend Billy-Bob, you're as thick as a pier piling,' Miss Legare said. 'Her Honour was giving us old-timey examples. Now where's my refill on the Scotch, Gunner?'

To shut the old bat up, Gunner poured her half a glass of the golden liquid. 'Let's not lose sight of our objective,' he said, 'and that is to bring tourists back to Tidal Shores, and maybe even – well, increase our personal fortunes, such as they are.'

'I'm all for that,' Ewell Saunders said. 'Out of all fifty states, South Carolina teacher pay ranked fortieth last year.'

'I want you all to imagine *your* future,' Hoyt said. 'When mermaid fever strikes Tidal Shores, everyone here stands to profit personally. Adam, your motel will have no vacancies. You'll probably want to buy the two that closed last year and remodel them. Tanya, you'll definitely want to serve more than just breakfast, and maybe branch out as well. Emmeline, you'll need to rent out some chairs in your beauty shop. Maybe hire some full-time manicurists.

'Ewell, a lot of folks who return to vacation here, having caught mermaid fever, will be tempted to make this their permanent home. They'll not only remember just how beautiful our coastline is, but they will be impressed with how mild our winters are compared to the northern states. And I daresay that a lot of these people will have children who will need your school. At the very least, they'll add additional dollars to our local tax base. A larger tax base means more money for teacher and staff bonuses, and that includes you.

'As for you, Your Honour,' Hoyt said to Adelaide Saunders, 'with a larger tax base, I'm sure that we can legitimately increase your salary, plus your discretionary fund will be larger.

'And speaking of larger, Reverend Billy-Bob, you will see your congregation swell, and with it the piles of money in the offering plates that are passed around in your church every Sunday. Surely you have heard that joke about the minister that throws the money in his church's offering plates into the air and tells God to keep whatever amount the Good Lord wants? All the money that falls to the ground the minister gets to keep.'

Everyone laughed except Reverend Billy-Bob. 'What percentage does God usually keep?' he asked.

'That depends on how high you toss the money,' Adam Patel said. 'I heard that it only works if you do it in a dark closet, so that you can't see how much God is keeping. In fact, if the closet is pitch-black inside, you just need to stand there with the offering plate, and God will reach down and take what is his.'

'Yeah, I heard that too,' Gunner Jones said, a smile playing across his handsome features.

'Y'all are messing with me, ain't y'all?' Reverend Billy-Bob Henderson practically wailed.

'Are we?' Miss Georgina Legare said and held up her glass for another refill.

'Well,' said Reverend Billy-Bob Henderson, 'the King James Bible does say in Matthew 6:6 that we should *pray* in our closets. With the doors shut. I suppose then that it would make sense to do the offering ritual in the closet as well, and since they didn't have electricity back in Bible times, I imagine that the closets were pitch black. Yeah, I'll try it. After all, God is all powerful. If He wants,

He can take all of the offering money. I'm giving Him a fair chance, ain't I?'

'Billy-Bob,' Principal Ewell Saunders said, 'your capacity for logical thinking is positively incommensurable.'

'Billy-Bob,' Mayor Adelaide Saunders said, 'this coming Sunday I'm going to listen to your sermon for a change. I reckon it will be a sight more interesting than the soft porn I normally listen to.'

'You too?' Miss Georgina Legare said. 'I'll trade e-books with you just as soon as I'm finished with *Donna Does Delaware*.'

'The *entire* State of Delaware?' Emmeline Davis asked, her eyes wide with admiration for the fictional Donna.

'It's a small state,' Miss Georgina Legare said, 'and Donna doesn't dawdle.'

'I knew it!' Sheriff Ryker Saunders said. 'I told my wife Willow that there ain't nobody on God's green earth that can sit through an hour of hail and brimstones with their faces fixed like the two of y'all's are.' Suddenly his demeanour changed. 'Hey,' he said, 'what about me? What do I get out of this so-called mermaid fever, except for traffic headaches and calls about drunks behaving badly on our beach?'

'I'll answer that,' Miss Georgina Legare said. 'You'll get to issue even *more* bogus traffic tickets to Yankees who are frightened by the stereotypical pot-bellied Southern Sheriff. As you well know, they'll be scared witless, so they'll offer you bribes, which you'll then pocket. *You* will be living high on the hog.'

Sheriff Ryker Saunders' complexion darkened further, but he did not object. Since none of the others laughed, it could be assumed that everyone present already knew that they had a crooked sheriff, and that they didn't mind just so long as he only soaked Yankee tourists.

'That's actually a terrible idea,' hotelier Adam Patel said softly. 'No one is going to want to visit, or live, in a town where they are constantly afraid.'

'Amen to that,' Gunner Jones said.

'Why don't you do just the opposite of intimidation?' Hoyt Hunter suggested.

'Say what?' Sheriff Ryker Saunders said.

'Direct your deputies to be the kindest, most polite lawmen the public have ever encountered. That will help Tidal Shores develop the reputation of being the most desirable place to live in all of the Southeast – maybe all of the country.'

'But don't overdo it,' Miss Georgina Legare said. 'A little fake kindness goes a long way.'

Hoyt Hunter flashed Miss Legare an unkind look that wasn't faked. 'As I was about to say, Ryker, if you are nice to people, that is a good way to get them into the Sand Bar. The last time I peeked into there, only Miss Legare was sitting at the bar – or should I say, *slumped* over the bar.'

'Hush your mouth, Hoyt,' Miss Legare slurred.

'Hoyt has a point, Ryker,' Tanya said. 'Your bar could be a big money-maker again, if you got folks to believe that you were a friendly man. I know that I would feel right comfortable frequenting a drinking establishment owned and operated by an officer of the law. Why, it would make me feel downright safe. And you know something, besides just shagging, you could introduce line-dancing. I saw that in a movie once, and it looked like so much fun.'

'Dancing is a sin,' Reverend Billy-Bob Henderson said.

'"Then David danced before the Lord,"' Gunner Jones said. 'That's 2 Samuel 6:14.'

'Show-off,' Reverend Billy-Bob Henderson said.

'What about you, Miss Legare?' Sheriff Ryker Henderson said. 'How will you benefit personally?'

Miss Georgina Legare threw back her head to laugh. The wattles on her neck vibrated with each sound that passed over her yellow, worn teeth. The smell of Scotch was practically strong enough to inebriate those next to her.

'I'll do just fine,' Miss Legare said. 'I'm going to convert the Den of Antiquity into the Mermaid's Merchandise Mart. It will be stocked to the gills – no pun intended – with everything that we plan to sell that has a mermaid theme. Mermaid swimming suits, mermaid pyjamas, mermaid backpacks—'

'But you can't do that,' Mayor Adelaide Saunders protested. 'We all have ownership in this – this creature that Gunner created.'

'Her name is *Miss Lucy*,' Gunner Jones said. '*Miss Lucy*. Now, Adelaide, you are correct in that I created her for the benefit of all of Tidal Shores, and I expected that we ten who share this secret would have a special claim to her, and the money that she brings in. Since Miss Legare's business is selling merchandise, and not a service, perhaps you can draw up a contract whereby she shares a certain portion of her profits with the rest of us.'

'Harrumph,' Miss Georgina Legare said, which suggested that either she'd been born in the nineteenth century or was the reader of British novels.

'Well, that settles it then,' Mayor Adelaide said. 'I'll draw up a contract tonight.'

'Wait just one cotton-pickin' minute,' Tanya Kitchens said. 'If Miss Lucy is going to be our salvation—'

'Only Jesus is our salvation,' Reverend Billy-Bob Henderson said. 'It says so in—'

'Shut up, Billy-Bob,' Miss Georgina Legare said. 'Tanya, go ahead and finish your thought, but make it a good one this time.'

SEVEN

Tanya Kitchens wasted no time. 'We have to all swear to not tell a single soul that this – uh, Miss Lucy, isn't real. That's the only way this is going to work.'

'I should think that's obvious,' Miss Georgina Legare said.

'Yes, but I mean that we can't even tell our spouses.'

At that, everyone but Tanya Kitchens laughed. Despite her rough appearance, the woman had been married and divorced three times, proving that being on the 'shady side of plain' was no handicap when it came to finding a husband.

'Tanya has a good point,' Sheriff Ryker Saunders said. 'From my experience, both as an officer of the law, and as a bar owner, the only way to keep a secret is to never share it.' He paused to look at his twin, Ewell. 'Not even to your brother. Or your mother, for that matter. The person whom you tell it to swears to keep it a secret but then tells just one other person, who also swears to keep it a secret, but by then the secret is twice removed from the source, and the genie is out of the bottle. What we need to do is sign a formal agreement that binds us to secrecy.'

'In the meantime, what do we do?' Emmeline Davis asked. 'Pinkie swear?'

This time everyone laughed except for Emmeline Davis. 'How about a blood oath?' Miss Georgina Legare said. 'That's what we did in my day; we pricked our index fingers and rubbed them together, mixing our blood.'

Reverend Billy-Bob Henderson rolled his eyes. 'But if someone *had* reneged on their oath, would you have run them through with a sword?'

'Only if they were a member of the clergy,' Miss Georgina Legare snapped.

'Touché,' Gunner Jones said. Despite the fact that his great-grandparents had been missionaries, and his parents attended Reverend Billy-Bob Henderson's church regularly, Gunner Jones made no secret of the fact that he held all organized religions in contempt. His feelings were not shared by most members of the Big Ten.

'How about this?' Mayor Adelaide Saunders said. 'In addition to an equitable profit-sharing document in regards to mermaid merchandise, I'll draw up a non-disclosure agreement. Whomever violates that agreement will have to pay each other member of the Big Ten the sum of one hundred and ten thousand dollars, for the grand total of a million dollars.'

'Whew!' Adam Patel said. 'You can bet that my lips will be sealed.'

'Well, that don't seem right,' Reverend Billy-Bob Henderson said. 'I ain't even signed off on this being a good idea. This thing is an abomination, pure and simple. Are y'all saying that I have to lie to my flock of little lost lambs when they ask me what I think about this fish-monkey?'

Gunner Jones glared at Reverend Billy-Bob Henderson. 'First of all, Miss Lucy's torso is that of an extraordinarily rare albino bonobo from what was then the Belgian Congo. That means that her top half was that of an *ape*, not a monkey. Look it up on any reference site.

'And secondly, you don't have to give your opinion whether or not mermaids are real. Simply tell your sweet little lambs what you've been telling us: that what we have here in Tidal Shores is an abomination in the sight of the Lord. Then expand on that subject. *Preach*, Billy-Bob. Tell your congregation that you can think of at least one degenerate in Tidal Shores who might even contemplate having intimate relations with mermaids – well, at least the top half – and that surely is a grave sin. Implore your flock to write to their congressmen, and women, to start enacting a law that prohibits such actions.'

'And then,' said Hoyt Hunter, 'while shaking your tiny fists aloft, as if in a holy rage, you declare in that quasi-feminine voice of yours that mermaids do not have souls.'

'Or if they did have souls,' Mayor Adelaide Saunders said with a wink, 'they couldn't count as much as a human soul.'

'But I'd still need to convert them, right?' Billy-Bob said. 'Because an *un*saved soul – even if it's just a half – is still going to Hell. And if I converted them, wouldn't I need to baptize them in a saltwater tank? Our baptismal tank is chlorinated river water.'

'Those are all great questions,' Emmeline Davis said. 'Now you're getting it. You see, Billy-Bob, if you sign this non-disclosure, and stick with the program, you'll have an endless supply of sermons.'

'Not to mention extra money in your offering plates,' said Tanya Kitchens. 'Because just before the offertory hymn is sung, you'll raise those tiny hands of yours as high as you can, and in that quasi-feminine voice of yours, you'll implore the Good Lord to soften the hearts of your congregation, and inspire them to open their wallets, in order to finance your mission to convert these fish-tailed heathens, and the subsequent need of a saltwater baptismal tank.'

'Oh, I declare,' said Miss Georgina Legare, 'never have I heard such fine oratory emit from the lips of a member of my own sex. Tanya Kitchens, if you lacked ten IQ points, and had a certain additional appendage, I would support you for the state legislature.'

'Miss Legare,' Gunner Jones said, 'shame on you for being a raving sexist.'

Miss Georgina Legare smiled. 'Gunner, darling, don't be cross with me. *You* do meet my requirements, and by a long shot, so I would support you, should you decide to enter politics.'

Everyone laughed, except for Reverend Billy-Bob Henderson, who was the penultimate prude, and who eschewed sexual innuendo. The standing joke in Tidal Shores was that he emerged from his mother's womb fully clothed, and that she changed his nappies while blindfolded.

What mattered most was that the next morning, over breakfast at the Pancake House, all the members of the Big Ten signed the non-disclosure agreement that Mayor Adelaide Saunders had prepared. The goal they set for the big reveal was two months out, which gave them time to prepare their respective places of business for the hoped-for onslaught of tourists.

Of course, Emmeline Davis needed to refine Miss Lucy's appearance by styling her hair, buffing her nails and shaping her eyebrows. Gunner Jones, on the other hand, plumped up Miss Lucy's breasts almost to the point of ripping her fragile old skin. He also filled in her existing ape nostrils, and created a new silicon nose that was a good deal narrower than her previous one. In addition, he gave Miss Lucy a proper pair of lips and a dainty prosthetic chin. Because Gunner Jones was such a skilled taxidermist, he was able to use his normal workshop paints to disguise the edges of his appliques and make them look at one with Miss Lucy.

The result was a mermaid that was far more presentable than

what the Big Ten had first laid eyes on. Now, few people would call Miss Lucy ugly as homemade sin. On the other hand, no one would call her beautiful either. The best that could be said about her was that her top half was convincingly human-*like*. What was especially important was that Gunner had done a masterful job of attaching her ape top to her fish bottom. There appeared to be a gradual transition between the halves, with a small number of scales continuing up her spine, and then stopping at a small dorsal fin halfway up. Who knew that mermaids had dorsal fins? Well, the world would know soon enough!

It was a Friday morning when the press releases went out announcing Miss Lucy's discovery and secret preservation. Early that same morning, Mayor Adelaide Saunders 'leaked' an email to Sheriff Ryker Saunders, her brother-in-law. In it she asked him to post an officer in the community centre to guard the mermaid that had been found floating in the shallows off Tidal Shores, and which the famed taxidermist Gunner Jones had preserved. The mayor believed that the townsfolk should be given a chance to view it before it was shipped off to the Smithsonian Museum in Washington, where it could be shared with the nation. This 'leaked' email went out to all town employees, as well as the mayor's friends, and everyone on the mailing list of the Tabernacle of Truth in Tidal Shores.

In no time at all, Sheriff Ryker Saunders had to send four additional officers just to deal with the chaos that the mayor's email had caused. No one had thought to cordon off the space directly surrounding the glass display case, so someone had to fetch a velvet-covered rope from the funeral home. And even though an admission fee of five dollars to enter the building had been suddenly, and arbitrarily, instituted overnight, no one seemed to object. There was a veritable logjam of would-be viewers at the main entrance.

The same scenario played out in the parking lot. Had the Big Ten spent any time thinking about local logistics, they could have blocked off both the entrance, and exit, to the community centre parking lot and charged a premium for parking. Instead, two officers had to deal with a snarl of traffic, amid the blaring of horns, and the shouts of aggrieved visitors. However, one thing was eminently clear: mermaid fever had struck Tidal Shores, South Carolina.

Not everyone who viewed Miss Lucy became an instant believer. However, buzz was definitely created, and the buzz spread far beyond the town limits of Tidal Shores. There was hardly a household in which at least one person did not know someone living in another town or city, or even in another state. After all, Americans are one of the most mobile populations in the world, with one fourth of the population relocating every year. By noon there were TV cameras from Charleston, Columbia and Myrtle Beach in South Carolina. By six that evening, the national networks had picked up the mermaid story as a bit of 'throwaway human-interest fluff,' as one producer put it.

But the 'fluff' stuck.

PART TWO
THE REPORTER

EIGHT

My name is Zoe Porter, and I was born and bred in Charlotte, North Carolina. Actually, let me take that back. I know what that expression means, but on the face of it, a foreign speaker of English could well assume that I had been bred – perhaps like a race horse – and that has yet to happen. I'll let you know when it does.

At any rate, I am a divorced working woman in my mid-thirties. You don't need to know the following information, but I'm happy to share it anyway. I'm a natural dirty blonde (which I'm willing to prove if I'm sufficiently motivated), and I have green eyes. I am of average height, and have an acceptable BMI, because I am a strict practitioner of the ELF diet. ELF, by the way, stands for *Eat Less Food*. I settled on the ELF diet because I am a lazy person. Exercise is a wonderful thing, and something that we should all engage in. However, one has to run about three miles to burn off the calories found in a slice of chocolate cake. I know myself, and I know that I'm never going to run three miles – ever! Case closed. No cake for me.

I'm a reporter/columnist at Charlotte's largest newspaper, *The Observer Today*. It's my job to find 'human interest' stories that can be fleshed out, and then turned into a series that appears in the Sunday edition over a period of several weeks. Sometimes the ideas for these stories are exclusively mine, other times they are supplied by my colleagues, or even one of the paper's editors. Often the idea begins very small – we call it a 'kernel' of a story – and then it grows. At other times it tanks, it goes nowhere. I don't mean to brag, but during the twelve years that I've been a feature writer, I've been nominated for three Pulitzer Prizes, and won two.

When I have copy to turn in, it goes 'to bed' Thursday nights, so that generally I have the weekends off. I live with my mother in her house on Providence Road, not because I have to, but because I actually enjoy her company. I started really liking Mama again when I divorced my philandering husband. Mama was there with two shoulders for me to cry on, and never once said 'I told you so.'

Both my parents *did* have unflattering things to say about Michael when I married him; however, I was eighteen then, and thought my parents were full of poppycock.

On weekends, when I'm home, I enjoy sleeping in with a short, dark, but very handsome male by my side. In Mama's house the only male I get to share my bed with is a nine-year-old rescue dog named Prankster. He is a black Labrador retriever mix. Prankster was supposed to be Mama's dog; she adopted him a year after Daddy was killed by a driver who was checking for 'likes' on something she'd posted on Facebook. At any rate, I couldn't help it that the four-year-old dog that Mama adopted preferred my bed from the start, but everything turned out OK because Mama soon adopted a middle-aged cat that just adores her. The feeling is mutual. I also like cats, and I believe that Prankster does as well, but so far Hairy has been very rude to the sweet Lab.

Now that Prankster is a senior citizen, he needs to be let out first thing in the morning to pee. My days of luxuriating in bed on weekends are over, until Prankster goes to that big fire hydrant in the sky. These days he nudges me awake, I let him out into Mama's fenced back yard for a few minutes, and then we both come in and eat before we walk. We *walk* – never run!

Prankster gets a bowl of carefully measured kibble that has been created just for senior dogs, and I get to sit down to one of Mama's extravagant weekend breakfasts. Mama does not follow the ELF diet, and thus is constantly searching for the newest fad, or pill, that will melt the pounds off her tiny frame after she's been binge-eating for several weeks. She's a huge fan of purges – toxins, that is, not ethnicities. The bone that I have to pick with Mama (pardon the food reference) is that she tries to sabotage my way of eating. She does this by cooking enormous breakfasts every weekend with all of my favourites: slow-cooked oatmeal served with brown sugar and raisins; eggs over medium with crisp bacon; grits with gobs of butter; cinnamon toast; pancakes with pure maple syrup and more gobs of butter melting down the stack of golden-brown discs. If I don't sample something from every dish that she's cooked, Mama carries on about how long she laboured in the kitchen cooking, working her poor fingers to the bone, and if that spiel doesn't work, she'll even go on about how long she laboured in hospital, pushing me out into the world. The second kind of labour ruined her wasp waist, and any excess weight that

The Mermaid Mystery

she carries now is a holdover from her pregnancy thirty-six years ago.

Because I usually just grabbed a bowl of cereal during the week before dashing off to my job, I was more than happy to spend a leisurely meal with my mother on weekend mornings. However, this Saturday I was going to have to wolf down my mother's cooking, or it was back to eating cereal. The evening before, the paper's managing editor had called, directing me to make the four-hour drive down to Tidal Shores, South Carolina, and get the scoop on 'this mermaid nonsense.' Luckily for me, it had been one Friday night when I hadn't had a date, which found Mama and me eating dinner over tray tables at 6:30 p.m. in the living room. We were watching the local news when the 'nonsense' aired about a mermaid found in our neighbouring state to the south. What my editor also referred to as 'a piece of fluff' had the potential to snowball into national news the following day, because already Dr Pat and Pal had announced that they were going to broadcast their morning show live from Tidal Shores the following day.

Dr Pat was not a medical doctor. His PhD was in English Literature, but you certainly wouldn't know it to hear him talk. He possessed the grammatical acumen of a five-year-old who'd been raised in isolation – or at best, by bonobos. Dr Pat purported to dispense marital advice (although he'd been divorced five times) and weight-loss solutions (although he was at least sixty pounds overweight). Dr Pat's 'Pal' were his guests, and they ranged from the Deli Llama (a chef in a llama suit *and* an orange robe), to Sister Bodacious (a whip-cracking nun with ginormous assets), who claimed to know what men *really* liked in the bedroom. Toward the end of each show Dr Pat would gaze tearfully at some product held in his well-manicured, but very small, hands and extol the wondrous properties of whatever it was that he was hawking. Finally, he would slowly shift his gaze, until he was staring directly into the camera – at you, the consumer – and pledge that 'some portion' of the proceeds would go to continuing the Lord's awesome work.

Frankly, Mama and I were not surprised to hear that Dr Pat and Pal planned to be in Tidal Shores to cover the mermaid story. That was just the sort of bizarre story that tended to appeal to him. On his most recent show he had a heart-transplant recipient who was a prominent atheist, but who had received a donor heart from a born-again Christian. Dr Pat demanded to know if the new heart had surgically created a Christian out of the heart patient. When the patient responded in the negative, Dr Pat harangued the poor man until he fled the stage in tears.

But when we heard that Dr Pat was going to be doing a story on something as ridiculous as mermaids, Mama and I looked at each other and rolled our eyes. Then we laughed so hard that we were compelled to cover our faces with our napkins, lest we cover each other with particles from our supper. This story was going to be a piece of cake for me – no food pun intended – and as it just so happened, Tidal Shores, South Carolina, was my old stomping ground. It had always been the Porter family's summer playground, and a place that we knew like our own back yard – because, in fact, it had once been Mama's back yard. You see, my mama, Beatrice Legare Porter, was a native of Tidal Shores. However, Daddy, aka Ogden Rutledge Porter, was a Charlottean, whose family had been vacationing in Tidal Shores for generations.

But Tidal Shores is where Mama met Daddy. They were probably toddlers at the time playing with their respective sand buckets and plastic shovels. Later on they probably splashed each other in the surf, but it wasn't until they were both teenagers, juniors in high school, that they really took notice of each other. I've seen enough photos of them to know that they were good-looking kids, but they claim to have instantly bonded over their mutual love of shagging one long summer night, and not over any physical attraction. Shagging, by the way, is the state dance of South Carolina, and does not have the meaning that those sex-obsessed Brits attach to the word.

At any rate, one dreary winter day, Daddy was killed in an automobile accident when a woman who was texting veered from her lane into oncoming traffic and hit him head-on. That was five years before the pandemic hit. He died immediately. We buried Daddy on a cold, drizzly day. Although I knew that it was only Daddy's physical shell that we left behind in the ground that afternoon, all evening – and sporadically throughout the night – I thought about him being cold and lonely up there on that hill.

Even though it was a terrible year for Mama and me, we still made our annual summer pilgrimage to Tidal Shores. For us it was an attempt to heal our broken hearts. But we weren't the only Charlotteans to spend our summers in this quaint little coastal town. Over the years many people from North Carolina had discovered that this little beach town was the best kept secret of the state to their south. Myrtle Beach, South Carolina, to the north of Tidal Shores, was too overdeveloped and noisy for them, and the Charleston area beaches to the south came with lodgings that were too pricey. Like the mama bear's bed in the Goldilocks' story, Tidal Shores was 'just right.'

The best way to reach the little beach was by taking a series of backroads, but the route had been imprinted on my brain while I was still buckled safely into my infant car seat. The long drive was actually enjoyable, once one left the city behind. The rolling hills of the Piedmont region were heavily forested with a mix of hardwoods and loblolly pines. Here the soil was clay. But halfway to the coast one crosses the 'fall' line, which cuts diagonal across the state. This imaginary line demarcates a drop in altitude, and the upland clay is replaced with the sandy soils of the coastal plain. With the slight drop in altitude, and the closer proximity to the Atlantic Ocean, the climate becomes warmer. An astute observer will notice that the vegetation is changing as well: the loblolly pines are gradually being replaced by longleaf pines, and as one gets within fifty miles of the sea, dwarf palms can be seen, sometimes by the hundreds, and often in areas of standing water. This region of South Carolina is appropriately called the Lowcountry.

For beach-loving families like mine, just crossing from the Piedmont region of the state, and into the Lowcountry, is enough to raise our spirits. Fond memories automatically come flooding back. For me, road trips, no matter how pleasant, always make me hungry. I'd read once that there was an evolutionary reason for this. According to the author, humans evolved to eat whenever food was available while on the move and away from a known food source, because there was no guarantee when our ancient ancestors would stumble upon new resources. Unfortunately for modern humans, we can carry huge amounts of snacks in our vehicle, and there are fast-food places, or petrol stations selling food, within an hour's drive of just about anywhere we choose to go.

On this particular day I stopped at a filling station in the city of Florence, South Carolina. Petrol was cheaper there than in Charlotte, so I topped off my tank, before going inside in search of something sweet. As I was perusing the racks of candy bars, I overheard a conversation between the clerk and a family that made my ears perk up. OK, call me an eavesdropper, but that's part of a good reporter's job.

'And she's a real, live mermaid too,' a girl of about eight said.
'Wow,' the clerk said. I could hear the boredom in his voice.
'She is real, but she's *not* alive,' an older girl said. 'She's – uh – Mama, what do you call it when they stuff you like that?'
'Mounted by a taxidermist,' the father said. 'And it was a pretty convincing job. I'm not one for believing in fairy tales, but I was able to talk to the fellow who found her – he's the sheriff, by the way – and he sounded awfully credible to me.'
'My husband is the sanest man you'll ever meet,' the wife said.
'No way!' the clerk said. He was just a kid in his late teens, but the sudden enthusiasm in his voice was intriguing.

I stepped quickly into view, my quest for a candy bar temporarily forgotten. 'Pardon me for interrupting,' I said. 'I saw that mermaid on TV last night, but in my opinion she didn't look like the stereotypical mermaid – from illustrations and figurines, I mean. Or from movies. The one that I saw on TV last night wasn't exactly pretty.'
'You're absolutely right, dear,' the wife said. 'I'd even go so far as to say that she looks like my mother-in-law on a good day. Like when she was much younger.'
'Honey,' the husband said with a groan, 'this woman is a complete stranger. Do we have to air our dirty laundry in public?'
'Mama and my grandma don't like each other,' the teenage girl said.
'Grandma calls Mama a golden digger,' the younger girl said.
'The word is "gold-digger,"' the father said. He turned to me, a pained expression on his face. 'The fact that this mermaid has a very unconventional appearance is one of the things that just might make me a believer. Any creature that evolved on a separate branch from Homo sapiens, to the extent that it retained a fish tail – well, one would expect there to be some incongruities with the human anatomy portion that this creature possesses.'
'My daddy is a smart man,' the little girl said proudly. 'He uses lots of big words. Sometimes he uses swear words.'
'Hush now, dear,' the mother said.
I couldn't help but smile. 'Please, sir,' I said to the father, 'could you elaborate on some of these incongruities?'
'Did you see her webbed fingers on TV?' the older girl said.
'You hush, too, Connie Sue,' the mother said.
The father put his hand gently on his wife's back. It seemed to me like he was telling *her* to hush as well.

'The mermaid,' he said to me, 'which they have named Miss Lucy, has arms that are proportionately too long to the torso – compared to a human, that is. Her cranium differs as well, as does her facial structure, but if I were to design a creature that evolved along a parallel track to Homo sapiens, it would probably resemble this Miss Lucy.'

'My husband is an anthropologist at the University of North Carolina in Charlotte,' the wife said.

'How very interesting,' I said. 'Sir, do you have a business card?'

'He's a professor, not a businessman,' his wife said.

'Honey, I *do* have professional cards.' He moved one from his wallet and handed it to me. 'Here, young lady. Are you interested in attending UNCC?'

'No, sir,' I said. 'Truth be told, I'm a reporter for *The Observer Today*, and I'm on my way now to do a story on this so-called mermaid.'

The woman grabbed her husband's arm with one hand and the younger girl with the other. 'Come on, dear,' she practically barked to her husband. 'You don't want this woman quoting you. The next thing you know, she'll have you on the *Dr Pat and Pal Show*, along with that thing! Now get that card back from her.'

'Nothing doing,' the professor said, but he allowed his wife to tug him out the door. Their teenage daughter shrugged and followed reluctantly.

'That woman is a real piece of work,' the clerk said.

'Yeah, I guess so,' I mumbled. Then to calm my nerves I selected two large bags of chocolate-covered peanuts. If I ate just one piece every mile, my chosen snacks might last until I pulled into Tidal Shores. My ELF diet be damned – well, just for that one day. My philosophy of life is: *moderatio omnibus et etiam moderatione*. That Latin phrase roughly translates as 'moderation in all things – including moderation.' In other words, it's OK to cut loose sometimes.

That said, I was five pieces of candy short before I even got within ten miles of the exit off Highway 17, and by then traffic was moving at a most uncharacteristic crawl. When I finally reached the two-mile-long road leading off the main highway, we'd come to a complete standstill. Folks in the South do not honk their horns in such situations. We either wait patiently for permission to move in *some* direction, or else for the Second Coming, whichever happens first. Today seemed to be the exception.

After waiting patiently for half an hour, like a good Southern girl should, I climbed out of my car and walked ahead to the car directly in front of mine. The elderly couple inside were singing along to Motown hits at the top of their lungs, as well as bouncing shamelessly around to the beat. At least they were polite enough to have their windows up, unlike some young men who insist on assaulting one's eardrums with the sound of their rap music and pounding bass. Thinking about the latter made me wonder if folks in the United Kingdom have to put up with such rude behaviour. At any rate, in the second car I came to, there sat a middle-aged trio of women, two in the front seat, and one in the back. All three of the women were busy scrolling through their phones, but all three also looked up when I approached. Thank heavens their windows were open, because I didn't relish the idea of tapping on glass to get anyone's attention.

'Good morning,' I said politely. 'How are y'all doing?'

'Burning daylight,' the front seat passenger said. She had a Deep South accent – possibly Charleston.

'Same here,' I said. 'This unexplained stoppage is really frustrating. Do you have any idea what's going on up ahead?'

'If you have to ask,' the driver of the car said, 'then you obviously haven't heard.'

'Heard what?'

'Dr Pat, from *Dr Pat and Pal*, are broadcasting this morning's show from Tidal Shores. Front and centre will be the mermaid.'

'Get out of town!' I said, feigning surprise.

The back-seat passenger laughed. 'So we did get out of town. We three are big mermaid fans – not that we think they're real, mind you – but we love the idea. So anyway, we're all three divorcees who used to vacation at Tidal Shores—'

'Before the pandemic,' the driver broke in, 'so we immediately called the one motel that we thought might still be in business, and we were able to get its last room. That's how fast other listeners thought to book rooms. As it is, we're all going to have to sleep in the same bed.'

'At least it's a king-size bed,' the front passenger said with a laugh.

'So then let me guess,' I said. 'All these cars are just people waiting to be let into town?'

They all three nodded glumly.

'Well, since y'all have a room already booked, why don't you just pull over more to the side of the road, turn off your engine, and walk into town? It's only two miles.'

'*Two* miles?' the back-seat passenger echoed, as if I'd suggested that she walk barefoot on broken glass. 'Young lady, haven't you noticed that it is mighty warm out today?'

'Yes, ma'am, it is, but it's not unseasonably hot, and it's possible that during the second mile you'll feel a soft ocean breeze.'

'But even so I might perspire. A *proper* Southern lady is only allowed to perspire in two places, and one is in her garden.'

'And the other place?' I asked, knowing the correct answer of course: in bed.

The proper Southern ladies laughed uproariously as I walked back to my car to turn off the engine and to grab my overnight bag. I certainly didn't intend to miss the taping of *Dr Pat and Pal*. And although I would have much preferred to stay at a motel, it wasn't necessary that I did, because I had an ace up my sleeve.

NINE

Business was so brisk at the Den of Antiquity that Miss Georgina Legare had hired two high-school seniors to help her. Both were male, and both were the sons of Sheriff Ryker Saunders and his wife, Willow Davenport Saunders. The boys weren't twins; they were in the same grade because Wade was a little thicker than his brother Wyatt – in all respects.

I'd been in the Den of Antiquity more times than I could count, but I had never seen it anywhere near this busy. The double doors to the shop had been blocked open, and there were three long tables in front of the store, piled high with merchandise. Customers filled the shop and crowded the tables. The two bags of chocolate-covered peanuts had yet to add any weight to my somewhat slim frame, thus I was able to thread my way to a table that sold dolls. *Mermaid* dolls!

The mermaid dolls came in various sizes, from six inches to three feet in length. But the remarkable thing was that these were not pretty dolls; the mermaid that they represented was not a Disney character, or an artist's fanciful vision of a mermaid with a glitzy tail. These dolls looked just like the poor creature that Mama and I had seen on television the evening before. This mermaid wasn't exactly ugly, but she was . . . more than a mite unattractive. She was ugly as far as mermaids went. If Daddy had been alive, he'd have described her as being 'as ugly as homemade sin.'

Why on earth would anyone want to buy such an unattractive doll? *Unless* the person who purchased the doll believed that her image represented an *actual* being, and not the figment of someone's imagination! If that was true, and judging by the number of dolls that were constantly being snatched from the tables, and the 'traffic jam' at the open doors, these customers all had to be believers. Or, at the very least, these people were immensely intrigued by what they had seen.

Now, I'd been raised to be courteous. I'd been taught never to shove another person, but it seemed to me that the only way I could gain access into the Den of Antiquity in a timely manner was to give a couple of folks an elbow to the ribs. As I stood contemplating such a barbaric move, I thought that I heard a giant bullfrog croak my name. Either that, I reasoned, or else I was suffering from delusions brought on by heatstroke as a result of my two-mile hike.

'Baby Child!' the frog croaked again, drawing nearer. 'Come give your old great-granny a hug.'

I tried peering between, and around, a well-fed couple whose fluffy body parts made the voice identification extremely challenging. I thought of jumping in place, since I'd been a fairly good basketball player in college, but in such close quarters I ran the risk of landing on someone's toes. Finally, when I was frustrated to the point of not caring any more about my deportment (although elbowing was still off the table), I ever so gently touched the fluffy woman's back.

'Spider,' I said loudly. 'There's a giant spider on your back.'

The large woman screamed and bulldozed her way through the crowd, which parted like the Red Sea. Instead of Moses standing high and dry on the other side, I beheld my great-grandmother, the formidable Miss Georgina Legare.

'Baby Child,' Miss Georgina Legare said, 'come give your Gan-Gan a hug.' Georgina Legare had always insisted that her great-granddaughter call her what Princes William and Harry had called their great-grandmother, the Queen Mother.

'But I'm all wet, Gan-Gan,' I said. 'I'm afraid that I've been perspiring like a football player in August who's been wearing his full gear. You see, I had to walk two miles just to get into town, because traffic is totally stopped out there.'

'Let's dispense with the hug then, shall we, dear? That traffic problem is all because Billy-Bob Henderson doesn't have the brains God gave a tadpole. It turns out that the community centre is far too small of a venue in which to tape a segment of the *Dr Pat and Pal Show*. And the parking lot only holds thirty cars.'

I frowned. 'So all those folks in their stopped cars are waiting futilely for something they'll never get to see?'

Before my great-grandmother could answer, a woman with a strong Yankee accent thrust a large mermaid doll between us. Strictly speaking, this item was more akin to a body pillow than a doll, and if the face on it hadn't been quite so unsettling, I might have been tempted to buy it myself – at a family discount, of course.

'How much for this?' the woman demanded.

'There is a price tag on it,' my gan-gan said. 'Whatever the tag says.'

'Maybe,' the woman said, 'but I don't have time to hunt for no tag. I don't want to miss the show. My husband is holding my seat, but he's a pushover, and just might give my seat away to a pretty blonde. So just tell me how much.'

'Your husband may be a pushover,' my gan-gan snapped, 'but I ain't. So look for the tag yourself, or else put that pillow back where you got it.'

'Lady, you just lost a sale,' the rude customer said, and inexplicably tried to make me take it.

I crossed my arms. '*I* don't want it,' I said.

'All right, all right, I'll tell you,' Gan-Gan said, sounding much aggrieved. 'It was originally a hundred and seventy-five dollars, but I'll let you have it for a hundred and fifty.'

'That's better,' the contentious customer said, and while managing to hold the mermaid body pillow, she fished a credit card out of a tan-coloured leather shoulder bag. 'I don't suppose I can have this gift-wrapped?' she said, when she was done paying for it.

'I'll have my team get right on it,' Gan-Gan said, 'just as soon as they finish gift-wrapping your car.'

'In that case I'm returning this pillow.'

'Sorry,' Gan-Gan said. 'You see those signs? They are on all three tables. This merchandise is on clearance, so no returns are accepted.'

'I could s-sue you,' hissed the angry woman.

'Please do,' my gan-gan said calmly. 'I welcome the publicity.'

As the enraged woman stalked off, I shook my head. 'Gan-Gan, I don't know why you even bothered to sell to that woman. She has the manners of a rattlesnake.'

'Don't be so charitable, Baby Child. Rattlesnakes usually warn one by shaking their rattles before they strike. That woman was in our faces from the get-go. But let's put that behind us, shall we? I need to call Billy-Bob and get him to open the church for the *Dr Pat and Pal* taping. The church has a huge parking lot, at least three times bigger than the one at the community centre. Also, Sheriff Ryker needs to solve the traffic problem. When the church parking lot fills up, he can always have his deputies direct cars to park on side streets, or even just close off the town altogether.'

'You mean like have an officer posted by the highway?'

'Exactly. Now if you'll excuse me, Baby Child, I have some phone calls to make.'

Baby Child! I was the youngest of my great-grandmother Georgina Legare's descendants, and she was my oldest living ancestor. We were not exactly a prolific family, so until I reproduced – or she passed – I was stuck with that nickname. Nobody knows for sure how old Gan-Gan is, although most of us dismiss the rumour that she dated two of the three Magi in the Christmas story, simultaneously, and then broke up with them when she learned that their gifts were not meant for her.

But while she may be ancient, Gan-Gan is still a mover and a shaker in her native Tidal Shores. In less time than it takes to cook a pot of grits from scratch (about an hour), she had both Reverend Billy-Bob Henderson and Sheriff Ryker Saunders on board with her plan. Within another hour I found myself sitting in the front row of the Tidal Shores Community Church between my great-grandmother (who smelled like perspiration and lavender soap) and a very handsome man, who Gan-Gan introduced to me as the taxidermist (who smelled just plain heavenly).

The church's pulpit, which was on castors, had been wheeled aside to allow everyone in the building an unfettered view of the stage. Now occupying most of the stage was the largest sofa that I had ever seen. The blue leather monstrosity must have required at least six average men, or four strong women, to carry it into the building and place it on the stage. Tucked into the right corner of the sofa was the diminutive Dr Pat.

I'd heard that the camera adds ten pounds, but I'd never heard that it added ten inches in height. Surely the show used camera tricks to make its host look larger, because Dr Pat, who I always assumed was a strapping six feet tall, could hardly be more than five feet. I guess it helped with the illusion that his sidekick, the Deli Llama, was also a tiny man. Or was the wise-cracking llama really a man? Those were remarkably wide hips under the llama suit and orange robe. At any rate, this being was seated on the far-left end of the world's longest sofa.

After both celebrities had been acknowledged with an interminable length of applause, a large object, about the size of an American refrigerator, was wheeled out on to the stage and placed in front of the sofa, halfway between them. This object, by the way, was draped in a heavy black cloth.

'My, my, what have we here?' Dr Pat said, as he rose to his feet.

'Maybe it's a vending machine,' a seemingly clueless boy said – although perhaps he wasn't clueless, but merely hungry. After all, it was mid-afternoon by then, and he might well have had to miss lunch.

Dr Pat was not in the least annoyed by the silly answer. 'Does anyone else care to guess?' he asked with a smile.

A very stern-looking woman, who wore her long hair swept atop her hair and held aloft with a million bobby pins, waved her arm wildly.

'Yes, ma'am?' Dr Pat said.

'Is it the truth-telling booth that you had on your show when you were in Atlanta?'

'Good guess. However, it is not. But boy howdy, I wish it was, because the truth is exactly what I came down here for today. So, thank you, ma'am, for starting our show off right.'

The stern woman was suddenly all smiles, which made me wonder if she was a plant. The Deli Llama nodded in approval. Lacking hands, he clapped his two front hooves together, which in turn got the entire audience applauding – well, everyone except Gan-Gan and me. Neither of us is easily swayed by the sentiment of the masses, or the clacking together of plastic animal feet.

Dr Pat was a master showman. It was like he had a clap-o-meter implanted inside his brain. He waited until the nanosecond the applause became less intense before he whisked off the black cloth that covered the mysterious object on the stage. The crowd gasped, just as he had intended it to, even if there had been nothing inside this box.

But, of course, there was.

TEN

The Tidal Shores Community Church was devoid of any fancy furnishings. Instead of wooden pews, worshippers sat on plastic chairs, which could be arranged in different configurations depending on the number of attendees and the purpose of each service. There were no stained-glass windows to distract one from the all-important sermons delivered by their carefully selected ministers. A simple wooden cross, 'three-quarters life-size,' stood at the back of the sanctuary. It was flanked by two enormous screens upon which the words of the hymns and responsive readings, if any, were projected. Seating for the choir was divided equally between stalls that flanked the sanctuary.

When the heavy black cloth was pulled off the refrigerator-size box on the stage, those audience members looking up at the screens had perhaps the best view of what the container held. However, from my seat in the front row, I had a mighty fine close-up view of the mermaid dubbed Miss Lucy. I will admit that for a while my eyes darted from the real thing to the projected image, until finally they settled on the screens, because on them I could see the details better.

'That is really cool,' I heard myself say aloud, to no one in particular.

But the handsome taxidermist heard me, despite the various exclamations erupting from the audience. He leaned in, flooding me with his scented pheromones. How much older than me was he? I wondered. And was it too much of a difference to prevent us from hooking up? I'd have to ask Gan-Gan later.

'Thank you for the compliment,' Gunner Jones said.

'She looks so lifelike,' I said above the muttering of the crowd. 'Whatever that thing is – well, someone here was certainly creative.'

Despite her advanced age, my gan-gan has the hearing of a wax moth, which has the best hearing in the animal kingdom. 'You have no idea how creative *some* people were,' Gan-Gan said, trying to whisper. Unfortunately, when one has a voice that sounds like a cross between a foghorn and a whoopee cushion, it's hard not to be overheard.

A second later Dr Pat shoved a microphone in Gan-Gan's face. 'Say it again, dear woman. Repeat for this assembled throng exactly what I overheard you say to this beautiful young woman sitting beside you.'

Gan-Gan pushed the microphone back until it was literally pressed against Dr Pat's nose. 'I have nothing to say, you charlatan.'

Dr Pat took a step back as he rubbed his schnoz with a child-size hand. 'Well! And here I thought that you Southerners were supposed to be so polite.'

'We can be,' I said. 'I mean that we usually are polite – unless someone treats us badly first.'

'Aha,' Dr Pat said triumphantly, 'so you admit that you don't turn the other cheek like Jesus instructed us to do.'

'No, sir,' I said. 'Sometimes, I do turn the other cheek. But bear in mind that God created each of us with four cheeks.'

Dr Pat took a step back. 'Ooh, I do believe we have a live one here.'

Gan-Gan heaved her tired old bones to her feet with a loud grunt. 'Darling,' she said to Dr Pat, 'you leave my great-granddaughter alone, before I slap the silly off your face.'

The crowd cheered and stamped their feet. Sure, they'd come to see the mermaid, but they'd also been hoping that Dr Pat would turn the mermaid's world debut into a show, and he was starting to deliver the goods for them.

Dr Pat chortled with delight. 'Ha. How refreshing, people, to see this dried-up old crone stand up and defend this nubile, voluptuous young temptress who is practically writhing in her seat with desire for the virile older man who so skilfully preserved the sad remains of the world's first documented individual specimen of *Homo oceanica*.'

Gan-Gan balled her liver-spotted hands into fists. 'Put up your dukes, you bilious bag of horse poop. How dare you call my Baby Child a Nubian! She was born at Presbyterian Hospital in Charlotte, North Carolina, so she's as American as you are!'

'Quiet, Gan-Gan,' I hissed without any 's'es, which is a trick that only *New York Times* bestselling authors and some centenarians can pull off. 'Getting a reaction from guests and audience members is exactly what this charlatan wants. That's what his show is about.'

Apparently, the Deli Llama had a keen sense of hearing as well.

He, or she – not that it mattered to me in the least – wagged a plastic hoof in my direction.

'We're also about selling our special herbs and spices, which are sourced from the Holy Land. We have a wide range of sauces and condiments from there as well. Our Dead Sea sesame salad dressing is to die for.'

'Oh, come on,' Gunner Jones said, as he hopped to his feet. 'This is ridiculous. Where's Sheriff Ryker Saunders? He's supposed to be on the show. After Reverend Billy-Bob found the mermaid, he immediately contacted the sheriff. And I'm the taxidermist who restored the poor thing – I mean *her* – to her former glory.'

The audience roared with laughter and stamped their feet again.

That was too much for Gunner Jones, who leaped gracefully up on to the stage, when he could have used the steps, and strode over to Dr Pat. Gunner Jones towered over the quack whose only doctorate was in American literature. What's more, Gunner Jones looked like the only sane person on the stage.

Dr Pat had the temerity to act as if he was totally unfazed by Gunner's action. He calmly extended his hand, and both men shook. To a sceptic, such as myself, it might even have appeared as if this interaction had all been planned.

'What the hell is going on?' I whispered to Gan-Gan.

'Shush,' she said, with definite 's'es.

Dr Pat had directed Gunner Jones to sit next to him on the gigantic sofa. The creepy Deli Llama kept to the other end. The fact that the confrontational taxidermist obediently sat so quickly, and without protest, seemed a mite choreographed to me. Then again, jumping to conclusions and running off at the mouth are just about the only two forms of exercise that I get.

Dr Pat smiled broadly at the packed church, revealing veneers that were blindingly white, and all the same size. The man had spent a fortune on his mouth, even though he'd received less than quality work. As if on cue, the Deli Llama smiled as well. However, take it from me, any member of the camel family, no matter how distantly related, is incapable of producing anything but a lecherous leer with its mouth. Then again, my judgement is based on a latex costume, and not the actual beast referenced.

'My, my, my,' Dr Pat said, 'if this isn't the best-looking bunch of people that I've seen gathered under one roof, then my name isn't Dr Pat.' He waited until the assemblage stopped cheering for themselves. 'Today I am pleased to welcome on the show this very attractive gentleman, mortician Gunner Jones.'

This time Gunner Jones waited for the applause to die. 'Actually, Pat,' he said, 'I'm not a mortician, I'm a taxidermist.'

Dr Pat frowned. 'Well, first of all, Gunner, it's *Doctor* Pat, not just Pat, and secondly, if you are not a mortician, what made you qualified to embalm this rare specimen of *Homo oceanica*? Do you not consider her top half to be human?'

The crowd murmured. When a packed church, with standing room only, carries on like that, it causes a lily-livered wuss like me to glance around for the exit signs. *Be Prepared and Carry On* is another one of my mottoes. I should probably try and protect that one with a trademark as well, before the Kardashians get to it.

Gunner sat even straighter in his chair and squared his broad shoulders. 'Well, Reverend—'

'That's Doctor,' the show's host snapped.

'I'm sure it is. Well, as I was about to say, it was immediately obvious to me, given Miss Lucy's bottom half, her fish tail, that the family *Homo oceanica* had split from that of ours, *Homo sapiens*, millions of years even before we and the great apes split from a common ancestor.'

'Are you saying that you believe in *evolution*?' Dr Pat asked in mock alarm. '*Here?* In a church?'

'What I'm saying—'

'Boo!' the crowd roared. 'Boo! Evolution is a lie!'

Gunner Jones stood and cupped his hands to his mouth. Then, rethinking that move, he turned, bent, and unclipped the microphone from Dr Pat's collar and clipped it to his own. When he straightened to face his antagonists, he looked like a Greek god. I mean that metaphorically, of course.

'People!' he shouted. 'I'm not up here to defend evolution. What I want to make clear, as someone who has degrees in both biology *and* anthropology, is that Miss Lucy here is both part fish and part mammal. I was merely presenting you with a hypothetical reason for her existence.

'Now, I am also a trained taxidermist, and as such, was called upon to preserve her before decomposition could set in. Based on my knowledge of vertebrate anatomy, I can only conclude that this marvellous creature that we have before us is what history has referred to – over and over again – as a mermaid.

'Forget the image in your mind from fairy tales, cartoons, Disney World, or the movie *Splash*. Go back and read the literature, the actual journals and accounts of sailors over the centuries. Some of the mermaids that they described were not all that beautiful. I'm sure you've heard the stories about the sailors who, when they first encountered manatees nursing their young, supposed them to be mermaids. Well, let me tell you something, either those sailors were blind as bats, or else their idea of what mermaids were like differed quite a bit from ours.'

No sooner had Gunner Jones unclipped the microphone from his collar than a pudgy man with wire-rimmed glasses clambered up the steps at the side of the platform and grabbed the device out of his hand. The audience held its collective breath. It took me a minute, but I recognized the interloper as Reverend Billy-Bob Henderson, Tidal Shores Community Church's pastor.

It was time for the real show to begin.

ELEVEN

'Good afternoon, ladies and gentlemen,' Reverend Billy-Bob drawled. 'Welcome to Tidal Shores Community Church. I'm the pastor, so I thought we'd take a step back, bow our heads, and have a word of prayer.'

'Boo!' That ugly response, or something worse, was uttered by at least three people. I couldn't believe my ears. According to Pew Research, forty-seven percent of South Carolinians and thirty-nine percent of North Carolinians attend church once a week. We're not heathens, like the Brits, who have a miserable five percent rate of forcing their butts into their pews – bless their god-forsaken hearts. Having said all that, a Carolinian of any stripe is always up for 'a word of prayer,' even if she knows it's going to be as boring as waiting for water to boil on an unlit stove. Prayer is the warp and weft of our life.

Reverend Billy-Bob Henderson was taken aback by the ugly response to his opening statement, and rightly so. Although I felt sorry for him, at the same time I must confess that I felt relieved. I'd heard him pray before, and a simple blessing over some food often segued into pleas for the Lord to heal Sister So-and-So's lymphoma, Brother Andy's gout, and fairly broad hints that parishioners should drop more money than they already did into the offering plates when they were passed around.

Well, it was still Reverend Billy-Bob Henderson's church, and even though this was supposed to be the *Dr Pat and Pal Show*, the good preacher was not about to be shut out of the action. After all, up on that stage is where he was the star every Sunday. He was not some charlatan with a furry friend sidekick that minced about on plastic hooves.

'Folks,' he said in a commanding voice. 'Listen up! I am here to tell you that this mermaid, Miss Lucy, as we in Tidal Shores have named her, is the genuine article. And I say that as an ordained minister, a man of God.'

The crowd murmured. Some people laughed, sarcastically to be sure, but that was to be expected. A few people quickly got up and left, but just as quickly others pushed their way into the building and filled their empty seats. However, on the whole, the assemblage appeared receptive to what Reverend Billy-Bob Henderson had said thus far.

'Now, some of you might be wondering why mermaids were never mentioned in the Bible,' Reverend Billy-Bob said. 'Well, if you are familiar with John 21:25, then you know it says that Jesus did so many things that if they were all written down, the entire earth could not contain all the books that they'd fill. So, you can infer from this verse that there are thousands of other details that the Bible didn't have room to include.'

'Preach it!' Dr Pat shouted from his seat on his super-size couch.

Reverend Billy-Bob turned. 'Say what?'

'You're on a roll,' Dr Pat said. 'Go for it.'

'Speaking of rolls,' the Deli Llama said, 'I recommend the pastrami today. On the other hand, nothing beats a good hard Italian salami.' He patted his necklace suggestively.

Reverend Billy-Bob frowned and plunged on. 'Some of you might be wondering how mermaids survived the Great Flood, when Noah built his ark. Water covered the earth so deep then that even Mt Everest was fully submerged. Perhaps you might be thinking that wasn't a problem, because mermaids are water-dwelling creatures who could swim until the waters receded. But let me dissuade you of that notion right now. Mermaids are semi-terrestrial. Contrary to mythology, and Hollywood, they do not possess gills. Later on, this afternoon, you are more than welcome to come up, in an orderly line, and take a closer look at Miss Lucy in person, to see for yourself that she does not possess these aquatic adaptations.

'But as I was about to say, mermaids need to rest periodically on a rock or a beach, or they will get too tired and drown. That, my friends, is what we surmise happened to Miss Lucy during our most recent storm. At any rate, unless Noah built saltwater tanks on the ark – which I highly doubt – he must have built shelves, or benches along the outside of the ark upon which the merfolk could perch and rest from time to time.

'And before any of you make up your minds about whether or not mermaids – and mermen – actually exist, I suggest that you consider the damage that a negative decision might do to their souls – nay, to their very salvation, by denying their existence. Consider this: Miss Lucy washed up on *our* shores, so that we who are a community of like-minded believers would be given this opportunity to witness to her fellow – uh – species. I mean, what if she had, perchance, washed up on the coast of Maine? Or Kansas?'

Dr Pat cleared his throat loudly, and the Deli Llama clicked his plastic front hooves together vigorously. Reverend Billy-Bob reluctantly glanced behind him.

'Kansas doesn't have a coast,' Dr Pat said. 'Perhaps you meant to say Connecticut. It has a coast.'

'A sharp mustard pairs well with many luncheon meats,' the Deli Llama said.

Reverend Billy-Bob plunged on even louder than before. 'We shouldn't be wasting our time talking about coasts and condiments. We have much more important issues to discuss. For instance, if a mermaid converts to Christianity and dies, does only the top half of her go to Heaven, and the fish half stays in the ocean?'

There were a few belly laughs from the crowd, which served to make Reverend Billy-Bob livid. 'I'm being serious!' he shouted so loud that his microphone squealed.

'Or, what if a converted mermaid wanted to marry one of us *homo* – well, you know – regular people? In the bonds of Christian marriage?'

'That's bestiality! That is clearly forbidden in the Holy Bible.'

I recognized the interrupter immediately as Sheriff Ryker Saunders.

'Aha, everyone,' said Reverend Billy-Bob, completely unfazed, 'this is the very man who discovered the less-than-lovely Miss Lucy bobbing in the waves here at Tidal Shores. Come up here, Sheriff Saunders, and join in the conversation.'

Sheriff Ryker Saunders, like the majority of Americans, had extra padding on his bones, so he had to use the stairs to get up on to the stage. Even then, he was huffing and puffing enough to have scared the three little pigs, when they still lived in their straw house.

'You're always quoting the Good Book, Reverend,' Sheriff Ryker Saunders finally gasped, 'so you know that it clearly says in Leviticus 18:23 that we are forbidden to have sex with animals.'

Reverend Billy-Bob Henderson clapped his hands to his cheeks in mock horror. 'Heavens to Betsy, Sheriff Ryker, I would never suggest such an abomination! What do you take me for? A Yankee Democrat? An Episcopalian? It was a theoretical question. Could the *homo* half of a merperson marry a *homo sapiens*? These are the type of ecclesiastical questions that are going to arise, and sooner rather than later. But of course, even before they can be addressed definitely, merfolk will have to clear all the legal hurdles.'

'Bravo, bravo!' Dr Pat said, rising to his feet.

The Deli Llama struggled to stand on his, or her, lower set of plastic hooves. 'Eat more cheese!' he, or she, said.

'Great discourse, you two,' Dr Pat said. He was beaming. 'Come and join us on the couch. Not you, Reverend, I mean the sheriff. You've already spoken your peace, so you're free to join my audience.'

Reverend Billy-Bob Henderson scowled, but he tottered off the stage. Unfortunately, he had not thought to save a seat for himself, which meant that the only available space was Gunner Jones' vacated space. Whereas Gunner had given off pheromones that sang of his virility and sexual availability, the good preacher smelled of overworked antiperspirant, and a suit that had been abused by dry-cleaning chemicals way too many times.

'Change places with me, Gan-Gan,' I whispered urgently.

'Nonsense, Baby Child. Maybe if you sit next to a man of God, a little of the Divine will rub off on you.'

'If it works like that, then we should *definitely* trade places; by the looks of you, you'll be meeting the Divine any day now.'

Gan-Gan had the nerve to pinch me between my armpit and bra band. She pinched *hard*. I couldn't repress a yelp, but I ducked low in my seat immediately following it.

Reverend Billy-Bob didn't miss a beat. 'Your great-granny's a hoot,' he said, as he patted my knee.

In the meantime, Gunner Jones had scooted down to sit next to the Deli Llama, who now had one furry arm draped around the taxidermist's neck as if they were good buddies. (Poor Gunner eyed the plastic hoof next to his face warily.) This forced the sheriff to sit next to Dr Pat, or else the crate containing Miss Lucy would block his view of half the audience – or more importantly their view of him. From his body language I got the distinct impression that Sheriff Ryker Saunders would have much preferred to lean into the ludicrous llama than engage directly with the wily spin doctor himself.

'Now, Sheriff, darling,' said Dr Pat, 'tell us exactly how you came upon this lovely maiden' – he paused for laughs, which he got in spades – 'and what first went through your mind.'

'First of all,' Sheriff Ryker Saunders said, 'don't call me "darling."'

Dr Pat threw up his hands in a gesture of mock surrender. 'Oh my, aren't we touchy today! But duly noted, sir. Now carry on, Captain, if you please.'

That earned Dr Pat more laughs.

'Don't eat fish,' the Deli Llama said, 'because a fish could be a mermaid's daddy.'

Gunner Jones shrugged off the Llama's furry arm. 'Actually, that's not possible,' he said irritably. 'They're not only different species, but they also belong to different families in the animal kingdom. Just like you couldn't very well be a chicken's daddy.'

Dr Pat chuckled. 'The truth is that this llama couldn't even be a llama's daddy.'

The crowd roared.

'But you can't beat my meat,' the llama said. As he spoke, he removed his sausage necklace, and then quickly slipped it over Gunner Jones' head. The taxidermist didn't bother to mask the disgust he felt by the indignity visited upon him by Dr Pat's sidekick. However, as a proper Southern gentleman, and guest of the show, he remained seated, but only because he had not been officially dismissed.

I wish that I could say that the faithful fans of merfolk were too chaste to pick up on the innuendo uttered by the weirdo in the camelid costume, but I was wrong. A dozen or so of the more conservative members of the audience – mostly women – got up abruptly and left. However, the majority of those present applauded loudly, and for such a long time that the lascivious llama stood and took a bow. I'm not at all a prude, but I found him and his fans downright appalling. In fact, I was halfway out of my seat as well, when I felt the vicelike grip of Gan-Gan on my arm.

'Stay!'

I did as I was told, but only because I was too tired to drive back to Charlotte that night, and Gan-Gan's guest room was where I planned to lay my head. Besides, I do believe in free speech, even if it is in poor taste.

Eventually Dr Pat motioned for the crowd to settle down. The way that he waved his hands, it looked as if he was patting two dogs on their heads, but folks knew what he meant because they shut up soon after that.

'OK, Sheriff Saunders, now that we've all had a few chuckles, I really would like to hear about the day that you discovered Miss Lucy, as y'all have decided to call her.'

Sheriff Ryker Saunders squirmed and fiddled with his badge before answering. 'Well, it was the day after Hurricane Ian had officially passed through, but we were still getting some unusually rough surf, with reports of some beach erosion. I'd been up all night tending to minor emergencies in town – garbage cans not secured, pets left outside, that kind of thing – but by first light I was finally free to head down to the beach to see what was what. That's when I saw what I thought was the body of a woman bobbing in the water. A dead body. A floater. A corpse. About a hundred yards out.'

The once unruly bunch in Reverend Billy-Bob's church were now so quiet that someone in the back row could have heard a mouse fart in the choir loft. Even though they could all probably have guessed the rest of the sheriff's story, I knew from experience as a reporter that a floating corpse is a sure-fire attention-grabber. The narrative was now his to lose.

TWELVE

Sheriff Ryker Saunders took a deep, dramatic breath. The man was acting; I was sure of it. We were all being conned, and my gan-gan was in on it. Well, good for Tidal Shores. If this little scheme worked to bring back the business that they'd lost because of the pandemic, I was happy for them. But they were naïve if they thought that this gimmick was going to be more than a flash in the pan. To quote Abraham Lincoln: 'You can fool all the people some of the time and some of the people all the time, but you cannot fool all the people all the time.' At some point this scheme was going to unravel.

'Well!' the sheriff said with an explosion of air that made Dr Pat lean away. 'I waded out into the pounding surf and grabbed that young lady – I mean that mermaid – by the hair and pulled her into shore. It was only when I got back to shallow water that I noticed her tail. At first, I thought that a fish had gotten a hold of her, and I started punching it with my fists, and then I saw that it weren't no fish.

'I said to myself, "What the hell, Ryker, this thing is either one of them damn fairy-tale mermaids like was in your daughter's toy box when she was growing up, or else she's the real thing."'

Dr Pat applauded, as did the ridiculous furry thing on the other end of the sofa. 'Go on, go on,' Dr Pat said. 'This is just too exciting. What do you think, Deli Llama?'

'I think I just wet myself,' he, or she, said.

'Then please excuse yourself.'

'Excuse me,' the Deli Llama said. They (as I shall now refer to them) stood carefully, crossed their legs, and hopped off the stage, including down the steps. They managed the steps so expertly, with their hooves crossed, that I was led to believe that either the person in the suit might really have lived in the high Andes mountains, or else 'accidents' were a common occurrence on the *Dr Pat and Pal Show*.

'Now, where were we?' Dr Pat asked with a coy, but well-practised smile.

The Mermaid Mystery

'Your ridiculous co-host just soiled my end of the sofa,' Gunner Jones said.

'Tsk, tsk, handsome,' Dr Pat said. 'Let's not be calling anyone names.'

'I was telling y'all how I fished Miss Lucy out of the roiling surf,' Sheriff Ryker Saunders growled.

'*Roiling?*' Dr Pat said. 'My, what a fancy word for someone of your ilk. But do continue.'

'Well anyway, as soon as I realized that the fish in question was Miss Lucy's tail, and not another fish chomping down on her, I whipped out my phone and called Gunner. I keep my phone in my breast pocket, so it wasn't wet. And when I say breast, by the way, I don't mean titty, but my chest, on account of I'm all man. But Miss Lucy here – well, you can see that she *does* have titties, even though they're small ones, and that's how come I knew that she was a mermaid, and not a merman with long hippy hair.'

Dr Pat giggled. 'Itty bitty titties. May I ask why no one has thought to put a top on her? At least a brassiere of some sort, if not an itty-bitty polka-dot bikini?'

'Why on earth would we do that?' Gunner Jones thundered. I found the man to be incredibly sexy when he was angry, which probably didn't say much about my emotional health.

Dr Pat recoiled as if he'd been slapped. 'Well, darling, what about the innocence of children? Surely you don't advocate perverting the malleable minds of our youngest members of society.'

'Now hold it right there,' Reverend Billy-Bob Henderson said. 'Ain't you putting the cart before the horses, Doctor? First the government needs to decide if Miss Lucy has the rights of an animal, or those of a person. If the Supreme Court decides that she's just an animal, then ain't no need to put no bra on her no how, because my dog, Francis, has her two rows of titties, now that she done have pups, and they're a sight bigger'n Miss Lucy's, and by law Francis don't need to wear no bra. There ain't nobody in this blessed world that can tell me that my hound dog needs to wear no brassiere. And that is final. Heck, half the men in here have bigger titties than Miss Lucy, and they don't wear no bras when they go to the beach.'

The crowd went crazy. Even though there were undoubtedly some folks in the church who were offended by the sight of Miss Lucy's bare mammary glands, there is nothing a true Southerner loves better than his dog – well, after his gun, and his family, and God, of course. Not necessarily in that order. Just sometimes. Plus, no one could argue with the fact that many of the men present were better endowed than the uninspiring mermaid.

In order to get the people to settle down, a stagehand of Dr Pat's had to vault up the steps and wave a red flag. That took a few minutes, and while it was happening, Gan-Gan leaned into me.

'You should see Billy-Bob without his shirt. It's plum indecent.'

'No thanks,' I said.

When at last he was able to get most everyone's attention, Dr Pat directed his attention to Gunner Jones.

'In your esteemed opinion,' Dr Pat said snidely, 'if the matter does eventually reach the United States Supreme Court, and if they should decide that merfolk are merely another species of animal – like cats, or dogs, like the good preacher's dog, Fanny—'

'That's *Francis*,' Reverend Billy-Bob snarled.

'Yes, whatever,' Dr Pat said. 'My question to you, Mr Jones, is do you think that it would be ethical for us humans to keep them as pets? Personally, I think it would be lovely to have an enormous saltwater aquarium installed in my living room, and stock it with a couple of these creatures. Of both genders, of course, as I don't believe in discrimination.'

Gunner Jones reached over Reverend Billy-Bob's considerable and righteous presence to shake a finger in Dr Pat's face. From the expression on Gunner's once handsome face I could tell that he would rather punch the charlatan than wag his index finger at him.

'Absolutely not,' Gunner Jones snarled. 'How would you like it if your children were kept as pets?'

Dr Pat giggled. 'I don't have any children, but I certainly wouldn't mind if my sister kept her kids in a giant saltwater tank.'

The audience gasped, and Dr Pat, sensing that he had gone too far, clasped his hands to his suddenly reddened cheeks. The cameras abruptly panned away from him.

'*People*,' he said, in his best Oprah imitation, 'that was a joke. I love the little no-neck rug-rats. I mean, Derrick, Michele, and what's-her-name. Now, if you'll look under your seats you'll each find a key for a brand-new Tesla.' He giggled again, but was soon brought up short when nearly a hundred quite gullible people started groping beneath their plastic chairs.

Gunner, bless his heart, came to the foolish man's rescue. 'That was another lame joke!' he shouted into his mic. Even then, not everyone turned around, and a goodly number got up and headed for the door.

Dr Pat shouted as well. 'Sex! Sex! Mermaid sex! That's what we're discussing next!'

After that announcement very few people, if any, made it through the door. My attention was certainly redirected back to the stage – and no, I did not find a key.

'What about mermaid *sex*?' Reverend Billy-Bob Henderson asked. 'Why would they even have sex?'

It sounded like it had never occurred to him that these creatures, even if they existed, procreated in some fashion, as did every other animal – and I do mean that term to include human beings. In my relatively short life as a reporter, I have come across people who have never given much thought about a cat or a dog having four limbs, a brain, liver, heart, kidneys, muscles, and blood, like we, their owners, do.

Gunner Jones sighed as he patted the preacher's knee. 'Billy-Bob, nothing on God's green earth, or in His deep blue sea, lives forever. Merfolk need to engage in the sexual act so that merbabies can be born.'

'Yes, but where exactly do the merbabies come from? I mean, I see Miss Lucy, right here in person on the stage – and up there on the giant screen – and I don't see any, well, you-know-what.'

The audience tittered.

Gunner Jones leaned far to his right to give Reverend Billy-Bob Henderson a playful tap on his shoulder with his fist. 'You mean a Mermaid hoo-ha, don't you?'

Reverend Billy-Bob coloured deeply. 'I suppose that's one way to put it.'

'Another way to put it would be vagina,' Gunner Jones said. 'But you're right, Billy-Bob, you can't see something that isn't there. If you were to view her from behind, you might see what is called a "cloaca." It's an all-purpose opening.'

Dr Pat shuddered dramatically. 'Ooh. Gross.'

'Chickens have a cloaca,' Gunner Jones said. 'That's where your breakfast eggs come from.'

'Speak for yourself,' Dr Pat said. '*Mine* come from the supermarket.' When almost no one laughed, he continued. 'Does this mean that mermen have ding-dongs?'

Gunner Jones shook his head in exasperation. '*Really*, Dr Pat? Are you asking if mermen have chocolate snack cakes for penises, or that they somehow manage to live forever, and that they don't need to reproduce? Because if it's the second option, your answer is right here on the stage.'

Dr Pat looked out at us audience members, desperately trying to gauge our mood. It was clear to me that he had not counted on having such a handsome, charismatic man going head-to-head with him. Privately, I would refer to Gunner as a stud muffin.

'Stop hitting on him in your mind,' Gan-Gan said.

'How can you read my mind?' I wailed.

Gan-Gan snorted. 'Small print is my speciality.'

Meanwhile, Dr Pat said nothing. This was a perfect opportunity for Reverend Billy-Bob Henderson to jump back into the conversation.

'For your information, ladies and gentlemen, nothing and no one lives forever. That is why y'all need to give your lives to the Lord right now. Jesus could return at any moment, and then where would you be, Dr Pat?'

'Right here,' the TV host said smugly, 'on this very expensive, not to mention expansive, sofa.'

Sad to say, that comment actually got a number of laughs, and not one negative reaction. I found that surprising, because a real belief in mermaids does contradict the Biblical story of creation, and deep down we Southerners are deeply religious. So far, I was under the impression that this mermaid craze was a fun fantasy, a way for adults to recover moments from their childhood, but not something to be taken seriously. However, the rapture was an important article of faith for many members of the audience, and I found the fact that they did not seem to be offended by Dr Pat's offhand remark rather troubling.

'What the heck is going on?' I said to Gan-Gan in a stage whisper.

'Shh. It means it's working, that's all.' Given my great-grandmother's low, whisky voice, a stage whisper is as quiet as she can go.

THIRTEEN

Reverend Billy-Bob Henderson was not about to let Dr Pat off the hook. 'If the rapture finds you sitting on the couch, does this mean that you're not saved?'

'Penises,' Dr Pat said, looking at Gunner Jones. 'You offered me two options before, and I meant the second. I call penises ding-dongs, which is also a type of chocolate snack cake. I wanted to know if a male mermaid has a penis.'

'If it doesn't,' Reverend Billy-Bob Henderson chimed in, 'then it can't convert to Judaism.'

'What the hell?' Sheriff Ryker Saunders said. 'Billy-Bob, I've known you all my life, and I come to this ding-dong church – I mean, dad-burn church – all my life, and I ain't never heard you say nothing anti-Semitic before!'

Reverend Billy-Bob Henderson turned on his friend. 'Don't you be swearing in here, Ryker – even if I did use a few of them bad words today myself. This is a church, and *not* the community centre where you are free to swear until the cows come home. I was forced to let y'all use my church because it was the only place big enough to accommodate this crowd. Besides, it would be unchristian of me not to reach out to these creatures' – the preacher pointed at Miss Lucy – 'if indeed they needed salvation.

'But the reason I said that they can't be Jewish, if they don't have you-know-whats, is because that in order to be Jewish, converts must be circumcised. It says so right in the Bible. In their Bible, and in our *Bible*.'

Gunner ignored the snickers and ploughed ahead. 'Well, I'm sorry but I can't give your question a definitive answer. This is the first physical evidence that we have of this astonishing life form, and it is quite obviously female. Having never even had a glimpse of a merman, I'm afraid that I can only offer my best guess.'

Dr Pat pretended to wring his hands. 'Oh, *please*, darling. Guess!'

'Well,' Gunner Jones said, 'this is purely speculative, mind you, but among many live bearing species of fish – and this is not to say that merfolk are fish – the males possess an appendage, a modified, but long, anal fin called a gonopodium, that substitutes as a penis for the transmission of sperm. This fin is inserted into the—'

'Blah, blah blah,' Reverend Billy-Bob practically shouted. 'Don't you realize that there are children present?'

Dr Pat pretended to shiver. 'Ooh, this is so exciting! You two are like my mommy and daddy the time I asked them where I came from.'

'From a nut house!'

I turned to face the rude man who was seated directly behind me.

'*What?*' he demanded of me. 'I came to see the mermaid and learn more about them. I didn't come to listen to these nut-jobs. They told me at the door that the only way I got to see her was if I paid my fifty bucks and took a seat.'

'Didn't your mama teach you any manners?' I said calmly. 'You're not supposed to use the word "nut" when you're inside a church; it makes folks hungry, and then they don't pay attention.'

The man grinned. 'All right, I promise to behave myself. I just want to get my fifty bucks' worth and see that gosh-darn mermaid up close. I'm a reporter from—'

At that precise a moment, two teenage girls burst through the front doors of the church, which had apparently been left unguarded. They were shrieking and hollering as if there were no tomorrow. Plus, they looked like a pair of drowned rats – drowned rats wearing the skimpiest bikinis I've ever seen, and I've seen some for the record books. When I graduated from college, Gan-Gan took me on a tour of Europe as a graduation present, and that tour included a trip to both the French Riviera and the Italian Riviera.

'We saw one!' the lead girl shouted.

'We saw a *him!*' her companion said. 'We just saw a merman.'

'A real merman,' the first girl said. 'And he was hot!'

'Now we're cooking with gas,' Gan-Gan declared under her breath. Her face was a wreath of smiles, her myriad deep-set wrinkles suggesting a tray of baklava.

I poked her bony ribs. 'What does that mean?'

'Shh, Baby Child! Just pay attention.'

Dr Pat, ever the consummate showman, immediately evicted Sheriff Ryker Saunders and Reverend Billy-Bob from the sofa and sent them both sauntering, and mumbling unhappily, to sit in the audience. In the men's places, he seated the two bedraggled teenagers. However, it became immediately apparent that even though

The Mermaid Mystery

Dr Pat had instructed the girls to keep their legs crossed, it wasn't going to happen. It was Gunner Jones who came up with the clever solution of having the young women don choir robes, not so much to preserve their modesty as the sanctity of the church – and, of course, to keep a good many people in attendance from committing adultery in their hearts. And with minors to boot.

'Now ladies,' Dr Pat gushed, when the issue of propriety had been solved, 'tell me about the merman you saw. Where did you see him? And have either of you been drinking?'

Dr Pat had the effrontery to lean into the girl sitting next to him and sniff her mouth. She jerked away and said 'Eew!'

If he'd done that to me, trust me, I would have hauled off and slapped him. I wouldn't have cared that he was a big TV star. If a fly, or another filthy insect, comes buzzing that close to my mouth, I slap it away. Case closed.

'No!' the other girl said. 'We had not been drinking. We are good Christian girls, and we're only sixteen. We'd rented a two-person kayak from that man down at the end of the pier. We'd paddled just beyond the buoy, when all of a sudden, up pops this mermaid – I mean, mer*man*.'

'Shut the front door!' Dr Pat said. He sounded genuinely surprised which, in turn, surprised me. 'What did this merman look like?'

'He looked just like you,' the second girl said. 'Well, maybe more like this taxidermist guy up here – no offence, you understand.'

Dr Pat pulled a long face, intended to get laughs, but none were forthcoming. 'No offence taken,' he said at last. 'What makes you think that this character was a merman, and not just some random guy that went out for a swim?'

The girls rolled their eyes in perfect unison. 'Geesh, how stupid do you think we are?' they said in unison as well.

It was the first girl's turn to speak again. 'Mermen have big, scaly tails. Real men don't. That's why.'

Dr Pat was now on the edge of his seat. 'And then what happened? Did you speak with him? *Could* he speak? Did he look afraid of you?'

'No,' she said, sounding bitterly disappointed. 'He just disappeared under the waves.'

'Yeah,' her companion said. 'You scared him, by shouting at him.'

'Damn!' Dr Pat said. 'Damn, damn, damn.'

'No cussing in my church, damn it!' Reverend Billy-Bob Henderson shouted angrily from his seat in the audience. When a number of people laughed, the good preacher turned and waved a fist in the air.

'I profusely apologize, Your Holiness,' Dr Pat said with his characteristic smirk, 'but I find this even more exciting than my first wedding night to the gorgeous Barbara Jane.'

Weak laughter followed. I had only watched his show once, but I'd have been willing to bet that his regular followers had heard that line before.

Dr Pat stood. 'Does anyone here have a boat that my crew and I can use?'

'I do!'

From my visits over the years to Tidal Shores, I was able to recognize Hoyt Hunter, the owner of Deep-Seated Attractions, a deep-sea fishing company. Before the pandemic he owned three boats, one of which he personally operated.

'Well, this will be interesting,' Gan-Gan growled.

I nudged her. 'What's really going on?'

'Oh nothing, Baby Child.'

'I want to rent your boat,' Dr Pat said, pointing at Hoyt Hunter. 'For me, and my camera crew.'

Gan-Gan also got to her feet. She moved slowly, of course, given that Plato was her first boyfriend.

'My granddaughter will be on that boat as well, Hoyt,' she said. 'Zoe is a reporter for *The Observer Today*, which is Charlotte's leading newspaper. She's here to do a feature on Miss Lucy, and I'm sure that she'd be delighted to also report on the *Dr Pat and Pal Show* excursion.' Gan-Gan fixed her beady brown eyes on me. 'Wouldn't you, darling, Baby Child?'

I popped to my feet. 'It would be my pleasure.'

'And she will be the *only* newspaper reporter on the boat,' Gan-Gan bellowed in a voice that startled the woman sitting to her left.

'Yes, ma'am,' Hoyt Hunter said.

'Hold it,' Dr Pat ordered in a surprisingly authoritative voice. 'I'm paying to rent this boat; I get to say who else gets to come along.'

'Well, it's my boat,' Hoyt Hunter said, 'and if Miss Legare's great-granddaughter doesn't get to come, and doesn't get her print exclusive, then I'm not renting it to you.'

'But I saw three boats bobbing out there in the water when we drove up—'

'And they're all mine,' Hoyt Hunter said, and crossed his brawny, tanned arms.

'Harrumph,' Dr Pat said.

I couldn't help but laugh. 'He used your favourite word, Gan-Gan.'

'It is *not*,' she said, and then stuck her tongue out at me as she sat down. I tell you, getting old has its privileges, but *being* ancient means that one can get away with things every kindergartener is taught not to do.

'Make up your mind, Dr Pat,' Hoyt Hunter said. 'The longer you take to decide, the likelier it is that the merman will have swum away.'

'My guess is that this merman might be related to Miss Lucy,' Gunner Jones said. His brow was lightly furrowed, and he was rubbing his chin as if he'd just concluded an important scientific question.

'No way,' one of the girls said. 'The mermaid – or merguy – or whatever you call him, was really cute. He didn't look anything like this freak!'

Even from where I sat, I could see the vein, which ran a jagged path along Gunner's forehead, begin to twitch. Apparently, he had grown fond of the chimera he'd either created, or merely embalmed. The jury was still out, as far as I was concerned. Nevertheless, I felt compelled to jump to my feet and stick up for Gunner. Maybe it was because he was so hunky, or maybe it was because that particular teenager had been so snotty, but it didn't matter.

'Miss Lucy is not a freak,' I said in my outdoor voice, so that everyone in that church building could hear me. 'If you look closely at the jumbotron, you can see that her features are symmetrical. Her eyes and nostrils – I mean nose – on the left side of her face align perfectly with the right side of her face. Her lips are symmetrical as well.'

'What there are of them,' some lout said.

I ignored that rude man. 'Throughout history,' I continued, 'the most beautiful women in the world have had perfect symmetry – like in ancient Egypt, Queen Nefertiti. Or in modern times, the actresses Sophia Loren and Audrey Hepburn. Then there's the most successful model of all time, Naomi Campbell—'

I felt Gan-Gan tug at my shirt. 'Sit,' she hissed.

'Feisty little thing, aren't you?' Dr Pat said. 'Meow! Welcome aboard S.S. *Dr Pat and Pal*, pussycat. Now, let me see who's all going to go on this little fact-finding cruise. I'll need my entire film crew – hair, makeup, the works. It's going to be windy, since I plan to stay out on the deck, and of course there will be glare coming off the water. So, my crew makes a total of eight, plus the Deli Llama, and then there is you, who looks every inch a skipper, and then that feisty – and dare I say, attractive – young woman in my audience, so that makes eleven. Although I assume that you have a qualified assistant – you know – just in case you fall into the water and start to drown or, God forbid, a passenger falls in, and needs a lifesaver thrown in their direction. Or do we all have to wear those horrid orange vests? Never mind, I know that the answer to that is yes. Well, I think that about covers it, so tell me how much it will be to rent one of those little tubs that I saw anchored out there in the harbour, and let's get this show on the road.' He chortled. 'I mean let's get this show on the water!'

'Think again, Patty Boy,' Hoyt Hunter said. 'Miss Legare's great-granddaughter ain't going to be sailing on any boat named Dr Pat and Pal, and neither are you. The particular boat that I am willing to rent to you today is named *The Reel Life*. Is that understood?'

'Aye, aye, Captain,' Dr Pat said, with just the slightest trace of mockery in his voice.

'By the way, the Deli Llama will not be accompanying us.'

Dr Pat seemed to suddenly stand three inches taller, and weigh twenty pounds more, as he puffed out his chest and his face reddened with anger. He strode over to the edge of the stage and put his hands on his hips.

'Just as long as I pay you, who I choose to bring along is none of your business, Mr Hoyt.'

'Sir, I'm not talking about who,' Hoyt Hunter said. 'I'm talking about *what*. I don't allow animals on my boats.'

'Animals?' Dr Pat said incredulously. 'None of my people brought their pets with them.'

'Well,' Hoyt Hunter drawled, in his distinctive country accent, 'what do you call a llama? It sure as heck ain't a human being. I don't care if it can talk and clap its front hooves together. My aunt Becki over in Florence, South Carolina, has one of them African grey parrots that knows almost one hundred words. It can even pray in two languages. But that don't make it a Christian, or a Catholic. It's still an atheistic animal.'

Dr Pat looked fit to be tied. 'Catholics *are* Christians, you ignoramus. And I *know* that the Deli Llama isn't an animal, because she's my wife!'

FOURTEEN

The collective gasp that ensued following Dr Pat's shocking disclosure that the Deli Llama was his wife practically sucked the oxygen out of that large space. Dr Pat's face went from red to chalk white in an instant, and from the direction of the pastor's study I heard the faint scream of a woman.

'Now look what you've gone and made me do,' Dr Pat moaned. 'You made me reveal that my wife is the Deli Llama in front of all these people, and this is going to destroy my ratings! You've ruined me, you ignorant, redneck racist. We have two children in college, and one who will be a senior in high school. Plus, our mortgage payment is out of this world, and on top of that I just bought the Deli Llama – I mean, Sophia – a new Lamborghini for her birthday.'

Hoyt Hunter started to shake with rage. '*Racist?* How dare you call me that! One of my best friends is one-eighth Gujarati from India, and I'm thick as thieves with Sheriff Ryker Saunders, who we're all quite sure is a person of colour – although no one, including Ryker, is sure who his mama slept with the night that him and his twin brother Ewell were conceived.

'And what makes you think that I care one whit about your financial situation? And who the hell, with two kids in college, and worried about their mortgage, would buy their wife a two-hundred-thousand-dollar car?'

'Don't be daft,' Dr Pat snapped. 'This wasn't one of their lowest priced automobiles. This was a Lamborghini Veneno, their fiftieth anniversary model, and I paid four million dollars for that beauty. That's how much I value my wife. How much do you value *your* wife?'

The crowd chirruped in delight at the exchange between the two men. Face it, they'd come to Tidal Shores craving entertainment, and that's what they were getting. Two shows for the price of one – it sounded like a winning combination to me. I'd never paid much attention to the *Dr Pat and Pal* television show before, but if today's taping was typical of the fare he offered, then I just might start watching – assuming, of course, that the show didn't go under because of his startling revelation. Perhaps he needed some help at this trying time.

'You could always get a new pal,' I shouted through cupped hands. 'We hoi-polloi have very short memories.'

Dr Pat looked at me with renewed interest. 'And who are you again?'

'I'm Zoe Porter, but my name isn't important. May I suggest that you have your wife wear a chicken suit, and call her Fred? Then every now and then, on the show, you and Fred could have these pretend disputes, and you could say: "What the cluck, Fred?"'

More than half of the room found that funny. Very funny, in fact. Both Dr Pat and Hoyt Hunter laughed.

'But Fred is a guy's name,' Dr Pat finally said. 'So shouldn't the chicken be a rooster?'

'No,' I said, 'because calling a hen Fred adds to the joke. It's unexpected. You could have a funny backstory about baby chicks all looking alike at birth. Anyway, at the end of each show, you could have Fred pretend to lay an egg. You could either save the eggs, and then after a while release a bunch of chicks loose on the stage, for laughs, of course, *or* you could pretend to crack open a plastic egg. Inside the plastic egg, which would be quite large, and cause Fred some discomfort to lay, would be a folded-up piece of paper highlighting the next day's show.'

Dr Pat jumped off the stage and made his way to me. It's not just because of the pandemic; in general, I am loath to shake hands. I find it an uncivilized custom. I prefer to fold my hands in greeting, like they do in Thailand, and would wager that the Thais pass along far fewer cold germs that way. But I try not to be rude, so when Dr Pat thrust his pale, clammy hand inches from my chest, I took it graciously. However, my fingers hung as limply as stalks of overcooked asparagus.

'Young lady,' he said, 'your creativity astounds me. Come work for me. I'll make you Vice President of Content and Programming. You can name your price – within reason, of course.' He lowered his voice. 'Keep in mind that you *are* a woman.'

I glared at him.

'Well, what do you say?' the clueless man demanded.

'I say that I just came up with another idea.'

'Yes?' He motioned for his sound man to hold a microphone on a boom next to my mouth. 'People,' he said, 'this brilliant young

The Mermaid Mystery

woman has just come up with another idea. So, Miss Porter, is this new idea in addition to, or instead of, your chicken named Fred idea?'

I turned slowly and waved at everyone in the church. 'Well, Dr Pat, this new idea of mine is totally independent of the chicken idea. You could use both on your show. What I'd like to suggest now is that you add a donkey character to your couch.'

'A donkey?'

'Yes, you know, an ass. That way, there'll be two of them on your show.'

Dr Pat looked as if I'd punched him in the gut. The huge church, which was jammed with people, several of them already suffering from summer colds, was suddenly so silent that one could have heard a dead man fart.

Gan-Gan grabbed my limp hand to offer me her support. 'It's because Dr Pat wanted to pay her less money because she's a woman,' the dear old woman said in a brave, loud voice. 'Now which of you ladies believes that you are worth less than a man? And I don't mean because the Bible tells you that, or because your husband tells you that, but because you came to that conclusion on your own. I want to see a show of hands.

'Raise your hands, ladies, if you honestly think that the meat-headed man whom you have to pick up after, every night, and whom you have to remind to take out the trash, and even to brush his teeth, has a mind that is superior to yours. But before you raise those hands, consider this: has there ever been a time when you even once stopped thinking about something? When your brain just shut down completely? I bet that the answer is "no." Now, have you ever gone on a long car ride with your husband, and asked him what he was thinking about, and heard him say: "Nothing"?'

Virtually every woman in the church nodded.

'Now raise your hands,' Gan-Gan said, 'if you honestly believe that men have more going on upstairs than women.'

Two women, out of perhaps three hundred, raised their hands. When those poor women saw how badly they were outnumbered, their hands came down immediately.

Gan-Gan, with a smirk on her face a mile wide, turned to Dr Pat. '*Mr* Pat,' she said, 'now offer my great-granddaughter that same position at a higher salary than any other vice president in your company, or I'll see to it that she sues you for sexual discrimination.

Refuse my offer, and it's a lose/lose situation for you. Accept it, and it's a win/win. What will it be?'

I'll say this for Dr Pat: he was capable of smiling wanly when backed into a corner. 'Welcome to the team, Miss Porter,' he said meekly.

'Thank you, sir, but no thank you. I'm a serious newspaper reporter. I'm all about ferreting out facts – real facts, as if there are any other kind. At any rate, I don't want a position on your show. But I would like the opportunity to appear on your show, and share what I've learned, when I feel the time is right.'

Dr Pat nodded. 'I understand. Well then, what are we waiting for? Let's go out on the water and gather facts.'

That's when Mayor Adelaide Saunders rushed from the sidelines and climbed precariously up the steps in her pink Louboutin heels. Because Tidal Shores cannot afford to pay its mayor a huge salary, Adelaide wisely shops in the upscale 'gently used' shops in downtown Charleston. These stores get their merchandise from the lucky folks who live in a neighbourhood called 'South of Broad' on Charleston's peninsula. It is one of the wealthiest neighbourhoods in America. That said, this schoolteacher's wife always looks like a million bucks.

Having once been a teacher herself, Mayor Adelaide Saunders is experienced when it comes to getting a room's attention. She gracefully took the handheld microphone from Dr Pat and, holding it at just the right position from her bright-red lips, began to speak in a cultured accent that was perhaps half a step higher than her actual position in Southern society. She may have married down, but she certainly didn't possess the lineage of Miss Legare.

'Welcome to Tidal Shores, y'all,' she said, as she flashed her perfectly straight, peroxided teeth. 'No doubt there will be many of you who wish now to adjourn to the beach, in hopes of getting your own glimpse of a merman. Others of you, however, might well wish to take advantage of the opportunity to come up here on the stage and view Miss Lucy.

'If seeing Miss Lucy up close and in person is what you prefer, then I ask you to remain seated until the beachgoers have exited the building. At this point I am going to ask our ushers to take their positions at the ends of each row. They will allow the rows to empty in an orderly fashion, as space in the aisles permits. Please do not stand, or move, until your usher indicates that you are permitted to do so.

'Remember, at the moment, they are only allowing guests out who prefer to go down to the beach, rather than to queue patiently in order to view Miss Lucy closely. Oh, and one more thing, our ushers today are high-school and college student volunteers. They are not being paid for their services, so I am sure that tips will be appreciated. Also, I ask that you treat them with respect.'

Without another word being spoken, approximately forty young men and women filed out of the pastor's study to the left of the sanctuary and took their positions at the ends of the pews. Bless their hearts, the poor kids were all sweaty from having been crammed into such a tight space. But on the other hand, being that age, and hormonally charged, they probably had a good time anyway. In fact, that is probably why some of them were so 'damp with dew.' (There are still a few Southerners from my gan-gan's generation who feel that the word 'sweat' is a bit vulgar, and prefer to use a synonym if possible.)

Sad to say, we Americans lack the 'queuing' gene. In the two hundred-plus years since we were a colony of Great Britain, the gene that would enable us civilians to stay in our place – whether in a line, or in a broader sense, socially – has been bred out of us. When told to stay put, some of us, like rebellious teenagers, can't help but push back. So it happened that I heard a lot of people saying 'excuse me' as they pushed past others, as well as a plethora of excuses for why they had to jump the line. The more people tried to cheat the system and get ahead, the more pushback there was, and soon no one was saying 'excuse me.' Soon all I heard was the din of angry voices (although I did make out the occasional cuss word), and what had once been a curious throng of mermaid-lovers was now a heaving, writhing mob of maniacs, each of whom thought that they were somehow being cheated out of a once-in-a-lifetime experience.

One would think that stopping this chaos would be in Sheriff Ryker Saunders' wheelhouse. If so, one would be wrong, because the town's lawman was nowhere to be found. As for Gunner Jones, he of the perfect features and flyaway pheromones, that hunk of burning flesh was studying his shoes as if he was perhaps trying to get them to levitate – with himself in them, of course. Forget about Dr Pat or his television crew being any help; they all shared the same look, which I took to say, loud and clear: 'This is not my circus, and these are not my monkeys.'

Except that it *was* Dr Pat's circus, and it *was* Gan-Gan's circus as well. Maybe neither of them had any choice in directly choosing the monkeys, but they both knew which 'jungle of crazy' that these simians would roll from. Once again, I felt that I had to take things into my own hands if I expected to get anything done, and by that, I mean write the feature-length story that I knew this could turn out to be. In fact, in my mind, I had already divided my story into three parts, to be published over three Sundays, and my head told me that if I followed my gut, this project could win me the much-coveted Pulitzer Prize.

Therefore, I had no choice but to take control of the narrative, and hang on to it, just as tightly as if I was hanging on to the mane of a wild mustang that I was riding bareback at a rodeo. If I fell off this horse I might get kicked in the head – hard – but if I hung on long enough, the reward could be life-changing for me.

'Gunner Jones, sir,' I said in my strongest, most authoritative voice. 'Please exit the stage right and go down the hall to the second door on your left. It's a closet that contains a set of hand bells. Bring as many as you can and pass them out to the ushers. Have them ring them as hard as they can.'

He hesitated, so I started climbing over the folks in my row, including Gan-Gan, who growled and spit at me like a cat when I clonked her on the knees with my right foot. However, when Gunner Jones saw that I was quite serious about my plan to restore order, he sprang into action. The choir master of Tidal Shores Community Church not only runs a top-notch group of vocalists, but his hand-bell ringers are exceptionally skilled at what they do. I have had to sit through many services at this church, and frankly, the only thing that makes listening to one of Reverend Billy-Bob Henderson's sermons bearable is that both the offertory hymn and final hymn are purely musical numbers performed by the hand-bell choir.

At any rate, we were back in the sanctuary in a matter of seconds with our arms full of bells, and we didn't even have to tell the stressed-out ushers what to do with them. If perhaps the clanging persisted a wee bit longer than was absolutely necessary in order to get folks stopped in their tracks – well, I'll take the blame. I've long fantasized about being in a bell-ringing choir, but I lack the will to attend church on a regular basis – although I still attend more frequently than most Brits.

I had in my possession the biggest bell with the largest clapper.

When I sadly realized it was time to give my new toy a rest, I turned it over to Mayor Adelaide Saunders.

'Thank you,' she whispered gratefully. Then she rang the large bell with deep sound three times. Hard.

All eyes were directed to the stage.

'Now then, people, listen up,' Mayor Adelaide Saunders said in a stern voice befitting a former teacher who'd once had unruly students, 'you are to return to your original seats. This time you will be obeying the ushers. If you don't, no one will be allowed on the beach, and neither will anyone be allowed up here for a closer look at Miss Lucy. Is that understood?'

There followed a chorus of 'yes ma'am.'

'Any questions?' Mayor Adelaide Saunders asked foolishly.

One hand shot up. The questioner was a young man who was too old to wear his baseball cap backwards, and too young to pull off a three-day beard stubble. He was, however, an expert at affecting a cocky grin.

'If we misbehave again, are you going to send us to detention, and assign us one hundred sentences: "I will behave in church"?'

Mayor Adelaide Saunders smiled. 'Everyone, this is my son, Drayton. He's our head lifeguard here at Tidal Shores. You folks that want to head down to the beach, squeeze politely past your neighbour and line up behind your usher. Drayton will take it from there.

'The rest of you, remain in your seats, and you will have a chance to see Miss Lucy up close. Believe me when I say this, what you see up here today will change the way you view the world. *Forever.* I promise you that.'

Only five people followed Drayton down to the beach.

FIFTEEN

I was privileged to stand at the apex of the prow of *The Reel Life*, like a real-live figurehead. I was sandwiched between Dr Pat on my left, and the manly Gunner Jones on my right. The sea was a mite choppy, and even though I had plenty of railing space to hang on to, I took advantage of several of the larger waves to lose my balance and fall against the chest of the handsome taxidermist. On the third such occasion he slid a muscular arm around my waist.

'I'm the queen of the world!' I shouted joyously into the wind. This last part was supposed to happen only in my head, but there was something about Gunner's strong arm encircling my waist, the salt air, and the sense of adventure – as sceptical as I was of its outcome – that created a disconnect between my mouth and my brain. Had I been a spy, and Gunner Jones a member of an enemy country, I would have spilled the beans in three heartbeats. The only torture involved would have been waiting for him to kiss me during interrogation.

'Shush! Please,' Dr Pat said, a bit snarky, if you ask me. 'You're going to scare off the merman. Besides, Kate Winslet you're not.'

'And you're no Leonardo DiCaprio,' I snapped. 'Although, if I'm being honest, with your longer neck, I find you slightly more attractive.'

'Stop flirting with my husband,' the former Deli Llama and future Fred said. She was standing directly behind Dr Pat, but I hadn't paid her any attention. In a T-shirt and shorts, and wearing sunglasses and a head scarf, she could have been any one of the female crew members, or perhaps even a movie star that Dr Pat had sneaked on board. The only reason I was sure that she was Dr Pat's wife was because this woman had a whiny voice. Every sentence she spoke ended on a down note. On that account alone, one could bet the farm that she wasn't Canadian.

I was about to explain to this poor misguided woman that Dr Pat had not, nor could he ever, enter even the outer rings of my planet's fantasy orbit, when Gunner Jones gave me a tight squeeze with one arm, and pointed straight ahead with the other.

'Look! Zoe, look, there's the merman!'

And there he was. A real, honest-to-goodness merman. It was immediately apparently that this creature was no one's cobbled together museum specimen. As *The Reel Life* shuddered to a stop, the merman swam toward us, using only his flukes for propulsion. His arms he kept tightly by his side. When he was only about twelve feet from the boat he stopped, and it appeared as if he was treading the water by gently moving his powerful-looking flukes ever so slightly, while he maintained an upright position. Then he smiled at us, and I would swear that his smile was directed at me.

'Hellooo,' Dr Pat called out. 'Do you speak English?'

'Don't be an idiot, man,' Gunner Jones muttered. 'How the devil do you suppose he would have learned that?'

'Good point,' Dr Pat said. '*Parlez-vous francais?*'

'*Oui,*' the merman said.

Had I been chewing gum, it would have fallen out of my mouth. '*Comment se fait-il que tu parles francais?*' I asked. '*Et que toutes les sirens le parlent?*'

'Oui, oui,' the merman squealed. 'Oui, oui, oui.'

'What did you say to him?' Dr Pat demanded. 'I used up practically all the French that I know.'

'I just asked him how he happened to learn French, and if all mermaids spoke it.'

'Hmm,' Dr Pat said. 'Well, I do know two more words. Bonjour,' he said, addressing the merman.

'Oui, oui, oui.'

'I'm sorry to burst y'all's bubble,' Gunner Jones said, 'but that doesn't sound like any French that I've ever heard. That sounds more like a cross between a pig and porpoise.'

'Yeah,' someone behind us said, and laughed. 'A porcine porpoise.'

'Oui!' the merman seemed to agree emphatically.

'*Hola,*' a cameraman said in Spanish. '*Como esta usted?*'

'Ouiiiiii,' the merman squealed again. Then he dove directly under our boat, *The Reel Life*, and as he did so, his beautifully scaled tail and massive flukes glistened in the sunlight.

I was reminded of the time that I went whale-watching in the Bay of Fundy up in Nova Scotia. Our first day whale-watching a humpback whale had swum alongside our boat and exhaled through its blowhole. To put it mildly, the humpback had very bad breath.

The following day, a humpback whale submerged beneath our boat, giving us all a thrill, but also setting nerves on edge for more than a few of us, given that the whale was almost as long as our boat. When the massive beast finally emerged a good way from the boat, I believe that even the captain was relieved.

The disappearing merman was another story. For one thing, his flukes might have been powerful enough to overturn a kayak, or even a canoe, but nothing larger. For another thing, he had been clearly happy to see us. True, there are animals that can appear to be smiling when they are stressed, when they are really feeling fear, or trying to mask aggression, but the top half of *Homo oceanica* was *Homo*, for goodness' sake – which meant that it was likely that his smile reflected a happy or at least pleased state of mind.

Perhaps his sudden disappearance merely meant that the merman had swum off to spread the good news that he'd discovered friendly humans to others of his kind. Gunner Jones, who was the closest thing to a biologist that we had on board, surmised the same thing.

'Look,' he said, 'we're dealing with an unknown species here; however, let's make some educated guesses from what we just saw with our own eyes. The merman had the bottom half of a fish, and fish often swim in schools. And of course he had the top half of a – well, he looked like a human, and we humans also tend not to be solitary, and we're capable of communicating complex ideas through language. I'd be willing to bet the store on the fact that the merman we just saw is capable of either saying more than just "oui, oui," or else we are incapable of hearing the nuances in the sounds he made. Perhaps he made many more sounds at a frequency we couldn't hear altogether.'

'Yeah,' Future Fred said, 'like elephants. I saw that on the Nature Channel.' I found out later that the woman's real name is Sophia Gluck, but she will always be Future Fred to me.

'Yes, like that exactly,' Gunner Jones said. 'That's a great analogy.'

I turned swiftly to catch Future Fred still smiling at the compliment, which shouldn't have irked me, but it did. What an idiot I was to have proprietorial feelings for a man that I had barely met, much less known for more than half a day. The only thing that I can say in my defence is that I was still in my early thirties, and my sexual drive was, supposedly, still on the upswing.

'I also watch the Nature Channel,' I said, perhaps louder than was necessary. 'Correct me if I'm wrong, but elephants rumble at frequencies that are too low for human ears, but that other elephants can hear from a mile away. On the other hand, dolphins, which are a marine mammal, emit sounds that are too high for the human ear to pick up. Since merfolk would appear to have a similar lung capacity as we humans, and they did indeed make inaudible sounds, would you expect these sounds to be low rumbles, or high-pitched squeaks?'

Gunner Jones gave me a half-body hug, which would have knocked the socks off me, had I been wearing any. Instead, I was wearing sandals, since as any self-respecting American will tell you, socks and sandals should never appear on one's body simultaneously. I mean, how else are we to spot Europeans at Disney World?

'You're a pretty bright girl yourself,' Gunner Jones said to me.

'And you're a clever boy,' I said. Of course, I was being sarcastic; the man was forty-five years old, if he was a day.

'Ahem,' Dr Pat said, 'maybe when you two are done flirting, Mr Jones can ask the captain to sail this tub slowly further out into the bay. From what I understand, merfolk prefer blue water, and this water is greenish-brown.'

'Whoa,' I said. 'How do you know merfolk prefer blue water? Have you polled them?'

Dr Pat snorted. 'Don't be so rude. You members of the press are all alike. I ask you, have you ever seen a picture, like a painting, or an illustration of some sort, of a mermaid in water that was this disgusting shade of greenish-brown? If you ask me, I'd say there's every likelihood that the mermaid back at the church died from a disease contracted in this soupy filth.

'Which brings me to a question I should have asked back at the church but didn't. Mr Jones, before you stuffed that rarest of creatures, like you were embalming someone's favourite housecat, did you see to it that a proper autopsy was performed? And I don't mean by you. I should imagine that what was needed was to have both a human coroner and a veterinarian performing this operation.'

'That's right,' Future Fred said. 'For a singular discovery such as this, only a collaboration of two trained medical professionals, from parallel disciplines, would have sufficed. Might we assume that this is the protocol that you followed? If so, I'm sure you wouldn't mind sharing the examination results with us. Would you?'

I glanced at Gunner Jones' face and could instantly tell that he was not pleased by this line of questioning. I knew that if I were in his shoes, I would appreciate someone coming to my rescue.

'I'm guessing that Mr Jones did follow that protocol, and that he would be more than happy to share those results with you – but at a later date. We in the media, and that includes y'all, as much as me, are prone to hyperbole, as well as jumping to conclusions. As we're dealing with a very new phenomena here, that being the discovery of a heretofore undescribed genus of animal, it is critical that we not put the cart before the horse.'

Gunner nodded vigorously. 'The lady is exactly correct. Caution rules the day in this case.'

'Who said anything about a damn cart or horse?' Dr Pat said. 'Can't you at least tell me that mermaid that you stuffed, like a Thanksgiving turkey, had two lungs, a heart, two kidneys, and two livers, just like I do?'

'Dr Pat,' Gunner Jones said, 'if you have two livers, then you have acquired one through surgery, or else you absorbed your identical twin brother in utero.'

'You don't make a lick of sense,' Dr Pat said.

'How many brains do you have, Dr Pat?' I said.

'Now you're just being mean,' Future Fred said. 'My husband was the highest-ranking student in the bottom third of his graduating class from our alma mater.'

'You're absolutely right,' I said. 'I was being mean, and I apologize to you both. But since y'all are not from around these parts, please allow me to explain the colour of the Atlantic Ocean here at Tidal Shores, as well as the coasts of North Carolina and Georgia.

'Our olive-green water is not a sign of pollution. It is because of the presence of phytoplankton, plus the size of sediments picked up by the waves. Phytoplankton are single-cell organisms that are an important part of the marine life food chain. Where they are found in abundance, one will find a large variety of fish, and therefore marine mammals such as dolphins, which are plentiful along our coast.'

'Well spoken,' Gunner Jones said. At that very moment the boat was rocked by a particularly large wave, and I almost lost my footing. Gunner, that sly devil, slipped an arm around my waist and held me tight against his side to keep me from falling when the vessel pitched the other way. I knew the feeling had to be one-sided, no pun intended, but I couldn't help fantasizing that this meant more than a simple act of kindness. Already in my pheromone-addled brain we were a couple on a date. Perhaps it was a 'three-hour tour,' and we would get stranded on a desert island for Lord only knows how long – but without Gilligan, the Skipper, and all the rest.

Alas, no sooner did the little boat right itself, than Gunner Jones dropped his protective arm, and inched away from bodily contact. To make matters worse, the voice of the real-life skipper of *The Reel Life*, the affable Hoyt Hunter, came over loud and clear on the public address system.

'Ladies and gentlemen, the sea is starting to get a bit choppy, and the latest weather forecast predicts the winds to pick up from the southeast, which will make the sea even rougher. Already I've had a couple of passengers complain of motion sickness. That said, I will be turning around to port now.'

A chorus of groans filled the air. It was clear that most of us were extremely disappointed that, having already spotted one live merman, we had to turn back. Besides, if we persevered in our quest, and the weather got truly horrible, who knows how much bodily contact I might enjoy from the hunky taxidermist? So yes, I was one of our number who expressed their bitter disappointment at having to return, but short of a mutiny, what else could we do?

SIXTEEN

There was a huge crowd on the pier awaiting us. Photos and videos of the merman had been texted to many of the landlubbers, and they were all dying to speak to an eyewitness in person. Unfortunately, the Tidal Shores pier was a relic of its past, pre-pandemic heyday, and it had slowly been deteriorating in the elements. The combination of hot Carolina sun and salt water had rendered even the pressure-treated pilings and lumber unsafe to that amount of weight. As more and more people surged forward on the rickety pier, it began to sway, which precipitated a reverse stampede. Shouts and screams of terror filled the air. Frankly, I couldn't imagine a more exciting morning.

I should hasten to say that in the end the swaying pier did not collapse and everyone made it off safely. The only casualties of the stampede were a number of cell phones and purses, all of which were collected later, and most of which were returned to their rightful owners pretty much intact. The real downside of the near catastrophe was that we passengers aboard *The Reel Life* were not allowed to disembark until Captain Hoyt was absolutely satisfied that it was safe for us to do so. This only happened after a cable had been fastened to the deck of the boat and strung along the pier until it reached a palmetto on the shore. There the cable was pulled taught and wrapped around the tree a gazillion times. Then, one by one, each passenger was strapped into a homemade harness which was then attached to a large swivel hook.

We have all heard the cliché about captains going down with their ships, but on this fateful day Captain Hoyt Hunter refused to allow a single one of his passengers to go down with the pier, unless he accompanied them. I had never witnessed such bravery until then and have never witnessed it since. Yes, he too was connected to the cable via a chest harness that Gunner Jones had helped cobble together, but it must be remembered that Hoyt Hunter was a married man with children. It certainly wasn't his fault that too many people, starved for a bit of fantasy to keep their minds off the world's troubles, had acted so irresponsibly. Believe me, I almost felt guilty when it was my turn to exit that little deep sea-fishing boat.

On the other hand, if I had postponed my exit, given my luck, it's likely that the pier would have collapsed just as I stepped on it. At the same time, the cable would either have snapped, or come loose from one of its moorings, and I would have been squished between the dock and boat. Then my poor widowed mother would have a flattened sardine for a daughter, and she never would have been able to enjoy the pleasure of vacationing in Tidal Shores again. And what about Gan-Gan? She'd never be able to even glance in this direction without being reminded of my grisly death. Therefore, I selflessly took my appointed turn, but after first requesting that it be Gunner Jones who escorted me to shore; after all, Captain Hoyt had to be plum tuckered after all those trips back and forth.

Gunner agreed without hesitation. In fact, instead of just pushing me along the cable in my sling, he cradled me in his arms. As the old saying goes, my "mama didn't raise no fools."

'Mr Jones,' I began.

'Please,' he said, 'call me Gunner.'

'And you can call me anytime.'

'I beg your pardon?'

'I mean, call me Zoe. Anyway, Gunner, the somewhat formidable woman whom everyone refers to as Miss Legare is actually my adorable great-grandmother.'

'Well, how about that! I thought the two of you were related, seeing as how you look so much alike.' He said that with a straight face.

I slapped him playfully. 'Gan-Gan is, like, one hundred-fifty years old, and I'm more like thirty-ish.'

'You share the same bone structure,' Gunner said, and a smile played across his perfect, symmetrical lips.

I took a deep breath and plunged on. 'So anyway, as I was about to say, I've decided to stay over tonight – at Gan-Gan's, of course – and how would you feel about coming to dinner with me? At her house? With her there, of course.'

By that time, Gunner had slid me safely along the cable, and to the land end of the pier. Without answering, he immediately began slipping the rope sling over my head in the most business-like fashion. I was flabbergasted. I am an attractive woman, if I do say so myself. By that I mean that I don't need to post photos of other women on social media to get blind dates – or even dates who can see.

'Gunner,' I said. 'Did you hear me? Free food.'

'Oh yeah,' he grunted, as he fiddled with the harness. 'Thanks, but no thanks. I already have plans for tonight.'

'Okey dokey,' I said flippantly, in an attempt to brush off his rudeness. But to be honest, my cheeks stung from that encounter, and I felt humiliated. Of course, it was my fault for thinking that he might be secure enough in his masculinity to not be intimidated by a woman extending a simple dinner invitation. *Or* – and this still gave me a sliver of shivering hope – perhaps it was the prospect of dinner with Gan-Gan that caused him to decline my innocuous invitation. Even though we had not been formally introduced inside the sanctuary, he'd seen me interacting with the woman whose bone structure I shared, so he must have guessed that we were related back then and had had time to think about the consequences of dating a relative of Tidal Shores' crotchety antiques dealer.

In any case, that was the end of my fantasy; there on the safe end of the pier, it crashed and burned. Not that I owe anyone an explanation for my behaviour, but in retrospect it might have something to do with the faint ticking of my biological clock. I'd always thought I would be married by age thirty and have my 2.3 children by age thirty-eight. The '.3' child in this scenario was a black Labrador retriever named Dark Vader, and my happy little family lived not in a vine-covered cottage with a white picket fence, but a Greek Revival mansion in the South Park neighbourhood of Charlotte where I grew up.

Even though I had my bubble burst, so to speak, I still had the presence of mind to call my editor at *The Observer Today* after I got back to Gan-Gan's. Randi Gillman not only trusts my instincts, but she often learns who my sources are before I do.

'Randi, you're not going to believe—'

'You saw a merman,' she said. 'How cool is that? Of course, you need to stay and flesh out the story. We'll make it a series, that's what we'll do. Did you get any photos? Did you film him?'

'Yes, but—'

'Good. I'm dispatching Fleishman down there tonight. He says he's OK with small boats. That's what it is, right? A mere tub – pun intended. Ha. Ha. Anyway, that's what all the videos show.'

'What videos?'

'Zoe, it's all over TV already. I assume that you *did* hear about the governor's visit tomorrow, so of course you need to make sure that you look your best for that. You still travel with a change of clothes, right?'

I gasped. 'Which governor?'

'The Governor of South Carolina, Wade Hubert Horatio Humphrey Harpootlian. He already made a statement saying that he'll be introducing a bill making merfolk South Carolina's state chimera.'

'What the heck is a chimera, and when did all this happen?'

'A chimera is half-beast, half-man,' Randi said. 'I thought you went to college.'

'I did.'

'Zoe, what have you been doing for the last three hours?'

'Licking my wounds,' I said. 'Taking stock of my miserable life.'

'Oh, I get it,' Randi said. 'Some handsome hunk resisted irresistible you.'

'You're a mind-reading witch,' I said. 'If you're going to yell at me for not reporting to you immediately, it's because I had a migraine brought on by the glare of the ocean, among other things, so I took a pill, and laid down in my gan-gan's guest room with a damp cloth over my forehead, and then I just sort of drifted off. Honest. That's where I am right now; I'm sitting on her guest-room bed.

'But, Randi, about sending Fleishman down here, currently Tidal Shores only has one motel, the Abide Awhile, and it's fully booked. This place is packed with people, they'll be sleeping in the streets, or in their cars.'

'Then see if Fleishman can stay at your cousin's,' my editor said.

'She's my great-grandmother,' I said, 'not my cousin, and strangers think that she's an ogre.'

Randi groaned. 'Then I'll tell Fleishman to throw a sleeping bag into the van.'

'And tell him to bring along a cooler with whatever he plans to eat while he's down here. There are public toilets at the community centre, and the library, but he would be wise to bring his own toilet tissue. This place is bonkers right now.'

'If it's really that crazy down there, I'll just keep Fleishman here. He's always been one of my more high-strung reporters.'

'Good call, Randi. It would be a shame if he had a nervous breakdown because the public toilets overflowed.'

'One of the TV networks has labelled it Mermaid Mania,' Randi said.

'Oh, that is so politically incorrect,' I said. 'The correct term is Merfolk Mania. After all, it was a merman whom we saw today.'

Randi laughed. Hers is a full-throated, generous laugh, the kind that makes one feel good just for hearing it.

'*Merfolk Mania!* I love that,' she said. 'That is going to be our headline tomorrow, and you are going to send me every photo on your phone, and a thousand-word article by nine p.m. tonight.'

'No way!'

'Way. Now get out your laptop and start typing, kid.'

Who, what, where, when, and why – those should be the basis of every good news story, but sadly, they aren't. In my assignment, the first four words were easily covered, and the topics padded for length, but the word 'why' was problematic. Why did merfolk show up conclusively at Tidal Shores? Or did they?

I had indeed been to college, and although I had a degree in journalism, my required science course had been biology. From what little knowledge I retained from those days, it still seemed highly unlikely to me that mammalian and piscine circulatory systems were compatible. Frankly, even though she'd been discovered dead, floating in the surf after a storm, the mermaid at the church was – let's face it – ugly as sin. I realize that was a mite harsh, considering all that the poor creature had gone through, but really, if I compared her to Daryl Hannah from the Tom Hanks movie *Splash*, this local gal would never get a date. Besides, when I enlarged my footage of the merman on my cell phone, it looked like they were two different species.

The merman was Hollywood handsome. By that I mean if he'd had legs, instead of a tail, he could hop on a bus, ride out to California, and maybe become a movie star. Although it might help if he didn't wear deodorant, because I read in an article that at least three very big Hollywood stars eschewed that stuff, and one even declines to use soap when he showers.

Now, this thought may seem a little far afield, but the merman was my Cousin Liam's doppelgänger. Liam might well have ended up in Hollywood, had he not gotten married at nineteen, and was blessed with five children by the time he was thirty. He might have gone on to father even more children had his wife not run away with a tourist from Ohio who sold roofing nails to big box stores. Tanya left all five kids behind but took the family dog.

Now, there was also the very slim possibility that the community of Tidal Shores had somehow gotten their act together and copied the very successful shows that have been put on daily at Weeki Wachee State Park in Florida since 1947, as well as many other places around the world. There, beautiful young women wearing 'mermaid tails' swim gracefully around in a large aquarium for the amusement of tourists. These women are experts at holding their breath under water and have been known to do it for as long as four minutes at a time. When I was nine years old, Gan-Gan took me, along with several cousins, including Liam, to Disney World, but on the way back we made a slight detour to see the so-called only live mermaids in the world. I remember being enthralled by the show, and when we returned to Tidal Shores, where we were spending the summer, every time that I went swimming, I kept my legs tightly together and pretended that they were a mermaid's tail. I even asked Gan-Gan to sew me a bathing suit like the one's we'd seen the real mermaids wear at Weeki Wachee, but Gan-Gan was too busy having her own grownup fun to heed my request.

At any rate, I knew what Randi wanted from me, which was a sensationalized story that would boost circulation. Therefore, I decided that at least in this instalment of her proposed series, I would pull out all the stops, and pretend that I had been convinced by what I had seen – no matter how improbable it was. In my defence, I believe various religions have been based on eyewitness accounts of events no less bizarre.

Having taken that approach, I was able to finish my assignment, and send it and my accompanying photos off to Randi by seven, which was the time that Gan-Gan called me down for dinner. Gan-Gan gave up cooking half a century ago, which doesn't matter because she has a live-in Russian housekeeper named Grusha who is a passable cook. I have a hard time guessing the ages of truly ancient people, but Grusha has been working as Gan-Gan's housekeeper for the fifty years since she gave up cooking, so she's no spring chicken. If only people were more like trees; one can tell a tree's age by counting the rings in its trunk after it's been felled. Wouldn't it be handy if one could tell a person's age by counting the wrinkles on his or her face – but without having to kill them first? Of course, Botox, fillers, and anti-wrinkle creams make that an uneven playing field. I'm just saying.

Anyway, I think it's a safe bet that Gan-Gan and her Russian housekeeper are lovers. For the record, they sleep in separate bedrooms, but then again, many married couples do as well, and for a variety of reasons, chief of which is snoring. For as long as I can remember Gan-Gan and Grusha have been going to great, and sometimes humorous lengths to convince guests that they are not lovers. In the meantime, no one who knows and loves my great-grandmother cares one whit what she does between her monogrammed silk sheets. At the same time, it is impossible for guests to ignore the tiptoeing between their two bedrooms after one is supposedly asleep, and for another, the fact that on Gan-Gan's bathroom vanity there are two electric toothbrushes, and no toothbrushes to be found anywhere in Grusha's bathroom. Of course, it is only fair to conclude from this observation that Miss Georgina Legare, she who is old enough to have played with God as a child, has one very snoopy great-granddaughter.

To my knowledge, Grusha has never caught me snooping around in what is supposed to be her bedroom. Even though I have dropped lots of hints that it would be perfectly fine with the entire family if the two of them came out of the closet, Gan-Gan's housekeeper has never warmed up to me. Perhaps she is still holding a grudge because, back when I was three years old, I asked if I could touch her moustache. '*Nyet*,' she said, and rather vehemently too, if I recall correctly. That seems to be one of her favourite words.

Gan-Gan is not religious, but Grusha insists on saying grace, which she mutters in Russian. After that ritual she glares at me, which means that I have to say 'amen.' As long as I don't, Grusha, who holds the serving utensils, will not relinquish them until I have done that. There have been times when I've been ravenous and jumped the gun with my 'amen,' uttering it during one of Grusha's lengthy pauses, instead of at the finale of her prayer. For that grievous sin I always earned the evil eye for the rest of the evening.

The evening of the big reveal, I was careful to time my 'amen' to the millisecond, which earned me a smile from my ancestor. That tiny bit of approval garnered a frown from Grusha.

'Well, this was really a big day for y'all,' I said, as I reached for the meat fork from Grusha.

The darn woman made me tug it out of her hand. '*Nyet*,' she said.

'*What?*' I turned to Gan-Gan. 'You had a fabulous turnout, and I saw the merman myself. He couldn't have looked more authentic.'

Gan-Gan stared at me. 'So, you know?'

SEVENTEEN

'What are you talking about, Gan-Gan? All I know is that I've written, and already submitted, a very exciting piece about the day's events. I have no doubt that my story will be picked up and reprinted by other papers all over the country. By tomorrow night, you're going to be all out of mermaid crap – I mean merchandise – to sell. And I hope that you have a well-stocked freezer, because the road into here is going to be one solid traffic jam for days. Maybe weeks.'

Grusha finally smiled and passed me the serving spoon for the mashed potatoes. '*Da.*'

'Thanks, toots,' I said, just to irritate her. 'Now pass me the gravy boat, please.'

'*Nyet.*'

'Well, in that case, *babushka*, I won't tell you the one big problem that I see looming on the horizon of y'all's scheme.'

The gravy boat came at me so fast that it slopped over the side. Fortunately, it was the kind that was attached to its own saucer, which contained most of the spillage.

'No more *nyet*,' Grusha said, wagging a crooked index finger at me. 'You tell everything, you skinny chicken-lover.'

'You want everything, you Muscovite maniac? Then pass me the green peas. And while you're at it, how about that basket of freshly baked bread, and that slab of room-temperature butter.'

The food piled up around my plate lickety-split. 'That's a sight better,' I said. 'And here's what I saw out there: that was no merman waving at us aboard *The Reel Life*. That was my Cousin Liam.'

Gan-Gan and Grusha exchanged horrified glances. '*Nyet!*' Grusha said as she grabbed for the peas. The serving bowl knocked over my water glass, the contents of which threatened to ruin Gan-Gan's two-hundred-year-old heirloom table. Supposedly Jefferson Davis, the first President of the Confederate States of America, had dined there on his way through the Carolinas at some point during the Civil War. Gan-Gan can't verify the exact date, although when she's had a tipple too many, she does claim to remember the actual visit.

I jumped up to get a roll of paper towels from the kitchen. The 'Jefferson table,' as Gan-Gan called this massive piece of furniture, was more precious to her than her last three husbands combined. I know that for a fact because she once told me so.

'Sit down, Zoe,' she commanded. 'Grusha, you sop up the water.'

'*Da*,' Grusha said, but glowered at her lover under black thickets that badly needed pruning.

'Zoe,' Gan-Gan said, 'where on earth did you get such a crazy idea, that it was your cousin out there posing as a merman?'

'The wonders of technology. I sent the pic of the merman to my laptop, then enlarged the photo, played around with it a bit, added some grid lines, and then compared it to one of Liam taken last summer at our family reunion. They were one and the same. Then I looked down at my legs to see if they were becoming fused, and possibly turning into a tail, with a pair of flukes at the end. Instead of flukes, guess what I found?'

'Very big feet,' Grusha said.

'*Nyet!*' I said. 'They're smaller than yours.'

'Still, very big feet,' Grusha said.

I gave her my version of the evil eye and ploughed on with what I'd discovered. 'Liam spends a lot of time outdoors in the summer, shirtless, as I'm sure you know, so he's got a deep tan. Even this early in the year. But when I examined the rest of the photo, I noticed a pale strip of skin around his waist just above where his scaly tail began.

'That got me to thinking, ladies. Now remember back when you were in college, or maybe even high school, and you got drunk and jumped into a swimming pool wearing all your clothes?'

'*Nyet*,' Grusha and Gan-Gan said simultaneously.

'More's the pity,' I said. 'The point I want to make is that wet clothes are heavy and produce a lot of drag. A lot of the guys had to hold their pants up with both hands when they climbed out of the pool, unless they didn't care about losing them altogether. Even some of the girls with slim hips had trouble keeping their britches up unaided.

'So, I got to thinking back to Weeki Wachee Springs in Florida and wondering just how those lovely mermaids managed to keep their tails from slipping. That's when I looked them up, and saw that they all have lovely round hips, the sort that movie stars used to have back in the 1950s. So, I'm assuming that whoever thought of copying their act up here didn't take this factor into account. Still, I have to give y'all props for having the ingenuity for sourcing the mermaid suit. However, it was a mer*maid* suit that you had Liam wear, and not a merman suit.'

'Don't be ridiculous,' Gan-Gan said, 'he was a merman!' Then, realizing her gaff, she clamped a gnarled hand over her mouth.

'Gan-Gan, dear, you were with me in church when Gunner Jones hypothesized that a merman had the same external sexual organ as live-bearing fishes. The gonopodium is a long anal fin that is very obvious on live-bearing fishes, such as guppies. Like I said before, I watched the footage I took of Liam at least a dozen times, and there wasn't even a trace of an anal fin to be seen. Y'all should have thought about that.'

Gan-Gan bit her lip. 'So, what do you plan to do next, Zoe? Do you plan to write an exposé that will pound the final nail into our coffin? Is it your intention to ruin the lives of everyone in this struggling town, the home of your ancestors, where you still have more kinfolk than there are leaves on a magnolia tree, and where you spent every dang summer of your blessed life, from the time you were a zygote, until now, with the exception of the pandemic years?'

'Vee should kill her,' Grusha said with a straight face.

'*Nyet*,' I said.

Gan-Gan patted her housekeeper's arm. 'That won't be necessary just yet, *devotchka*. We can still use her to get some good publicity, and as they say: there is no such thing as bad publicity. Right, Zoe?'

'*Da*, Gan-Gan.'

Grusha glared at me. 'I keep eye on you; then vee see.'

'Gan-Gan,' I wailed. 'You weren't really serious about having me whacked, were you? You know, deep-sixed. After all, I'm your own flesh and blood. The fruit of your shrivelled loins.'

The old crone smiled. 'Don't be ridiculous, Zoe. You're my favourite grandchild. Tell me that you were joking – if not, I'm insulted.'

'Of course I was joking,' I said. Except that I was not. Many a truth has been said in jest, and I am a cynical woman. My career as a reporter has exposed me to every sort of scheme imaginable, and even though I don't cover the so-called 'hard news,' I do read virtually every story that comes over the wires. I am sadly cognizant of the fact that great-grandmothers do exist who would kill their descendants if the right set of circumstances demanded it. I am a young woman – compared to Gan-Gan – but I am not naïve.

'Then eat up, dear. Grusha has been slaving over a hot stove all afternoon.'

'*Da*, I vork for your gan-gan like slave in de gulags.'

My great-grandmother cackled and patted her housekeeper's arm affectionately. 'Don't be silly, *zaya*. You're going to give Zoe the wrong impression.'

'Gan-Gan, I'm not as stupid as I look; I can see that the two of you have a special relationship, and I don't give a damn if you insist on keeping it a secret.'

My great-grandmother let go of Grusha and grabbed my forearm with her other hand. Then she proceeded to squeeze it with nails as sharp as lion's claws. She might have been a centenarian, or merely just a nonagenarian, but she had the grip of a male college student – but that's just a guess, mind you, as it had been years since a male college student had grabbed any part of me.

'Ouch!' I said.

'My personal life is none of your business,' Gan-Gan hissed.

'That's right,' I said. 'And bravo to you for hissing a sentence that uses the letter "S" in it. There were three of them, in fact. So many *New York Times* bestselling novelists hiss long mouthfuls of ear-grating dialogue that don't contain a single letter "S," and still their book reviewer gives these novelists rave reviews. Should I cite you an example?'

'No, you've whined long enough. Question: do you think anyone else suspects that Grusha and I are – uh – well . . .'

'Lovers?'

My use of the 'L' word left both women looking so stricken that I almost felt sorry for them. I might even have tried to take it back – *somehow* – but Gan-Gan was too quick on the draw.

'Why, you impertinent little bitch! I should wash your mouth out with soap!'

'*Da*,' Grusha said vehemently. 'Soap veet lye.'

'What is *veet*?' I asked innocently.

'She meant "with,"' Gan-Gan snapped. 'Tell me, why are you making fun of Grusha's accent? Is it because you think that she is more than my housekeeper?'

'No!' I snapped back. 'I don't care what she is to you, and I wasn't making fun of her. I honestly didn't understand her – although one would think that after fifty years in this country, she would sound more American. But saying that I should wash my mouth out with lye soap, that's just plain rude.'

'Look here, missy,' Gan-Gan hissed again, although thankfully her claws retracted a mite. 'English is a very difficult language for foreigners to pronounce correctly. This may come as a shock to you, as it did to me, but even many Brits find the English language hard to master. Take the name of their most famous river, the Thames. Do you suppose that they pronounce it as it is written? No, Baby Child, they pronounce it *Temz*. So, if even the British cannot pronounce the "th" combination of letters correctly, how on earth are we to expect immigrants to our country to perfect that sound?'

'Point taken,' I said. 'When I was an exchange student at Oxford, I dated a guy whose family name was Featherstonehaugh, but they pronounced it *Fanshaw*.'

Gan-Gan nodded. 'How long did that relationship last?'

'Well, his parents didn't approve of me.'

'That long, eh?'

I attempted a pleasant smile. 'Now, if you two ladies will excuse me, I believe that I will toddle off to bed. Unless, of course, you offer me an after-dinner libation. In that case, I shall tipple before I toddle, and hope that I don't topple down your impossibly steep stairs. Really, Gan-Gan, you might consider installing a lift; Cousin Liam has a lift in his house, because like yours, it's two stories, and set up on pillars to protect it from storm surges.'

'Vee haf tree stories,' Grusha said.

'Oh really?' I said. 'Are these stories about palm trees, or oak trees, or pines? I'm very fond of trees.'

'Don't be rude, Zoe.' Gan-Gan growled. 'She meant that this is a three-story house. We have a finished attic that is essentially a third story. In the olden days, before the Late Unpleasantness—'

'You mean the Civil War in the 1860s when six hundred and twenty thousand soldiers died? That's more than died in the Revolutionary War, the Mexican War, the Spanish American War, World War One, World War Two, and the Korean War combined.'

'Oh, Zoe, you can be so harsh at times. I was merely explaining that the attic, which has a leak-proof roof, was where certain members of the house help stayed back in olden times. Although admittedly, it can get a little warm up there in the summertime.'

I nodded. 'I'm sure. But by *house help*, you were referring to *enslaved* persons, am I right?'

Gan-Gan flushed. 'Contrary to public opinion, that was before my time. Now, back to the present – to the future, actually. You did bring a frilly frock in that bag of yours, didn't you?'

'Pardon me?'

'For your interview with Governor Hubert Horatio Humphrey Harpootlian,' Gan-Gan said, and then grinned. For a broad that old, she had a remarkably full set of teeth. Sure, they were practically worn down to the gums, but what remained of them were stained a very pleasing shade of brown.

'*What?*' I responded. 'Were you spying on me? Were you eavesdropping on my phone call to my editor?' I said.

'Vee haf our veys,' Grusha said, and grinned as well. Perhaps the gulags had been hard on her, because I could count only four teeth. Again, I'm just a reporter.

'Gan-Gan, for the record, no one says freaking "frilly frock" anymore.'

'Well, I do, and this is my house, so I can say what I want. Anyway, I just wanted to give you a heads-up, so you'll look nice. Governor Hubert Horatio Humphrey Harpootlian will be bringing his own camera crew for a live telecast, but you're to be the only representative from the "fake news" allowed to interview him.'

I shouldn't have been surprised; Gan-Gan can pull more strings than a skilled puppeteer. Instead, I bristled at the words 'fake news.'

'I'll have you know,' I said, 'that unlike the reporters on the networks that you watch, I stick to the facts. Nothing but the facts.'

'*Da*,' Grusha said, 'altoinative feks.'

'That certainly could have come out worse,' I said, 'but no, they're just regular "feks" – I mean, facts! I stick to the truth. There is only one way to tell the truth.'

'*Nyet*,' Grusha said.

'How can you possibly disagree? Is that what they taught you in Communist College?'

My great-grandmother reached out with both spindly arms to grab us simultaneously. 'Ladies, perhaps we should agree to disagree.'

'I think not, Gan-Gan. I cannot agree with stupidity.'

Grusha wrenched her arm away from my great-grandmother and pointed at me. '*Zasranets!*'

I smiled at the enraged Russian. 'Same back at you, sweetie.'

'Why, Zoe, what a kind woman you've turned out to be, after all,' Gan-Gan said. I could only assume that the dear old woman did not speak a word of Russian, because Grusha was certainly not placated by my response.

'Dis voman must go tonight. I demand.'

'*Nyet*,' Gan-Gan said. OK, so maybe she spoke *one* word of Russian.

'*Da!* Must go!' Grusha stomped a foot so hard that my sweet tea sloshed over its glass.

'This is still *my* house, Grusha, darling,' Gan-Gan said softly.

'Ladies,' I said, 'why don't the two of you come out of the closet and get married?'

'Ha!' Grusha said. 'Den vee get arrested.'

'Arrested for what?'

'Den you know nuss-ing,' Grusha said triumphantly. 'Dis illegal.'

'Gay marriage has been legal since 2015,' I said. 'Don't you read the papers? Watch TV? Listen to the radio?'

'Fake news,' Grusha said, and folded her arms.

'Gan-Gan, have you been keeping her locked up in the house, depriving her from any sort of input from the outside world?'

'It's a cruel world out there,' my great-grandmother said. 'Besides, she's a natural born sceptic who doesn't know how to read English. I see it as my Christian duty to protect her from the slings and arrows of the twentieth century.'

'Gan-Gan, you are aware that we are now well into the twenty-first century, aren't you?'

'Don't be silly, Zoe.'

'Well, *aren't* you?'

'Of course I am, dear. I'm a savvy businesswoman. In fact, I'm the founding member of the Big Ten . . . nis Club.'

'I beg your pardon,' I said. '*You* play tennis? Forgive me for sounding surprised, but isn't falling in your demographic particularly dangerous? I read somewhere that broken pelvises amongst women of a certain age can sometimes mean that they will never walk again, which can, in some cases—'

Gan-Gan tossed what remained of her sweet tea into my lap. It was a direct hit, so I know that she did it on purpose.

'Oops, my hand slipped,' she said. 'That happens sometimes to us women of a certain age.'

'I'll take that as my cue to leave, ladies,' I said, as I stood. 'Good night. And Grusha, no need for you to tiptoe to my great-grandmother's room tonight. Walk there proudly; I'm perfectly fine with the two of you being lovers. But when you get there, ask her to fill you in on the dissolution of the Soviet Union.'

'Zoe!' Gan-Gan shouted. 'That's enough!'

But it was too late. The lit match I'd thrown had already started a small fire.

'Vhat eez dis about de Soviet Union?' Grusha demanded to know.

'The Soviet Union is no more. It collapsed in 1991, like a soufflé when the oven door is slammed while it is still baking. But don't look so downcast, your Mother Russia still exists; she just isn't as powerful as she once was.'

Grusha turned to Gan-Gan. 'Eez true?'

Gan-Gan shrugged. 'More or less. Maybe more. I was going to tell you eventually. When the time was right. You know – when you were in a good mood.'

'You lie like a bug!' Grusha screamed, knocked over her chair, and ran into the kitchen. 'I am finish wiz you.'

'The expression is "lie like a *rug*," dear,' Gan-Gan said. Her eyes were spilling over with tears. Because of the myriad well-defined wrinkles on her face, the tears flowed down in alternating directions, and suggested some of the old games that I used to play in amusement park arcades when I was a girl. In Gan-Gan's case, tears from both sides of her face met at the middle of her chin where they combined into a steady trickle of water. It was a most disconcerting sight. Who would have thought that a dried-up old crone – and I mean that lovingly, as I will be one as well someday – could contain so much liquid in their tear ducts? Also, as far back as I could remember, I had never seen my great-grandmother ever shed a single tear.

Even at my granddaddy's funeral, Gan-Gan had sat on the folding chairs by the grave, looking stone-faced. Then again, she may have been shit-faced. I was eight years old then, and wasn't into smelling anyone's breath, except for Bobby Johnson's. However, every time I tried to kiss Bobby, he ran away screaming, and carrying on about how yucky girls were.

'I'm so sorry, Gan-Gan,' I said. 'I should have left well enough alone.'

'No,' she said. 'It was time I levelled with Grusha. I guess we weren't fooling anyone, were we?'

'No one in the family. But I'm sure that you got everyone else fooled. I mean, who would think that the grand dame of a small Southern town would turn out to be a liberal lesbian with a Russian lover?'

Gan-Gan shuddered, and then wiped her chin on her fine linen napkin. 'Oh, Zoe, please don't use the "L" word.'

'Which word? Lesbian, or lover?'

'*Liberal*. I'm anything but. I'm an old-fashioned, Conservative woman. I've voted Republican my entire life, straight down the ticket, and I attend church every Sunday, even though Billy-Bob's sermons bore me to distraction. Publicly I look down my long patrician nose at same-sex marriage, but privately – Zoe, tell me honestly, what would be the consequences of Grusha and I finally tying the knot?'

My pulse raced with excitement. 'Is she even an American citizen?'

'*Da* – I mean, yes. We had to see to that decades ago; it was too much trouble trying to renew her Green Card.'

'Look, this is the way I see it. There may be a few stick-in-the-muds who express negative views, but so what? You've been alive a lot longer than anyone else in town. Maybe in the county. Maybe in the state. It's what you think, and believe in, that matters. So go for it. March into that kitchen right now and tell Grusha that you want to make an honest woman out of her – whatever that stupid old expression means. And while you're at it, tell her that you're sorry for keeping her ignorant, but you did it only because you were afraid of losing her precious love.'

Gan-Gan stared at me. 'Zoe, you should write the inside of greeting cards.'

'Yeah, Gan-Gan, if I wanted to starve to death. Who sends cards anymore?'

'Then you should write lyrics for songs.'

'And not sing the lyrics as well?'

My great-grandmother shook her head. 'I love you dearly, kid, but I heard you singing in the shower earlier.'

'Good night,' I said, then kissed her on the cheek before heading upstairs. For my kindness, I was repaid with a mouthful of saltwater.

EIGHTEEN

The following morning when I came down to breakfast, Gan-Gan and Grusha were sitting at the table, placidly chewing Grusha's homemade biscuits. Their faces bore not a hint of expression; they might as well have been a pair of cows chewing their cuds. Were they trying to hide the joy that they felt at finally being able express to their love freely – I had heard no tiptoeing during the night – or was it rage that they were concealing behind their leathery masks?

If it was rage that they were feeling, then perhaps I was the object of it, for exposing my great-grandmother's multitudinous lies. If this was the case, I could understand why both women would be pissed with me. Gan-Gan stood to lose her lover who she'd tried so hard to isolate from the world, and Grusha had been stripped of innocence, and essentially lost forty years of her life.

If it was joy on Grusha's part, knowing that she could at last become an official wife to a woman that she'd hopefully come to love, then I had to rethink her origin story. Perhaps she wasn't Russian after all, but merely British with a speech impediment. What else could explain the fact that she looked as inexpressive as a *moai*, one of the iconic statues on Easter Island? Still, I could only hope that at any second they would set down their biscuits, throw up their arms, and shout something like: 'Hurrah! We're finally out of the closet!'

But when they'd finished with their biscuits, they polished off the last of their bacon and eggs, drank another cup of coffee, ate another biscuit (who said old ladies can't eat?), sighed heavily, and then finally pushed back their chairs.

'Governor Hubert Horatio Humphrey Harpootlian will be landing in sixteen minutes,' Gan-Gan said. 'Don't be late – but do brush your hair first. It looks like a rat's nest.'

'What do you mean the governor will be *landing*? Tidal Shores doesn't have an airport.'

'Helicopter, Baby Child. On the beach.'

'Shut the front door!'

'De door eez shut,' Grusha said in a monotone, while avoiding eye contact.

'That's just an expression, darling.'

'I am not your darling. *Da?*'

'*Da*,' I said, and dashed upstairs to brush my teeth again and touch up my lipstick. However, I did *not* brush my hair. My hair was supposed to be worn slightly messy; that was the style I'd chosen. Besides, getting anywhere near the helicopter as it landed, or even near the ocean, was just going to mess it up all the more.

By the time I clattered downstairs, the house was empty. I was surprised to see that the breakfast things had not been cleared from the table. It was not like the Grusha I'd known virtually my entire life to not immediately do the washing-up after meals. Then again, Governor Hubert Horatio Humphrey Harpootlian's visit was undoubtedly a big deal for her, not to mention his arrival by helicopter.

In the three plus decades that I'd known the woman from Russia, I'd never encountered her outside the confines of Gan-Gan's house. Frankly, I couldn't help but feel proud of myself, as if in a way I'd been her liberator. In 1597, in *Meditationes Sacrae*, Francis Bacon wrote that 'knowledge is power.' I had, after all, ripped the blindfold off Grusha's head and made her aware that there was more going on in the world than what my great-grandmother was allowing her to know. One might say that I'd filled Grusha's head with power, and now she'd been freed from a life of indentured servitude.

Thus, feeling smugly satisfied with myself, as many do-gooders are wont to do, I practically skipped my way to the beach. By then, thank heavens, the helicopter had already landed. Trust me, only a masochist would voluntarily get within a hundred feet of a helicopter landing on a sandy Carolina beach when it hasn't rained for several days. If one really did have rats in their hair, the sand kicked up by the rotors would either kill the little varmints by asphyxiation or send them flying off into the next county. Although, to be honest, there was one woman who got a little too close for comfort and said that the sand blasting against her face did more to smooth her acne-pocked complexion than three acid peels from her dermatologist. Still, she would not recommend it, because she lost her wig during the incident.

At any rate, it was only after the rotor blades slowed to a full stop that Governor Hubert Horatio Humphrey Harpootlian stepped from the helicopter. The governor was an enormous man. His office listed him as six foot five inches and weighing 285 pounds. In my opinion, someone in his office, maybe the governor himself, shaved a good fifteen pounds off his official weight. It wouldn't be accurate to say that his eyebrows each weighed a pound, because he only had one brow, a black hedgerow that grew across his forehead, practically from temple to temple. Frida Kahlo would have wept with envy had she lived to see photos of Governor Hubert Horatio Humphrey Harpootlian.

The only other significant feature of South Carolina's most powerful elected leader was that he had an astonishingly high, and seemingly perfectly round pair of buttocks. When viewed from the front, Governor Hubert Horatio Humphrey Harpootlian appeared to be just another overfed and under-groomed American who'd won the lottery pool when it came to height. But when viewing him from the side, or from the back, the casual observer might be forgiven for assuming that the politician had been born with a totally flat derriere and had stuffed a pair of basketballs into his jockey shorts to compensate for the deficiency in natural padding.

The optics of Governor Hubert Horatio Humphrey Harpootlian walking, with his enormous and perfectly round butt cheeks bobbling in the air, had never ceased to cause great amusement amongst the good people of South Carolina. Fortunately, we Southerners are a polite people, and we ridicule our public figures only in private. Besides, the governor had no choice over his genetic inheritance, although there are some small-minded folk who say that a man with his physiognomy should not have run for such a visible office.

By the time I arrived at the scene, which was to be the permanent home of Miss Lucy the mermaid, I was huffing and puffing. Already the governor Hubert Horatio Humphrey Harpootlian and my gan-gan were involved in a tête-à-tête conversation adjacent to the preserved remains of the mermaid. Both the governor's aide and his security agents were standing at a discreet distance, and when I tried to approach my great-grandmother, a frowning man in dark glasses waved me off.

'Stand back, miss,' he barked.

Gan-Gan looked my way. 'Oh, she's all right,' she said. 'She's family. I invited her. She's doing a piece for *The Observer Today*.'

'Fake news,' Governor Hubert Horatio Humphrey Harpootlian said.

'That's a matter of opinion, isn't it, sir?' I said, as I stepped quickly up.

'Are you one of my constituents?' he asked.

'No, sir, I live in North Carolina.'

'In that case, you're dead wrong. *The Observer Today* publishes only fake news.'

'In that case you're a bully and a buffoon, and I won't include your visit in the article that I'm writing.'

Gan-Gan gasped. 'Zoe! I'm so proud of you. I didn't think that you had that much spine.'

'*Me?* After everything I said at dinner last night?'

'Yes,' Gan-Gan agreed, 'but that was only with family. But now you've just told off this big buffoon – who, by the way, is your second cousin. His great-grandmother, Lorraine Legare, was my oldest sister.'

'Shut the front door!'

'Eventually, Zoe, Baby Child, you might do well to shut your mouth before a fly finds its way in.' Gan-Gan turned to Governor Hubert Horatio Humphrey Harpootlian. 'H,' she said, 'meet my favourite great-granddaughter, Zoe Legare Porter. Her Mama was Beatrice Legare.'

The governor extended a meaty hand. 'Cousin Zoe,' he said, with a slight nod of his head.

'Cousin H,' I said, with a slight nod of my own head.

'That's *Governor* Hubert Horatio Humphrey Harpootlian,' he said.

'That's *Reporter* Zoe *Legare* Porter,' I said.

'Children,' Gan-Gan said, 'enough! Now play nice, you two, or I'll have a word with y'all's mamas.'

'Yes, ma'am,' South Carolina's chief executive and I said in unison.

'Good,' Gan-Gan said. 'Now, H, what do you think of our little lady here? Pretty remarkable, isn't she? Think of all the tourism she'll bring to the state.'

'She's a beauty,' Governor Hubert Horatio Humphrey Harpootlian said. 'She'll do just the trick.'

'Trick?' I said.

'It's just an expression,' Gan-Gan said.

'Hmm. Governor,' I said, 'do you really think that Miss Lucy is a beauty?'

Governor Hubert Horatio Humphrey Harpootlian took a couple of steps in my direction and loomed over me, like a building, or a large tree, that was in danger of falling. The black hedgerow that was his eyebrow had buckled in the middle by the force of his scowl.

'That too was just an expression, girly.'

'Well, I should hope so,' I said. 'Instead of putting lipstick on a pig, as the saying goes, I'd venture to say that someone put lipstick on an albino ape, attached it to a fish tail, and voilà, we have Miss Lucy, the soon to be legendary mermaid of Tidal Shores.'

Governor Hubert Horatio Humphrey Harpootlian had the audacity to throw back his massive head and let loose with a full-throated laugh. What's more, it wasn't that he'd found my observation humorous; he'd found it preposterous. Meanwhile Gan-Gan had turned chalk white, and she'd suddenly developed a twitch at the left corner of her mouth.

Had I accidentally stumbled on to something? Perhaps Governor Hubert Horatio Humphrey Harpootlian wasn't laughing at my hypothesis; maybe he was trying to distract me from pursuing that train of thought by shaming me with his laughter. Maybe I should be giving more credence to Gan-Gan's pallor, and sudden onset of a facial tic. The last couple of years had seen an avalanche of conspiracy theories unleashed upon the public, and a good deal of them had emanated from duly elected government officials. How was one to discern the truth?

Mama says that in 'her day' she could look things up in books called encyclopaedias, and that their contents had been vetted by scholars, and one could trust that they were indeed facts. Mama also said that American television had only three networks, and the nightly news programs delivered unadulterated news – again facts. Or *were* they? I mean, isn't everything filtered through somebody's bias? But come on, an ape top, and fish bottom, if that's indeed what this was, how stupid did they think the American public was?

'Well then,' Gan-Gan growled, 'it's time you took the boat tour, Governor Hubert Horatio Humphrey Harpootlian. Perhaps we'll see a live mermaid. Maybe even a merman.'

'What a great idea,' I said. 'May I come too?'

'Absolutely not,' Gan-Gan said. 'You're a fake news reporter.'

I felt as if my face had been slapped. My great-grandmother has always been supportive of my career and has never once criticized

The Observer Today. I had, however, heard her criticize Governor Hubert Horatio Harpootlian's views on social issues, as well as gerrymandering. Voting districts in South Carolina are established by the dominant party in the state legislature, and at first glance make as much sense as a Jackson Pollock painting.

'But, Gan-Gan,' I protested, 'you know that I research my stories diligently.'

'Maybe too diligently, sometimes,' she said with a toss of her hoary head. 'If you get my drift, Baby Child. I reckon it's time you drive back up to Charlotte. Give your mama my love, of course. And your brother, if you see him. Lord knows I haven't seen hide nor hair of him for nigh on thirty years. Not since he dropped that piece of jam bread, face down, on my new white sofa. Blackberry jam it was. And after I told him a hundred times that eating was to be done only in the dining room and kitchen.'

'But, Gan-Gan, in all fairness, if memory serves me right, Lofton was only two at the time. At least that's what Mama tells me. I mean, what do I know, I was just four.'

'Well, they never should have let him out of his highchair, and he never got a whipping.'

'Gan-Gan, one doesn't whip a two-year-old.'

'Spare the rod and spoil the child,' Governor Hubert Horatio Humphrey Harpootlian said. 'It's in the Bible.'

'No, it's not,' I said.

'Zoe,' Gan-Gan snapped. 'Out!'

'Pardon me, Governor H,' I said, 'I must bid you *adieu*.' Then I was out of there faster than a dog that stumbled upon a colony of feral cats.

In fact, I charged out of there so quickly, and I was so annoyed, that I didn't pay no never mind – to use a colloquialism – to where I was going. The fact that I smacked full-on into a very hunky man, almost knocking him over, was completely accidental.

NINETEEN

The evening before, as Gan-Gan and I had walked the short distance from her antique/souvenir store up to her house, I'd queried her about Gunner Jones' romantic entanglements – if any. Gan-Gan firmly believed that Gunner Jones 'batted for the other team.' Her opinion was based on rumours, and the fact that the man was not known to date any women who lived in Tidal Shores. In my estimation, all that said about Gunner Jones was that he was a wise man who didn't want old gossips like Gan-Gan actually knowing the details of his love life.

When I smacked into Gunner Jones that morning, we instinctively clutched each other to keep from falling over. A rational person might suppose that our embrace would have lasted a nanosecond, and then we would have pulled apart while mumbling words of apology. Or at least I would have apologized. Instead, we stood perfectly still, locked in each other's arms, like two pieces of a puzzle that had never quite been separated. I breathed in his smell, felt his body heat, and heard the thump of his heart.

It was Gunner Jones who disengaged from our inadvertent embrace. 'Whoa,' he said. 'Maybe we should take things a little slower at first. You know, like dinner, or a movie. Or not. Or we could just fall into the sack if that's what you were signalling. To be honest, I'm not up on the latest lingo that you kids use these days.'

I shrugged. 'What's "lingo" mean?'

'Oh my God,' Gunner Jones said. 'You don't own a *lingo*? I thought that everyone in your generation owned a lingo.' He said that with a straight face.

'I'm not exactly a kid, and I know what *lingo* means, you *dingus*. And dingus, for your information, is slang for a dim-witted, silly person, but not meant in a mean sort of way. But yeah, dinner and/or a movie would be nice, except that I'm headed up to Charlotte this morning.'

'Why?' Gunner Jones said.

'Because that's where I live, and that's also where I'm gainfully employed.'

'Doing what, if I might ask?' he said.

'You might,' I replied, 'but if I told you, I'd have to kill you.'

I was merely stalling in order to brush hair back from my face using my fingers. I even had to pull a few strands out of my mouth. If only I'd listened to Gan-Gan, it wouldn't look quite this messy. But how was I to know that I would collide with someone?

'I'll take the risk of you trying to kill me,' Gunner Jones said. 'So, spill; what is it that you do, up there in Charlotte?'

'I'm a features reporter for *The Observer Today*.'

Gunner Jones smiled. Believe me, he was devilishly handsome when he did so.

'So you write fake news for a living?' Gunner Jones said.

'Not you too!' I wailed.

His smile widened. 'I'm just yanking your chain. It saddens me that so many newspapers are going out of business or being forced into only online versions. I read the print version of *The Observer Today* every time I come up to Charlotte, which is about every three or four months, and it has always seemed to me to be very even-handed. Therefore, I'm sure that your articles are well researched, and that you too try not to show any bias.'

I was standing way too close. Ever so slowly as I spoke, I inched backward, out of my arm's reach, lest I grabbed the hunk with both hands by the collar, and plant one on him. After all, Me Too cuts both ways.

'Frankly, it's almost impossible *not* to show bias,' I said. 'That's because I have to start with a point of view. Let's take the mermaid series that I'm doing here—'

Even when Gunner Jones frowned, his perfectly sculpted face had its own peculiar attractiveness. 'Wait! You're doing a series on my Miss Lucy?'

'So, she's *your* Miss Lucy, is she?' I said.

'That's not what I said,' he protested.

'That's exactly what you said. I'll have you know that I did not fall off the turnip truck last week; you can't pull the rug over my eyes.'

Gunner Jones let loose another full-throated laugh. 'Wow! Two metaphors, one of which includes a reference to your great-grandmother's generation. Turnip truck! You're an absolute delight.'

'And you're as irritating as a power outage on the hottest day of the year,' I said. 'What I initially wanted to say – what I insist on saying now – is that I don't for a minute believe that the *thing* that y'all refer to as Miss Lucy is, or at any time was, an actual mermaid.'

'Oh really? What makes you say that?' Gunner Jones' eyes were sparkling. He seemed intrigued, perhaps even amused by my declaration. He certainly didn't seem upset.

'Listen, Mr Jones, I am an educated woman. I have a Bachelor of Arts degree from the University of North Carolina at Charlotte in journalism, with a minor in biology. For the longest time I toyed with the idea of becoming a foreign correspondent – the ones who visit war zones, or third world countries where famine and disease are rampant. I thought that all those courses in biology, and having to dissect pig foetuses, would inure me to gross things, but I found out the hard way that they didn't.'

I paused.

'Go on,' Gunner Jones said. 'You can't stop there with your story. What happened to make you change your mind?'

'It was the aftermath of a car accident. That's all I'm going to say. Anyway, my point is that I know enough science to say that there is no such creature as an actual mermaid. What you, my great-grandmother, and the rest of the Tidal Shores city council are perpetuating is one huge hoax. To y'all, this may be a hoot, and for now it certainly seems to be a draw for tourists, but it is immoral.'

Gunner Jones looked as if I'd slapped him. '*Immoral?*' He grabbed my hands and pulled off to the side, where we were less likely to be overheard. 'Even if it is a hoax – and I'm not saying that it is – what makes it immoral?'

I shook my head. 'That you even have to ask that, Gunner, tells me everything I need to know. Where's your moral compass? You're lying to all these people, for heaven's sake. My great-grandmother is selling merchandise out the wazoo, all based on a lie.'

Then Gunner Jones, the undeniably handsome stud muffin, brought my hands up to his lips and kissed them. 'Zoe, what we're really doing is selling happiness. For young and old alike. That, and saving a community that once thrived on this very spot for almost three hundred years. Is that so bad?'

I snatched my hands away from his searing lips. 'So *y'all* are the real purveyors of fake news!'

Gunner Jones shrugged his broad shoulders. 'Are you thinking of children around the world, for whom the discovery of mermaids is a thrilling confirmation of their deeply held beliefs?'

'Those are fantasies, Gunner,' I said.

'Yeah, like Santa Claus. Are you in favour of pulling back the curtain on Santa Claus now for children under the age of five?'

'That's not fair,' I said.

'What if a sick child – no, make that hundreds of very sick children, and adults too – in hospital wards all around the world can have their spirits lifted by the confirmation that mermaids really exist. Would you really deny them that? What would be gained by your version of the truth?'

'My version of the *truth*?' I asked incredulously.

'Well, isn't the truth always in the eye, or ear, of the beholder?' Gunner Jones said. 'Let's say that you witness an altercation between two people – maybe two kids on the playground. They each have different stories, and what they have to say differs from what you saw.'

'But then there's the absolute truth,' I said, perhaps a tad pompously. 'By that, I mean what *really* happened.'

'Zoe, the statement that a square is not a circle is an example of the absolute truth. Would you care to give me some other examples, without delving into religion?'

I stamped a foot with frustration. 'You are so maddening. So what are you suggesting? That I let you guys perpetuate a preposterous myth, to maybe millions of children, just to bring tourism back to little old Tidal Shores, South Carolina?'

'Exactly that,' said Gunner Jones with his sexy grin. 'And remember, even though you were born up in Charlotte, North Carolina, your mama was born down here in Tidal Shores, South Carolina, as was her daddy before her, and his daddy before him, and who knows how many generations before that.'

'I do. It was six generations.'

'There. See? You can't let your heritage – this town where so many generations of your family were born, diapered, drooled, teethed, crawled, walked, schooled, worked, wed, mated, birthed, parented, suffered debilitating diseases, were diapered again, drooled again, and then died – this place with so much of your personal history, you can't let it disappear off the map.'

'You forgot the part about my ancestors owning and abusing enslaved persons.'

'Oh yeah, that too,' Gunner Jones said. 'I just didn't want you to feel guilty; you seem like a sensitive woman.'

'And you didn't need to mention drooling even once,' I said.

'I thought you were a realist, Zoe.'

'OK, OK,' I practically screamed. 'I'll play it cool for six weeks. That's *six* weeks. Y'all can have y'all's fun for that amount of time only. Then I'm pulling the curtain back and revealing your scam for what it is: a scam. *Capiche?*'

Much to my delight, and to my surprise, Gunner Jones grabbed me and kissed me. Of course, I am under no obligation to say more; nonetheless I would like to divulge that the kiss was returned, and was not a mere pressing of lips against lips. There were other shapes involved, one of which was quite impressive.

Of course, since we were in a public place, our inappropriate contact, if any, was of a brief duration. It was, however, of sufficient length to convince both of us that we needed to reunite as soon as possible.

'What does your schedule look like?' he asked, as he walked me out to my car. By then any thought of saying goodbye to Gan-Gan had flown out of my head.

I sighed. 'I'm supposed to do a human-interest piece about a prostitute over in Raleigh, North Carolina. I need to interview her and, more importantly, her sister.'

'No kidding,' Gunner Jones said. 'What's so interesting about a prostitute in your state's capital? Is she sleeping with prominent politicians?'

'No,' I said. 'This prostitute is a conjoined twin. The interesting thing is that her sister is a virgin. At any rate, after I interview those two women, I'm scheduled to go up to Boone, North Carolina and interview a ninety-year-old couple who found a gem-quality emerald the size of a goose egg in their back yard. They've been offered fourteen million dollars for it, and some chump change. What they're hoping to do with the money is buy a small island somewhere that comes with titles – like Baron and Baroness, or some such. I plan to ask them, why don't they buy a desert island that nobody cares about, and declare themselves monarchs? Why settle for being lower-ranking aristocrats when one could be top dog?'

'Why, indeed,' Gunner Jones said. 'I've always fancied myself as a benevolent dictator.'

'Oh really?' I said. 'Who would you dictate to?'

'A dictation machine. The whole thing was just a joke, by the way.'

'That's too bad,' I said. 'Because I wouldn't mind following your orders.'

'Zoe—'

'I was only teasing. For goodness' sake, I'm outta here. Like now. Listen, if it's all right with you, I'll give you a call when I'm done with the Boone trip. Who knows, they might not even live long enough for me to get up there, given their age. I hope that the island they want to buy has a helicopter pad, in case they need to get evacuated for medical treatment.'

'On the other hand,' Gunner Jones said, 'maybe Lord and Lady Whoever plan to be buried on the premises of their manor home. Maybe that's their goal. In that case, I think it's rather romantic.'

'Hmm,' I said. 'You really are a romantic man, aren't you? First a fake mermaid, for which you stand to profit less than your friends, and now bought titles, and lonely burials on a remote island. It doesn't get any more romantic than that.'

We'd reached my car by then, but Gunner Jones pulled me into the shade of a live oak. 'What did you mean by that? About me profiting less than my friends?'

'Gunner,' I said, 'I'm actually cleverer than I look. I'm well aware that the town council of Tidal Shores is comprised of its major business owners. I can see that you're an excellent taxidermist, but I doubt that you can do the volume of sales that my great-grandmother can, because your work involves precision. Likewise, you can't rent your extra chairs to other beauticians, like Emmeline Davis, or schedule more harbour tours like your good buddy Hoyt Hunter. You know what I mean.'

'Maybe I do know,' Gunner Jones said, 'or maybe I don't. After all, according to you, Zoe Porter, I know more about the true anatomy of Miss Lucy over there than anyone else in Tidal Shores. In my book that's worth a whole lot more than any one member of the Big Ten's share of the profits.'

'*The Big Ten*,' I said. 'I love it. It sounds either like a sports league, or the heads of powerful criminal families.'

'Loose lips sink ships,' Gunner Jones said, 'so allow me to seal yours with a kiss.'

TWENTY

A year later , , ,

'**M**ermaid Day!' Mama said in disgust. 'What's this world coming to? I can't believe the President of the United States of America officially declared Mermaid Day an official holiday!'

'Mama,' my brother Lofton said, 'you voted for the man. Besides, what choice did the president have? It was nearly a unanimous vote in the House of Representatives, and it was a unanimous vote in the Senate. It's what we, the people, wanted.'

'Don't be a jerk, Lofton,' I snapped. 'You know how Mama and I feel about it.'

'I do,' said my jerky brother, 'but that's only because the two of you can't see all the good that belief in mermaids has done for this country. For a while there it looked like we were facing a political divide that was going to shatter our democracy. Truly, it was about to become an uncivil war: brother against brother, sister against sister, mother against son—'

'We get the picture,' Mama said, as she handed her twenty-nine-year-old son a plate of country-fried steak with red-eye gravy, mashed potatoes, English peas, collard greens, and light-as-air biscuits. Mama cooks up a storm when her 'baby boy' stops over for dinner, even though he is a well-to-do banker, who can afford to eat at the most expensive restaurants in Charlotte.

I got up to fix my own plate, because Mama does not wait hand and foot on me. However, I have every confidence that Mama loves me as much as she does Lofton. Mama is an old-fashioned Southern woman. The takeaway is that Lofton is helpless around the house when there are females present. Still, he somehow manages to care for himself when he is not at home visiting her, or when he is between live-in girlfriends.

'What's really sad,' Mama said, as she poured fresh coffee for Lofton, 'is they say that now nearly half as many people believe that mermaids are real, as believe that God is real.'

Lofton snorted. 'Who is *they*?'

'You know,' Mama said, 'the hosts of *Get Up, America*. The show that I watch every morning with my breakfast. They've interviewed experts on the subject. Lofton, it's not just little kids who believe that mermaids are real, it's their parents too. It's being taken as a fact.'

'So?' my stupid brother said. 'You can't prove that mermaids are *not* real, just like you can't prove that God *is* real.'

Believe it or not, Lofton's not just a banker, but one of the vice presidents of a major chain of banks that spreads across the nation. Lofton is a financial wizard *and* a moral moron.

'Lofton, you *dingus*,' I said, 'I watch *Good Night, America* on the same channel whenever I get a chance, and I've heard there have been close to a hundred mermaid sightings in just this one year since Miss Lucy went on display.'

'You're behind the times, Sis,' Lofton said, as he slathered the top half of his biscuit with unsalted butter. 'The number just reached one hundred and thirty-four. The last sighting was yesterday evening near Durban, South Africa.'

'How odd,' I said, 'that mermaids should be lollygagging about where great white sharks abound.'

Lofton slammed his knife petulantly against his plate. 'What do you know about Durban, South Africa and sharks?'

'Zoe dated a nice young man in college who was from there,' Mama said gently. She picked up the bottom half of Lofton's biscuit and began buttering it for him. 'His name was Greg, wasn't it, Zoe?'

'Greg*ory*,' I said.

'That's right, dear. Anyway, Lofton, your sister's boyfriend had vicious scars on his left thigh from a shark attack. I'm surprised that you don't remember him. He came down to Tidal Shores with us on summer break for a week, and Zoe got all out of sorts because her gan-gan wouldn't let them share a room.'

Lofton smirked. 'I remember the dude now. Skinny, big ears, buck teeth. Zoe was so pissed that the two of them weren't allowed to shack up that week that she kept slamming doors until Gan-Gan finally asked us to leave. Weren't we originally supposed to stay two weeks?'

'You're evil, you know that?' I said to my brother.

'Children,' Mama said, 'now behave. Zoe, I realize that you and

I tend to think a lot alike when it comes to politics and religion, but Lofton makes a lot of sense as well.'

'He *does*? Mama, I've taken you to see Miss Lucy; you've seen for yourself that she's a fake.'

Mama plopped globs of strawberry jam on Lofton's biscuit halves and spread it around for him as she talked. 'Zoe, don't get me wrong, darling. I still think that an imaginary creature should not be given a national holiday. However, why, in the grand scheme of things, does it matter if Miss Lucy is a fake, just as long as she is bringing hope and happiness to people who have been through some very trying years? Honestly, dear, I'm afraid I'd endorse Bigfoot if it would step up and get the job done – pun intended.'

'Ha, ha, Mama. Mama, the United States Supreme Court just last week, in a five-to-four ruling, declared that *merfolk* have the same rights and privileges as *Homo sapiens*. Think how ridiculous this is, Mama! There aren't any such creatures as merfolk, and it took almost eighty-nine years for the last enslaved Americans to be officially emancipated after our nation declared its independence from England. Until then they were counted as only three-fifths of a person for tax purposes.'

'You see, Sis,' Lofton said triumphantly, with jam oozing from his stuffed mouth. 'That proves that we've come a long way!'

'Think of how much more fun cruises will be,' Mama said, 'with merfolk swimming alongside the ships. Not at a distance, like they do now, but close up, like the one that you took me to see from Hoyt Hunter's boat at Tidal Shores.'

'That was no mermaid, Mama. That was your nephew, Liam Legare.'

'Zoe, dear, don't be such a spoilsport. Allow an old lady her fantasies – if only for a day. It's been an especially difficult year for me, as you well know.'

Indeed, I did know. Shortly after the supposed mermaid, aka Miss Lucy, had been reportedly discovered bobbing about in Tidal Shores' bay, Mama's geriatric dog Prankster had to be put to sleep. Even though the black Labrador often slept with me, during the day he was Mama's constant companion whenever she was home.

'You're not that old, Mama,' I said gently. 'But I guess it is OK to dream. Just don't expect your church to approve of inter-species weddings anytime soon.'

'I don't see why not,' Mama said crossly. 'The Episcopal church has always been on the cutting edge of social equality. We do perform LGBTQ+ weddings.'

'I know, Mama. That's where Gan-Gan and Grusha got married. Who knew that they'd actually come out?'

'You forced them out of the closet, dear,' Mama said. 'That's why they didn't invite you.'

'And that still hurts,' I said. 'Did you even suspect that they were lesbians, Mama?'

Mama snatched a piece of bacon off Lofton's plate and held it up to his open mouth. He practically inhaled it. They reminded me of a nature special I'd watched, in which a tiny songbird unwittingly feeds the much larger chick of the cuckoo bird.

'Zoe, I was raised not to interfere in other people's lives,' Mama said pointedly. 'I didn't concern myself with their somewhat unorthodox arrangement, or what I suspected might be going on behind closed doors whenever we stayed over.'

'Mama, all I did was let Grusha know that gay marriage was legal. It was unconscionable that Gan-Gan was keeping her in the dark about that.'

'Your great-grandmother had a phobia about marriage, that's why. It didn't have anything to do with Grusha per se; it was marriage in general that she feared. She was never married, you know.'

'*What?* Do you mean to say that Grandpa Legare was an – uh – illegitimate son?'

'Good for Gan-Gan,' Lofton said. 'And by the way, Mama, Zoe meant bastard, but she was afraid of offending you.'

'Tattle-tale,' I whispered. 'Suck-up.'

'And now she's calling me names,' Lofton said, and opened his mouth again to be fed. My sweet grieving Mama obliged her baby boy by holding another piece of bacon up to his waiting lips.

'Look at it this way,' I said. 'If I hadn't said anything, then poor long-suffering Grusha would probably never know the bonds of sacred matrimony, or the satisfaction of being known as Grusha Legare. That has a certain ring to it, don't you think?'

When Lofton opened his mouth to speak again, I had the brief satisfaction of shoving a particularly long strip of bacon down his greasy gullet. Instead of being irritated by what I'd done, he looked pleased.

'More,' he said, with his mouth full. He clapped his pale banker's hands as he didn't have baby bird wings to flutter.

I turned my attention to Mama. 'Getting back to the subject of your church: given that it's Sunday, why aren't you there right now, praying for the souls of your wayward children?'

'Zoe, darling, was that sarcasm really necessary? I have every confidence that my two little pollywogs will forge their own special relationship with God, in their own time. And you know very well that I go almost every Sunday, but sometimes I like to take a little break – especially when my back is acting up. I just can't sit still as long as I used to. And anyway, for when I don't go, there is always a church service on TV that I can tune into.'

That said, Mama took the television remote from her apron pocket, and the kitchen set came to life. Immediately a church service already in progress filled the 65-inch screen. Her quick action surprised me, so it took me a few seconds more than it should have before I recognized the show. It was *Guns for God*.

'Jesus was the Lamb of God!' Reverend Givmemore shouted at his studio audience. 'And what colour are lambs, folks?'

'White!' the audience roared.

'So then what colour was Jesus?'

'White!' the audience roared again.

'Was Jesus the Son of God?' Reverend Givmemore shouted.

'Yes!' the audience roared and stomped their feet.

'So then, what colour is God?' This time the reverend practically screeched his question.

The studio audience was on their feet. 'White! God is white! With God's might, we'll make this country white.'

I snatched the remote out of Mama's hand and turned off the TV. 'Mama, I'm ashamed of you! How can you watch that racist trash?'

Mama wiped her hands on her apron. 'I don't. I'm just as appalled as you are. Someone must have switched channels on me.'

We both looked at Lofton. Mama's look was questioning; my look was accusatory.

'It's free speech,' Lofton said with a smirk. 'Isn't that what you two are always going on about?'

'Yes,' I said, 'but this is different. What Reverend Givmemore said was incendiary.'

'No, it wasn't,' Lofton said. 'I didn't hear him mention violence.'

'You didn't hear it *then*,' I said, 'because I turned the TV off. But Reverend Givmemore has been quoted as saying that AK-47s should be given to every child between the age of four and seven, in order to protect the "white Christian minority from the dark hordes."'

'I read that article, *Glocks for Goldilocks*,' Lofton said smugly, 'and I'm telling you, that was a prime example of fake news. It appeared in the same newspaper that quoted a woman who was supposed to be one of the world's top geneticists, and she said that she could prove that there were no such creatures as mermaids. *Prove*. That, by the way, was before the last fifty or so mermaid sightings happened. I bet you that woman is looking for another research position now. Probably wishes she'd done the sensible thing and stayed home and raised her kids. Right, Mama?'

'Lofton, you are both a racist and a misogynist! And Mama, how could you raise a Neanderthal like this? We didn't grow up in the 1950s!'

Tears sprung to Mama's eyes. 'Zoe, darling, Lofton was only six years old when y'all's daddy died. On account of that, I may have spoiled him a little, but I didn't mean to turn him into those shameful things that you said.'

'Mama, you didn't spoil Lofton a little, like he's a pint of milk gone bad; he's so spoiled that even bacteria avoid him. I'm not accusing you of turning him into the racist that he appears to be, but you are responsible for turning him into a man who believes that we women were born to serve men.'

'Nonsense,' Mama said, as she used a corner of her apron to wipe the grease from around her baby boy's mouth. The overgrown baby banker who pulled six times the salary that I did, and who still brought his socks and underwear home to be washed. Fortunately for Mama, Lofton sent his shirts out to the cleaners for a professional pressing.

'Give me a break,' I groaned.

'Misogynist, am I?' Lofton said angrily. He jumped up and grabbed the TV remote from my hand, and before I could react, the audience on the *Guns for God* Sunday morning worship show were singing their closing hymn.

Onward Christian soldiers, marching off to war!
With the guns for Jesus, blasting down the door!
Christ the Major General, leads against the foe,
Forward into battle, see his big guns go!

'Turn off the television, Lofton,' Mama said. After he did so, she patted him tenderly on the shoulder. 'But I don't get it. Whose door are these people blasting down?'

'That's what bothers you about this song?' I said.

'Well, darling,' Mama said to me, 'aren't you always going on about how context is everything. Maybe in this hymn it's Satan's door that they're singing about.'

'Yeah,' Lofton said, and belched, whereupon Mama patted his back.

'You know what?' I said. 'I'm going for a walk. Mama, text me when your favourite child has gone back to that fancy new high-rise apartment of his that cost over a million dollars.'

'Zoe, darling, don't be that way. You know I love y'all equally.'

'Really, Mama? How many bacon strips did you dangle in front of my beak – I mean lips?'

'Your mouth wasn't open, darling. Besides, you live here with me – when you're not on the road – but I only get to see Lofton occasionally. You and I talk all the time. In fact, Zoe, I bet I see your boyfriend more often than I do your brother.'

'Mama,' I said, 'Gunner Jones just turned forty-nine years old. Surely that makes him a man friend, instead of a boyfriend. He also happens to live four hours away, whereas your baby boy banker here lives four miles away.'

'It seems to me that Gunner Jones is robbing the cradle,' Lofton said. He got up and put his arms around our mother's still tiny waist. 'Mama, fry me up some more bacon, will you? Remember that I like it real crisp.'

'Spoiled and demanding,' I said, and headed out for my walk. A long walk.

TWENTY-ONE

I am not one for telling tales out of school, but I feel compelled to state that Mama is prone to exaggerate when she feels threatened. I'd obviously gotten under her skin when I'd accused her of being partial to Lofton. To set the record straight, Gunner Jones had driven up only twice to see me in Charlotte, and I'd gone down there only once since we'd met.

Although we were initially quite attracted to each other physically, we soon recognized that our age difference, plus our moral outlook, were not going to mesh neatly in a long-term relationship. Well, those two issues, and the fact that Gunner Jones already had a lady friend down in North Charleston. That by the way, is where he snuck off to every week. She was a bartender in an 'itty-bitty-titty' bar, as Gunner Jones called it. He swore that *she* kept her top on, but he didn't want anyone else in Tidal Shores finding out about their relationship, so that's what all the secrecy was about. As one might suppose, Gunner Jones didn't think that even I should be aware of Candy's existence, and vice versa.

Despite everything that was said during our breakup, Gunner Jones and I remained friends. OK, maybe we weren't exactly friends so much as allies. You see, during the year since Gunner Jones had introduced his creation, Miss Lucy, to the world, he had come to regret the ramifications of this act of deception. What was meant to bring economic recovery to Tidal Shores infected almost half of the country with a disease of the mind: a mass delusion. I am, of course, referring to the belief in something that does not exist: the belief that merfolk were real.

Both Gunner and I were baffled by the fact that so many well-educated people, governors, senators, even doctors and university professors either professed a belief in merfolk, or refused to deny their existence. What kept these supposedly rational people silent? Were they afraid of losing their supporters, their patients, or their funding, as the case may be? Were they afraid of being ridiculed by the man on the street? Gunner Jones and I could prove that the emperor had no clothes, in this metaphor, so together we set out to do so.

The Sunday following Mermaid Day, I saw to it that a long interview with Gunner Jones was published in *The Observer Today*. Included in the interview were what should have been damning photographs taken by Gunner Jones himself. There were pictures of both the female bonobo, and the goliath fish, while they were being stuffed and mounted in their original forms. Then there were pictures of the two animals as they were being dissected, stuffed again, and the two halves were eventually expertly glued together. Gunner, like many creative geniuses, liked to keep a detailed record of his work in progress.

Any rational person, any thinking person, anyone who was not a complete idiot, anyone who was not a full-blown blithering nincompoop, who happened upon my article and even just read the photo captions, could not possibly put the paper down and still believe that Miss Lucy had been a real mermaid. Unfortunately, to my deep dismay, and yes, to my horror, I quickly realized that my article did not move the needle one iota toward the side of reason. Yes, I realize that I've just accused nearly half the country of being idiots and nincompoops, but on the other hand, did they not assign themselves these distinctions by refusing to be anything but cretins?

It's been said that no good deed goes unpunished, and I was just trying to do a good deed by saving America – the entire world, actually – from mermaid mania. What a lot of people don't know is that the ancient Amorites worshiped a god called Dagon that was a fish from the tip of his tail up to his navel, and then shaped like a man from his waist up. To put it bluntly, the god Dagon was a merman. Today we would call the worship of Dagon idolatry. While I am not equating the worship of this half-fish deity to mermaid mania, I am stating that the parallels between that culture and ours should be carefully considered by people who would sooner welcome large saltwater tanks into their churches than share their pews with parishioners of a different colour.

The punishment for my good deed was swift, and odoriferous. Within an hour of my copy of *The Observer Today* landing on Mama's front walk, a bucket of fish heads and entrails was thrown against her front door. The smell of this piscine gift was such that we could immediately determine that their previous owner had been collecting them for several days. This informed us – and the police – that there had been malice a-forethought, or at the very least, the perpetrator was a lazy fisherman who couldn't be bothered to throw out his fish waste on a daily basis. Either way, I was not amused, and Mama was even less inclined to find the situation smile-worthy.

I cleaned up the mess, of course. There was garbage, graffiti and eggs to clean up on the next three days, but Thursday morning found me in New York City where I was a guest of the nationally syndicated television show, *Get Up, America.*

The show was live, airing at seven in the morning, but I had to arrive two hours early to endure a 'pre-interview,' have my hair and make-up 'done,' and wait nervously around in the green room with three other guests who were scheduled to appear on the show that morning. Coffee, tea, juice and a large variety of pastries were made temptingly available to us, but we'd all been warned about the likelihood of having our lipstick worn away if we indulged, or possibly appearing on camera with wads of dough wedged in the gaps between our teeth. (This last bit of information did not apply to native-born Americans, as everyone knows that we all have perfect teeth with no spaces between them.)

Apparently, my segment was considered the most provocative, because it was the lead story. Having had to drag myself to the studio at such an ungodly hour, I hadn't had a chance to have breakfast, so when the producer came to fetch me, she found me chomping on a bagel. I had chosen this Jewish gift to the world because it is the antithesis of the similarly shaped doughnut, although I do prefer the latter for its sweetness. A proper doughnut is light and airy, and I could quickly chew and swallow even a large bite in seconds. The denser bagel is more filling, but it also needs more chewing. However, my need to masticate mattered not one whit, because live TV runs on a very tight schedule wherein every second counts.

'And we're delighted to have with us this morning,' the host of *Get Up, America* said, in his neutral television accent, 'that brave little reporter from Charlotte, North Carolina, Miss Zoe Porter.'

At that point the producer shoved me out on to the set, and I immediately stumbled on a large television cable. The jolting forward motion caused me to expectorate the wad of sodden dough that was in my mouth, as I am in the habit of often chewing with my mouth open. Much to my embarrassment the ball of wet bagel landed on the host's shoe, as he had risen to greet me, and was faced in my direction. On the plus side, I had not lost my balance completely, and thus I had not fallen on my face. On the negative side, I thought that perhaps I could save face by making that awkward entrance appear intentional, as if it was part of a deep curtsy.

This all happened in a split second, mind you, so I didn't have time to think things through. Just why a cud-chewing American woman would curtsy to an American television host was beyond the ken of most of that morning's viewers, and understandably, it was offensive to most of *Get Up, America's* Anglophile watchers as well. But you know what they say about no publicity being bad publicity. *Get Up, America*'s viewership shot up by twenty percent the following day, and when it was announced that I would appear on *The View from Here*, that show as well had a much larger market share.

At any rate, the handsome host of *Get Up, America* laughed briefly, and thanked me for treating him like royalty. Then, as valuable seconds were ticking away, he got me seated and we hit the ground running.

'In a minute we're going to show the pictures that you took of Miss Lucy, but first I want to give you a chance here, in front of all America – and much of the world – to double down on that claim you maintain in your newspaper column. So here goes: is Miss Lucy a mermaid?'

'No, Mr Anderson, she is not a mermaid.'

'Uh-huh.' Greg Anderson lightly drummed his fingers on the desk in front of him. 'Then what is Miss Lucy – if not a mermaid?'

I took a deep breath and looked straight into Camera Two, as directed. 'The *thing* known as Miss Lucy is, as we will see in the picture, the top half of an ape sewn to the bottom half of a fish. Plus silicone, a human hair wig, and a really professional paint and makeup job.'

I didn't know where they got the studio audience from, but a good portion of them had no idea what they'd been in for. I heard gasps, groans, and even a few swear words directed at me. The last really surprised me, because until then, I'd always thought that New York City was a woke place, somewhere one might expect fairy tales to remain the province of small children – or at the very least, a city where different viewpoints were respected.

'Now come on, folks,' Greg Anderson gently remonstrated his audience, 'Ms Porter may not be a biologist, or a scientist of any kind, but she did see the mermaid in person. And since the taxidermist himself, a Mr Gunner Jones, backed out at the last minute, I'm afraid that we're going to have to take her word for it. Her word, and the pictures that I am about to share with you.

'But first, Miss Porter, in your opinion, why is it that Gunner Jones refused to appear on the show with you this morning? Weren't you two an item at one time?'

At that revelation, several members of the audience hissed. So much for wokeness.

'I can't answer for Gunner Jones,' I said. 'But I can see now that he made the right choice.'

'Boo!' some shouted.

'Case in point,' I said. 'Mermaids are a biological impossibility. We humans are warm-blooded animals, and fish are cold-blooded animals. We have different circulatory and nervous systems. And anyway, despite the depiction in books and art of mermaids having breasts, would any man – would *you* – want to have sex with a slimy, scaly, fish bottom? In fact, I challenge every one of you, male or female, who still believes in mermaids, to stop by a fish market on the way home and purchase the biggest fish that they have. Take it home to bed—'

'Uh, I'm going to have to stop you right there,' Greg Anderson said. 'I'm afraid that the network has decency regulations. We're not cable TV, and we're not France. There are small children watching at this hour. Pre-school children, and children who might be home sick in bed.'

For the most part, the studio audience seemed shocked into silence. However, some of them were tapping intently on their phones. I could only hope that they were calling their local fish market.

'I think your expression just said it all,' I said. 'Mermaids have always been a fantasy. The vision of mermaids that Disney has put in our children's heads differs starkly from the mermaid in the original version of Hans Christian Andersen's story. In the original story, the witch cut out the mermaid's tongue, and when she got her legs, each step was like stepping on knife blades. Also, she never got to marry the prince; instead she got turned into sea foam.'

'Boo! Boo! Shut her down! Get her off the stage!'

Studio audiences are handpicked, and very small, so the rudest of my detractors were immediately located by security and escorted out of the room. One of them was wearing a mermaid tail skirt, with only a small opening at the bottom for her feet. She could barely shuffle out of the studio, and once fell head-long into the couple in front of her. Thankfully, they were average Americans, and thus amply padded, and they suffered only minor injuries when they hit the studio floor. Nonetheless, I was quite shaken by the treatment I'd received, and since the show was transitioning to a commercial, I was fixing to leave as well, when I felt the surprisingly strong producer push me back down in my seat.

'Stay!' he hissed. 'We've bumped the next segment, and we are putting you in that spot. You're much more interesting than the celebrity breakup special in our line-up.'

'Really? Which celebrity couple is that?'

'It's the couple who claim to bathe only once a week, if you can imagine that. No wonder they're breaking up.'

'Oooh,' I whined. 'But I wanted to meet them; I love English people!'

'Too bad. I've already sent them home with his and hers swag bags. OK, now on the count of three . . . one, two three!'

'And we're back,' Greg Anderson said. 'This morning we're honoured to have the controversial mermaid-denier, Zoe Porter from Charleston, South Carolina.'

'Actually, I'm from Charlotte, North Carolina.'

'But you deny the existence of mermaids. Despite the fact that they seem to be popping up all over the world.'

'Look,' I said curtly, 'none of these claims have been authenticated. In not one of these sightings has an actual mermaid and a person been close enough to shake hands.'

Greg Anderson chuckled. 'Oh no? Then look at this. Roll footage,' he said to his crew.

Immediately, on every monitor in the studio, and on millions of television sets around the country, possibly even the world, a lovely nymph of the sea could be seen reaching up to, as the Brits would say, snog a boy in a skiff. Their kiss soon grew inappropriately passionate, until the mermaid wrapped her arms around the lad's neck, and pulled him overboard. Then amidst a swirl of bubbles the two of them disappeared. The camera lingered on the approximate spot where they had last been seen for approximately two more minutes, before the film clip ended and Greg Anderson turned back to me.

'That evidence was taken in the Mediterranean. Yesterday. Just off the island of Majorca. What is your response to this?'

I ignored the cameras and looked Greg Anderson straight in his Mediterranean blue eyes. 'My response is that you're ambushing me. *Get Up, America* has always been known as one of the few shows where sane people can, without resorting to vitriol, rebut the inane theories that pop up as regularly as worm castings after a summer rain.'

'I beg your pardon?' Greg Anderson said. 'Your quaint Southern metaphor eludes me.'

'Piles of worm poop. And it's only Southern because I'm Southern. The point I'm making is that there is more and more crazy stuff being said on the internet, and videos appearing on it that are totally bogus, and I thought that y'all were too smart to be played, or, at the very least, too honourable to sell out to the dark side just for a ratings boost.'

No one enjoys being chastised, least of all alpha male television hosts – especially not by a woman guest, when the show is being aired live. Greg Anderson's brow lowered, his jaw clenched, the corners of his mouth twitched, and his chest strained against his three-thousand-dollar suit when he inhaled. However, I had momentarily silenced him. I'm sure that this awkward state of affairs did not go unnoticed by his millions of viewers.

I was not a mean person, but now that I was in the catbird seat, and had a national audience, I thought it my duty to sing a little longer. Given that *Get Up, America* was the most even-handed of all the talk shows currently on network television, if I couldn't get my point across in this venue, then perhaps the America that I loved was doomed.

'Good people of America,' I said, 'if mermaids are indeed real, then that footage that you have just seen, from Majorca, shows a mermaid drowning a boy. She was not pulling him underwater to join him, like Tom Hanks joined Darryl Hannah in the movie *Splash*. In the movie, Tom's character followed the mermaid into the sea; he wasn't dragged under. To sum it up, folks, mermaids are both sex offenders and dangerous killers, who drown children – that is if they are indeed real. Who knows to what extent mermen will go to seek vengeance for all the times that their kind were hauled up in fishing nets or shot for sport in past centuries.'

Greg Anderson was fully recovered by now. 'Hold it right there! You can't be hurling libellous allegations on live television! You're not allowed to call someone a sex offender or a murderer unless you have proof.'

I smiled smugly. 'You just showed the proof. No, wait! That boy's parents didn't report him missing, did they? It was all a ruse, wasn't it?'

Then Greg Anderson's classically handsome face coloured. 'I bet you think you're so clever.'

'Well, which is it, Mr Anderson?' I demanded. 'Are mermaids capable of murder, or is *Get Up, America* in the business of peddling fake news? Don't equivocate, sir, because millions of people are listening.'

Greg Anderson chuckled through clenched teeth. 'While I ponder your question, young lady, we will be heading to commercial. I've got to make sure this network has enough money in case mermaids really do sue us. Ha. Ha.'

The second he got the signal that the commercial was being shown, he became a raging bull. 'Get that damn microphone off her blouse! Get her off my set! And no, don't give her a swag bag. Nobody makes a fool out of Greg Anderson on air. Oh, and by the way,' he shouted at my retreating back, 'I'm cancelling your limousine back to your hotel. If I could, I'd stick you with the hotel bill, *and* the airfare, but they've been prepaid.'

I smiled. Hearing that the hotel had been prepaid was good news. By the time I checked out in three hours, the mini bar was going to be emptied.

TWENTY-TWO

Charlotte Douglas International Airport had always been my favourite airport. If you guessed that the reason for this was because it was my home airport, then you'd be wrong. However, if you guessed that it was because this airport contains a Cinnabon restaurant in its main lobby, you would be correct. These giant cinnamon rolls with their gooey centres and cream cheese icing are my comfort food. I bought three of these, on account of I needed a lot of comfort just then. Also, because I'd had an extremely stressful day, I stopped by a nearby shop to purchase a strong drink to go: a large coffee latte with a double shot of espresso.

Mama was picking me up, and we had arranged to meet near the bottom of the escalator by the baggage claim. Besides being an international airport, this one is a hub for many regional, as well as national flights, so it is always busy. When I arrived, late afternoon, the baggage claim level was crowded, and it took me several minutes to spot Mama. When I finally located her, she looked as if she'd lost her best friend – not in a crowd, but to the Grim Reaper.

'Mama!' I exclaimed in alarm. 'What is it? Did Gan-Gan finally decide it was time to let go?'

'Let go of what, darling?' Mama said. 'The card with the number to her Swiss bank account? No, I'm afraid this is about that stud muffin that you used to date.'

'Which stud muffin was that?' I said in all innocence. 'I'm afraid you'll have to be a little more specific.'

'You know, darling, that gorgeous hunk who was old enough to be your father? Even smelled a mite like your daddy too.'

'Eew. But again, you're going to have to give me more details.'

'For heaven's sake, Zoe,' Mama said, her voice rising so high that it practically melted the wax in my ears. 'I mean that tanned and toned taxidermist from down in Tidal Shores. That muscular slab of prime beef whom I was nailing, and who is responsible for starting this mermaid mania.'

Even as she spoke, a teenage girl pushed by, carrying a huge mermaid doll made of fabric and stuffed like a body pillow. Although

I tried to duck out of the teenager's way, the tail of the obscenely large toy slapped me in the face. Like I said, I desperately needed those three humongous cinnamon buns – maybe if not to eat, then at least to launch at the next passenger who assaulted me.

I dragged Mama outside where things were less chaotic and where it was easier to hear. 'Mama! Did you just say that you were "nailing" Gunner Jones?'

'Well, that's going to stop now, isn't it, darling?' Mama burst into tears. Having faked a fair share of crying episodes in my relatively short life, I'm somewhat of an expert on real, versus fake, crying jags and I could tell quickly, and conclusively, that she was really upset.

'Mama, you're not making a lick of sense. One minute you're talking nonsense about doing the beast with two backs with the bod from the beach, and the next minute you're boo-hooing.'

'That's because Gunner Jones is dead, darling. My lover man is dead.'

'He's *what*?'

'Dead. Can't you hear, darling? Don't they have real news programs in New York City anymore? Or is it all fake news these days?'

'Mama, I've been on a plane for the last two hours, and after that I've been focused on nurturing my soul, because apparently nobody cares about the truth any longer. So, why don't you fill me in? When did Gunner die? *How* did he die?'

Mama wailed loudly for a minute or two before responding with words. 'I was watching *News at Noon* while eating my sandwich and apple, and my full cup of milk. It's important to get enough calcium to keep your bones strong when you're my age.'

'Especially if you're going to be bonking the bod from Tidal Shores,' I said.

'Zoe, don't be rude. At any rate, I am partial to peanut butter and jelly sandwiches, as you know, and I'd been particularly generous with the fillings on this one, so I was wiping my mouth off with my serviette – that's what they call a napkin in the UK, isn't that classy – when I saw my darling Gunner's face pop up on TV.'

'OK, Mama, stop there. I mean, don't stop walking altogether; just stop with your story. Where are you parked?'

'Short-term parking, of course,' Mama said. She surged ahead, and I followed, like a duckling behind *its* mama.

'Mama,' I called after her, 'is this stuff about you and your darling Gunner a fantasy, or could there possibly be some truth in it? I know that's a ridiculous question, given that you're twice his age, and you couldn't possibly have been carrying on an affair behind my back – I'm not blind, you know – but on the off, off, *off* chance that such a thing could really happen, I just want to make sure that I'm not shown up to be a complete fool at some point.'

Mama stopped walking and turned to face me. Huge tears streamed down her cheeks so fast that they puddled in the indentations formed by her clavicles. The poor dear would need to replace her electrolytes if she kept this up for long. When she calmed down a bit, I thought that I might suggest a light sprinkling of salt on a hard-boiled egg.

'Zoe,' Mama said, sounding anything but calm, 'I am not twice his age! The span of years between Gunner and me, is exactly the same as that between you and him. And anyway, that's not relevant anymore. I've been trying to tell you that Gunner Jones is dead. He was murdered. They're saying that it happened late last night, or in the wee hours of this morning.'

Although I hadn't been dating the man for several months, still my brain had a hard time processing what she'd just said. I would much rather have listened to her recount sordid details of her affair with him, than any details that corroborated his death. Unfortunately, my training as a reporter overrode my feelings as a friend and ex-lover.

'How was he murdered, Mama? Who killed him?'

'They don't know who killed him,' Mama sobbed. 'Just that he was shot twice. Once in the shoulder, and once in the neck. The neck wound was the fatal one, as it hit an artery.' Having imparted that much information, Mama threw herself into my arms, almost knocking me over.

Frankly, I didn't know which was more shocking: Mama's sordid confession, or the murder of Gunner Jones. And to think that just five minutes earlier, disproving the existence of mermaids was the single most important thing in the world to me. But oh, how foolish and naïve of me to have thought that way. Ever since the day that Daddy was killed in an automobile accident by a drunk driver, I should have known better. One's world can turn on a dime at any moment. Truly, tragedy is just a phone call away, or a mother waiting to greet you at the airport.

I looked around for a place to sit, but there are no benches between the terminal and the parking garage. So, with Mama still clutching me, we managed to shuffle along to her car – although we paused a half-dozen times so that she could blow her nose on my sleeve, since neither of us had any facial tissues with us. Thankfully, she insisted that I drive home.

As soon as we got inside the house, I fixed her a gin and tonic, and a whiskey, straight up, for me. I gulped my drink, and then I called Gan-Gan.

'Just so you know, I'm not taking your calls,' Gan-Gan said when she answered after the first ring.

'Then why are you talking to me now?'

'Because this is a special occasion. Well, at least I think that it is,' my great-grandmother said. 'I mean, why has it taken you so long to call and find out the details of your lover's death?'

'For your information, Gan-Gan, I was on a plane back from New York City when Gunner's death was announced. I didn't hear about it until Mama picked me up at the airport. And by the way, Mama was beside herself with grief, because it's Mama and Gunner who were lovers. I haven't dated Gunner in a month of Sundays.'

'Good grief,' Gan-Gan said. 'That's just about the most disgusting thing I've ever heard.'

'Don't be so judgemental, Gan-Gan,' I found myself saying. 'The age difference between Mama and Gunner was almost exactly the same as between Gunner and me.'

'Don't be silly, Baby Child,' my great-grandmother said. 'It's not the age thing. It seems that neither of you have even half the brains of an inbred squirrel. Y'all are descended from one of the South's proudest and most noble families. Jefferson Davis, the President of the Confederate States of America, was my great-great uncle. However, Gunner Jones is descended from Yankee carpetbaggers.

'Just the thought of you dating Gunner Jones was enough to make my dinner repeat itself, and when I picture the two of you knowing each other in the biblical sense – arms and legs thrashing about every which way, the two of you panting like marathon runners, sweat seeping from every pore, juices seeping from orifices, loud cries – no, make that screams of gratification during the act of culmination – I feel like marching right over to Gunner Jones' taxidermist shop and putting three more bullets in his head myself. Of course, I would never do that, because I am such a staunch pacifist that shooting even a Yankee corpse is against my principles. You do remember me telling you that I protested against the Vietnam War, don't you?'

'Yes, Gan-Gan,' I said. 'Didn't you protest against World War Two as well? How about World War One, or the Civil War?' To be honest, I was being sarcastic. I saw it as payback for both her disparaging comments about Gunner Jones' heritage, and her disgusting, not to mention presumptive, description of our sex life.

'Are those trick questions, Baby Child? Fighting Hitler was the moral thing to do.'

'Gan-Gan, unless you can give me any more details regarding Gunner Jones' death, I need to get off the phone.'

'OK,' she said, 'but you aren't going to like what I have to say.'

'Out with it,' I said wearily.

'*You* killed Gunner Jones. Baby Child, you're the one who took the life of one of the kindest, most generous men who ever called Tidal Shores home – even if he was a damn Yankee.'

TWENTY-THREE

'Now you hang on,' I ordered my great-grandmother. I set my phone on a side table as I poured myself another drink and swallowed the scorching liquid in three gulps. 'I'm back! Now, how could this have been my fault when I was in New York City when it happened, not in Tidal Shores?'

'Baby Child, did you just down yourself some liquor?'

'*What?* How did you know?'

'Because I can smell your breath over the airwaves, that's how. Or maybe it's because that's what I would have done if someone would have laid into me like I just laid into you. Anyway, now that you're all liquored up, I can tell you that it's your fault because you betrayed Gunner Jones' confidence. And in doing so, you made him the villain in your silly and ill-advised attempt to disprove the fact that mermaids are real.'

'But they aren't,' I said, 'and it isn't a fact.'

My great-grandmother must have sighed loudly and for a long time, because I heard a great deal of static on my phone. 'Baby Child,' she said after quite a while, 'when one gets to be my age, one comes to the realization that the truth is like the elephant in that Indian parable.'

'Elephant?'

'Yes, I'm sure you've heard it. Six blind men are walking along together through a forest when they encounter an elephant standing in their path. What is it? they wonder aloud. Meanwhile each of them has grabbed a hold of a different body part. The man who has the tail believes that the elephant is a rope. Another man grabs the trunk and thinks that he is holding a large snake, so he quickly backs off. One man touches the elephant's broad back and believes that they have encountered a wall. The man who touches a leg thinks that they have walked off the path and into a tree, while the sixth man is convinced that the sharp tusk is a spear. Each of the six men describes an attribute that they believe to be true, and it is their truth. None of the men are lying; it's just that none of them are privy to the whole truth.

'You see, Baby Child, one never has the whole of the story, does one? You might believe, deep down to the marrow of your bones, that mermaids don't exist, but until you've drained every ocean, and every connecting sea, of every drop of water, you can't prove conclusively that mermaids don't exist in some corner of the globe. Even then, you can't prove it without a shadow of a doubt, because for all we know, mermaids might have the power to make themselves invisible. So, there you have it, only God knows for sure if mermaids do, or don't, exist.'

'Hmm. Well, I would suppose that since you played with God as a child, you might be able to coax the answer out of Him.'

Gan-Gan guffawed. 'Good one! Zoe, God and I were never chums; we were merely passing acquaintances. However, King David and I were thick as thieves, until he saw Bathsheba bathing naked on a rooftop. Frankly, I don't know what he saw in that woman. She had thick ankles, you know. "Cankles," I believe you young people call them, on account of one's ankles and calves are all of a piece, with no discernible transition between them. And before you judge me too harshly, Baby Child, you need to know that it was my night to bathe naked up on that roof, not hers! If that bitch had waited her turn, then I would have been Queen of Israel.'

'Gan-Gan, surely on some level you realize that you are delightfully off your rocker. You might look twenty-five hundred years old, but that is not your chronological age, and even if it was, it most assuredly would not be healthy to hold on to resentment for two and a half millennium.'

'Why, I never!'

'Gan-Gan, do you love me?' I asked plaintively, but with an agenda, of course.

'Now that's a silly question; I love you more than all the rest of my many descendants combined.'

'So, you love me even though I was on national television exposing your fake mermaid?'

Gan-Gan laughed delightedly. 'That's precisely why I love you: the fact that we don't see eye to jaundiced eye. Everyone else in the family is afraid of me. But not my Baby Child. In fact, I love you so much, that even though I'm a happily married woman again, I'm leaving you half of my estate. And trust me, Zoe, it's a lot more than you think.

'I now own a chain of Mermaid memorabilia shops,' she continued to brag, 'and they are named, appropriately, Mermaid Memories, and can now be found in seven coastal states. And that's not counting the two right here in Tidal Shores. Oh, Baby Child, you won't believe how this place has grown since Hoyt Hunter found that poor little mermaid's body floating out in the harbour, and—'

'Gan-Gan, again my jaundiced eye doesn't see what your eye sees when it comes to Miss Lucy's corpse, which was, granted, cunningly contrived and cleverly constructed. But never mind that – for the moment. Since you love me so much, am I still welcome as your houseguest?'

During the ensuing silence, babies were born, grew up, married and raised families, and died. Comprehensive peace came to the Middle East twice, but sadly failed. Ocean levels had risen to the point that water was lapping at the door of 10 Downing Street and the White House lawn when Gan-Gan at last spoke.

'Of course, Baby Child, you're always welcome to stay here. With me. And my wife, Grusha. However, surely you must be aware that thanks to the very rude, practically vicious, way that you forced her out of the closet, she doesn't love you quite as much as I do. She may spit in your food.'

'Gan-Gan, please tell your wife that I am truly sorry that she felt I was forcing her out of the closet. At the time, I believed that I was liberating her. Of course, Grusha's liberation was none of my business. But in my own defence, it didn't seem to me then – and still doesn't seem that way to me now – that Grusha is the type who can be forced into anything. And anyway, I always had this suspicion that Grusha had a scimitar hidden somewhere on her person, and that she was just waiting for a chance to jump out of the shadows and slit my throat while shouting *huzzah*!'

'What a clever girl you are, Baby Child, to figure it out! She keeps it strapped to her girdle. One really can't tell that she's wearing a scimitar under that thick black peasant dress and starched linen apron that is her uniform.'

'No, y'all are the clever ones,' I said. 'Y'all are probably the two smartest women whom I've ever met,' I said, laying it on a bit thickly. 'Now, Gan-Gan, I need to go, because I have another important call coming in. Of course, it's not as important as talking to you, but I do have to answer it. Please remember to give Grusha my love, but save the lion's share for yourself. Bye-Bye.'

Gag me with a spoon, I thought, reviving a crude expression

from back in Valley Girl days. Give Grusha my love? I'd sooner put milk and sugar on a bowl of grits than say any words of endearment to that mean old crone. However, Gan-Gan and I were blood kin, and in the South those ties might as well be made of steel. Plus, I needed a place to stay while I investigated Gunner Jones' murder, because that is exactly what I intended to do next – after I got the OK from my publisher and caught up on my sleep.

It's been said that there is no rest for the wicked. If that is true, then surely I am one diabolical woman. My publisher was more than fine with me doing a little investigative reporting on Gunner Jones' murder, but no sooner did I hang up with her, than I felt Mama tug on my sleeve.

'Darling, we need to have a serious talk.'

'Mama, I just ate thousands of calories in carbs, drank two days' worth of caffeine, and my thoughts are already swirling around like a dust devil.'

'But this is important, Zoe. I won't be able to sleep tonight unless I get this off my chest.'

Right then is when I knew Mama had been lying about her affair with Gunner Jones. To what end she'd done so, I was still unsure. What mattered was that she was going to pay for the sin of lying to her firstborn, and most especially for carrying on so in a public place when I'd already had such a hard day.

'Listen, Mama,' I said sternly, 'I'll forgive you for lying to me, if you come with me down to Tidal Shores.'

Mama recoiled in surprise. 'But there's been a murder down there.'

'Exactly. You don't want me going alone, do you? I need an extra pair of eyes and ears to keep me safe. It will be fun, the two of us working together, a pair of super sleuths. Like in the movies.'

Mama's face brightened. 'Can we pick names for ourselves? If so, I'd like to be Nancy Drew.'

'Why not Agatha Christie?'

'Because when I was a girl – wait just one cotton-picking minute! You're trying to slip one by me, aren't you, Zoe Legare Porter. How did you know that I was lying? I mean, what makes you *think* that I was lying about my relationship with Gunner Jones?'

'Because it occurred to me that the woman who can't even bring herself to use adult nomenclature to refer to human sexual organs would not engage in the sort of rumpy-pumpy that you described.'

Mama smiled wanly. 'That depends, darling. What is rumpy-pumpy?'

'It is a British expression, which sounds very vulgar to American ears, once you learn its meaning.'

Mama turned borscht red. 'Oh my. Just so you know, darling, I haven't really been pumped in the rump since your father passed.'

'Eew, Mama,' I said, 'that's gross. I don't want to hear that.'

'But you just said—'

'Stop it, Mama, *please*. Just agree to come with me, Nancy Drew. It will be lots of fun, I promise. We'll sneak around like a couple of real detectives. We can skulk in the shadows, loiter in doorways, and prevaricate at parties – in other words, do whatever is needed to uncover the identity of Gunner Jones' killer.'

Mama clutched her string of Chinese cultured pearls, and freshwater ones at that. 'But, Zoe, that sounds so dangerous!'

'I was just being dramatic, Mama. You don't have to do all those things; you can just sit on the beach and read the latest book by Mary Alice Monroe. I just said those things because I thought that you might enjoy living dangerously, because I thought that maybe you were – uh—'

'Bored? Oh, Zoe, you can't believe how bored I am! I'm so bored that some days, when it's sunny out, I just sit on the veranda, wearing a muumuu and flip-flops, to watch my toenails grow. So, believe me, I would dearly love to skulk, loiter, and prevaricate, and possibly even a few more nefarious things. Is there anything that we can do that will put us in the pokey? Here I am, in my seventh decade, and I've never once been arrested – hells bells, I've never even received a speeding ticket.

'I am a curious woman, and I think that it would be interesting to spend a little time in the slammer. It would be good for my memoir, don't you think? Do you think I would be lucky enough to get a prison wife? If I have any choice in the matter, I would prefer someone of a different race, on account of I've never had that experience.'

'Mama, you're completely bonkers. You know that?'

She shook her head sadly. 'Mind your language, Zoe. Here in the South, we say that someone is "eccentric."'

'Sorry, Mama. You are charmingly eccentric.'

She smiled gratefully. 'So, when do we leave, Agatha?'

'First thing in the morning, Nancy. Tonight, Agatha is going to get her sleep.'

TWENTY-FOUR

Mama is Gan-Gan's youngest granddaughter, and a Legare by birth, so she is also a favourite of my great-grandmother. However, as long as I can remember, Mama and Grusha have never exchanged even one civil word. Mama refused to tell me what their conflict was all about, so eventually I gave up asking. Then the wedding happened – the one that excluded me but included Mama – and now everything seems to be hunky-dory between the two of them. Of course, I am curious about what their original disagreement was about, and what was said, or done, to heal their relationship, but I have finally come to realize that the information will either be volunteered, or forever withheld. Mama's mouth is like Fort Knox, and no one can unlock that vault unless she is part of the process.

At any rate, on account of Mama's new relationship with Gan-Gan's wife, Grusha welcomed Mama warmly. I, however, got the stink eye.

'Listen, dear,' I said to her, as soon as I could get the Russian American alone, 'I doubt if you'd be Mrs Grusha Legare today if it weren't for me pushing you gently out of the closet. Not that it was my business, of course. I only did it for your happiness.'

The furrows in her forehead deepened to the point that one could plant corn in them, and her beady black eyes narrowed to mere slits. She was setting the table for lunch, and she slapped a plate down with such force that it broke, sending a sizable piece skittering across the dining-room floor.

'Now see what you do?' she snarled.

'Mrs Legare,' I said calmly, 'I am so sorry that I broke that plate. I am also sorry for your happiness with my great-grandmother. Believe me, if I had the power, I'd send you back to Mother Russia and the most remote gulag in Siberia that ever existed.'

The furrows on her forehead relaxed – a little – and her beady black eyes opened just enough to reveal a glint of light. While she didn't actually smile, at least her mouth assumed a straight line.

'*Da?*'

'Oh, *da*,' I said. 'I would even see to it that you were beaten on a daily basis, and that your rations were never more than stale bread and water – although on Sundays you would be given a smear of lard for your bread.'

At this point Grusha's face underwent a total transformation. She literally beamed as she flung open her arms.

'Come to me, my Little Cabbage. Your Auntie Grusha wishes to welcome you into the family.'

Quite frankly, I am not a casual hugger. And anyway, her statement confused me. 'Into which family are you welcoming me?' I asked.

Grusha laughed heartily. 'The Legare family, *da*?'

'Well, that's silly,' I said. 'I've always been a member of this family. Ever since I was a zygote, I was a Legare.'

Grusha's face darkened again; her furrows grew deep enough to conceal pinecones; her beady eyes became slits that healed and disappeared altogether. Boy was I in for trouble!

'The gulag,' I said. 'Hourly whippings with a cat-o-nine-lives. No lard on Sundays. They'll force you to listen to Captain and Tennille's "Muskrat Love" twenty-four hours a day.'

'You're wasting your time,' a familiar voice said.

I whirled. Then I looked down. There stood Gan-Gan – all five feet of her. Had she been this short the last time I checked in with her? I realize that people lose height as they age, but I couldn't remember my great-grandmother being so short that my chin could practically rest on top of her head. Then again, perhaps my memory of her was skewed because she had always been – and still was – such a vibrant and powerful woman in the community of Tidal Shores and in our family, that I just naturally put her on a pedestal. Even a large doll can be noticed across a room if it's stood on a high enough pedestal.

'What you don't seem to understand, Baby Child, is that Grusha's problem with you is simply one of jealousy.'

'She's jealous of little ole me? Whatever for? I'm a divorced woman, in her thirties, who still lives with her mother. Yes, my car is paid off, but it's ten years old.'

Gan-Gan wrapped me in her wrinkled arms. 'My wife is jealous because you've always been the apple of my eye.'

'*Da!* Apple!' Grusha glared malevolently at me.

I wiggled free from my great-grandmother's embrace. She smelled cloyingly of lavender bath salts.

'But I'm a rotten apple,' I protested. 'I rarely come down to visit you. When I do, it's mostly just to take advantage of your hospitality, for a free place to sleep.'

Gan-Gan smiled, revealing butterscotch-coloured teeth. 'That's all true, Baby Child, but when you took your first step, it was to toddle into my arms. Your first words were "Gan-Gan." You etched yourself so deeply into my heart by your first birthday that there is no one in the world that is more important to me than you, and Grusha has always known that. She also knows that the two of you are the only beneficiaries of my will, which is to be divided with you receiving sixty percent of everything that I own, and she the remainder.'

I gasped and looked at Grusha, who stuck her tongue out at me. I returned the favour.

'Oh, my sweet girls,' Gan-Gan said, and enveloped me in the cloying scent of lavender again.

'What's going on?' Mama asked as she walked into the room.

'What's going on is that your grandmother is leaving me the lion's share of her estate in her will. That explains the reason why her wife hates my guts and is probably why she didn't want me at the wedding.'

'*Da, da,*' Grusha said, nodding her head vigorously.

'Why, I'll be dippity-doodled,' Mama said. 'Why on earth would you do that, Grandma?'

'Because I want to. Because I can. And maybe because Grusha, like me, will most probably be dead in ten or fifteen years, whereas Zoe is a ne'er-do-well who works for a fake press that still uses paper, and which will undoubtedly go kaput in less than a decade.'

'Ne'er-do-well?' I said.

'Why don't I rate?' Mama demanded. 'Granddaughters are more closely related than great-granddaughters!'

'You see, Beatrice,' Gan-Gan said, 'you were never very nice to me as a girl. As a toddler, you bit me several times. Hard. Then as a teenager, you and your cousins made fun of my clothes. I made them myself, you know, and I was quite proud of them. In fact, I had a reputation for being quite the good seamstress. But you and your cousins called me the Ugly Granny – just not to my face.'

Mama blanched. 'Maybe just that once. And Sharon started it.'

Gan-Gan laughed raucously, and patted Mama on the shoulder with a liver-spotted hand. 'I just bet she did; that Sharon was always a spunky child. What a shame she decided to celebrate her fiftieth birthday by sky-diving. Anyway, it's time to eat lunch. Grusha has made us her favourite Russian dish: boiled potatoes and cabbage. However, to add a little extra flavour to it, she waved a chicken over the pot – twice.'

'Was the chicken dead or alive at the time?' I asked.

'Always with the jokes,' Grusha said. 'This one doesn't cook, so she doesn't really want to know.'

I shot her a dirty look, one that could have choked a chicken had it been anywhere near. How dare she comment on my state of mind?

'Grusha also made us a loaf of her delicious peasant black bread,' Gan-Gan said pleasantly. The so-called loaf was round and black, with a domed top that was blistered. It looked like something one might expect to see on top of a volcano.

'So, what do you ladies plan to do this afternoon?' Gan-Gan asked, as she plonked a ten-pound hunk of black bread on to my butter plate.

Mama and I exchanged worried glances. Consuming a hunk of Grusha's homemade black bread is somehow the equivalent of downing two fifty-pound bags of cement. Just like cement, it seems to harden in its new location. Unless I remembered to smear an entire stick of butter on my slice of Grusha's bread, I'd be dragging that thing along in my lower GI tract for the next six months.

'We thought we'd head down to the beach. Right, Mama?'

As Gan-Gan's eyes turned to Mama, I heaved the twenty-pound slice of bread into my lap.

'Is that a man at your window?' Mama asked, as she wrestled with her own hunk of bread.

When both Gan-Gan and Grusha turned to face the dining-room window, I slid the twenty-pound hunk of bread from my lap and into my open pocketbook. I thought I heard it land there with a *thunk*, but I can't be sure, because my heart was beating so loudly I could scarcely hear anything else.

'Well, lookee here,' Gan-Gan said presently. 'Both of my ladies love your bread so much, Grusha, that they are just dying for another hunk.'

Mama and I jumped quickly to our feet, like deer that had been resting in the woods and then suddenly startled. Mama knocked over her water glass, but it was already half empty. I, however, spilled an entire glass of sticky sweet tea on Grusha's crisp white tablecloth.

'Thank you for a fabulous lunch,' I said, 'but we must be off!'

'Yes, dears, time and tide wait for no woman,' Mama trilled.

Having grabbed our handbags, off we ran.

TWENTY-FIVE

Mama and I both like to plan ahead, and both tote around enormous handbags, so we already had everything we needed with us. Of course, at the moment everything was beneath several tonnes of Grusha's black bread. Now, I am not by nature a cruel woman. I feed the feral cats in my neighbourhood, and if I can, I try to carry insects outdoors rather than smack them with a rolled-up newspaper. However, I see it as my patriotic duty to control the starling population on the North American continent.

In 1890, a group of misguided literary enthusiasts attempted to establish in America breeding colonies of every bird mentioned in the works of William Shakespeare. To that end, these folks released 100 starlings in New York City's Central Park. Today there are 200,000,000 starlings in North America, more birds than any other species, and they have caused many native species to go extinct.

'Mama,' I said, when we'd reached the sidewalk, 'tip that slab of lava out of your pocketbook. Crush it under your heel, if you can. Maybe some starlings will find it, eat it, and be unable to achieve lift-off afterward.'

'Good thinking, Zoe,' Mama said. 'And by the looks of how prosperous Tidal Shores has become, I think that they can pay to fix the sidewalk if these slabs create divots.'

That said, we happily junked the chunks. After jumping on them several times, we skipped giddily down the street toward the beach. Before Gunner Jones (may he rest in peace with his two bullet holes) constructed Miss Lucy, one could hear the ocean shortly after leaving Gan-Gan's house and spot its soupy water just a block further on. How things had changed in just a year.

The town was so jam-packed with tourists now that a roar emanated from the beach. Also, a hideous pavilion in the approximate shape of a reclining mermaid blocked our view. The tail end of this giant wooden structure housed a number of shops, which sold mostly the same sort of things: mermaid tails that one could wear in the water, regular swimwear, goggles, swim fins, sunglasses and sunscreen. And of course, snacks. However, none of these little shops sold merfolk dolls; all dolls and merfolk replica had to be purchased in Gan-Gan's shop.

The quality of the merchandise in the shops varied considerably. Amateur mermaid tails were priced between $60 and $200. Professional tails ranged from $1,300 to $5,500. The most expensive of these were made of silicone and the scales were individually articulated. There was a boardwalk in front, with signs posted that gum-chewing was not allowed. Nonetheless, the once beautiful white painted planks were marred by the flattened pieces of chewing gum that had been spat out by people too lazy to look for a rubbish bin. Again, I am not a mean-spirited person, but every time I step on a wad of someone's expectorated gum, I have the desire to seek out the culprit (by some magical means) and put a massive wad of gum in their hair just before they step out to celebrate an important event in their life.

Mama and I managed to weave our way down the entire length of the boardwalk without once stepping on one of these sticky reminders of how uncouth society has become. However, there are advantages to being forced to look down when one is at the beach – at least in the United States. I have seen movies set in the 1950s in which beachgoers had bodies where their flesh conveyed the general shape of the skeleton beneath it. Mama says that back in those days, people spoke of dieting in preparation for 'swimsuit season.'

These days, people have no shame, and whether or not that's a good thing, I leave that up to you. But when we reached the end of the boardwalk, I looked up and saw a woman who'd been ahead of us continue to walk on. She was wearing a thong bikini, which all but disappeared into the crack between her buttocks. South Carolina is not the French Riviera, and the good folks of Tidal Shores stopped burning harlots at the stakes a few years ago, but such exhibitionism is usually not tolerated. It was clear to me that there was a new mindset amongst the powers that be. What I beheld was fascinating, as well as disgusting. I was torn between looking away and staring at her backside.

'Stop!' Mama hissed. 'Eyes on the ground. Have I raised you no better than that?'

'Huh?' I said.

'That woman is Dolly Henderson,' Mama whispered conspiratorially.

'Is that supposed to mean anything to me?' I asked.
'She's Reverend Billy-Bob Henderson's wife, that's all.'
'*Our* Reverend Billy-Bob Henderson?'
Mama nodded vigorously.
'Get out of town and back!' I said. I might have been too loud, because the woman being discussed turned and glanced back, before ambling on her seductive way. Unfortunately, Dolly Henderson had given me another eyeful to behold. Her enormous breasts virtually spilled over her itsy-bitsy polka-dot bikini top. The left one came perilously close to escaping its bondage and displayed part of an aureole as a sign of its independence.

'Her hypocrisy just burns me up,' Mama said. 'When your cousin Liam was a baby, your aunt Margaret took him to church to be christened. When Liam started crying, Margaret took out one of her God-given milk dispensers and fed the poor child. Well, Dolly was fit to be tied!

'Dolly called Margaret a whore, a slut and a slattern. Right in the middle of the service. She stood up, pointed a finger, and screamed like a fishwife. And all because Margaret was using her mammary glands for their primary purpose – to produce milk for human infants.'

Mama was panting with emotion. I couldn't remember ever seeing Mama so worked up about anything. Even when Lofton smuggled a girl into his room for a sleepover his senior year of high school, and Mama didn't find out until the next morning, she hadn't been this upset. Then again, Mama tended to glide over Lofton's indiscretions. She squinted when it came to his iniquities, as it were. For Lofton, such was one of the perks of being Mama's favourite.

'Mama,' I said, 'was Margaret being discreet when she nursed Liam? Did she have a cloth covering her chest?'

'No,' Mama said peevishly, 'and why should she? One could see less of her breast than we just saw of Dolly Henderson's breast, and she didn't have a little human being attached to the end. Zoe, this is a crazy, mixed-up world, in which lies become the truth just because they've been repeated enough times.'

'Mama,' I said sadly, 'that's not something new. Adolf Hitler understood that concept and utilized that method extremely effectively.'

We held hands as we stepped off the boardwalk and approached the water. At one end of the beach, a section had been cordoned off and named Mermaid Mer. The word 'mer' means 'sea' in Latin, French and Spanish. Here one could rent mermaid 'tails' to wear over one's legs, and splash about in the shallows. A cheaper tail, with printed scales, and inflatable flukes, rented for fifty dollars for half an hour. The better suits with articulated scales and hard plastic flukes cost a whopping eighty-five dollars an hour, and one had to be twelve years of age or older to rent one of those babies.

There were lots of rules, and of course, waiver forms to sign. One girl recently had an eye gouged out by one of the rigid plastic flukes. A small boy almost drowned when he broke the 'no diving' rule. His buoyant flukes floating on the water's surface held his head under water, and he was barely able to right himself in time. Then there was the issue of folks who neglected to pay strict attention to the instructions on how to put on the tails. There were several instances when the wearer, upon emerging from the water, would regrettably slip right out of the heavy wet suit. This issue was particularly problematic for men and boys, who tended to have narrower hips. One elderly gentleman, with extremely narrow hips, was also impressively endowed, and quickly became a favourite amongst the 'widow crowd.'

'So,' I said, 'we've seen the beach, and now let's get out of here and start our investigation.'

Mama patted her pocketbook. 'It's about time. I brought a large magnifying glass, a pair of binoculars, two torches, a Swiss Army knife, three bobby pins, two Snickers bars, a credit card, and a roll of duct tape. Oh, and a few of my prescription sleeping pills.'

'Good Lord, Mama. What do you plan to do with the duct tape?'

'Oh, Zoe,' Mama said. 'Did I somehow give birth to a Yankee? Every Southerner knows that if it can't be done with duct tape, then it can't be done at all. Why, I plan to tie up the guilty party once we ascertain who it is. With your help, of course.'

'Right.'

Mama dug into her massive handbag and retrieved the binoculars. They were pink and had flamingos printed on the sides. She scanned the beach in both directions.

'OK, I see Dolly and her three bratty kids frolicking over there on the right. May I suggest that we begin our investigation by putting the screws to her husband, Reverend Billy-Bob Henderson? That man is a bigger hypocrite than his wife. Have you ever seen their house, Zoe?'

The Mermaid Mystery

'Yes. It's nothing special.'

'No,' Mama said. 'Not their house *here*; their house in Charleston, down along the Battery. They paid eleven million dollars for it. Reverend Billy-Bob has always kept one hand in the offering plate, but your great-grandmother tells me that Billy-Bob's learned a new way of dispersing Sunday-morning gifts to the Lord. Now he simply throws the money into the air, and lets God catch what He can.'

'Shut the front door!' I said, laughing. 'I bet that God is all fumble-fingers – no disrespect intended.'

Mama laughed as well. 'Yes, sad to say, the Lord should stay out of major league sports. Come on, dear, let us make haste over to the church office and see if we can catch Hypocrite Henderson before he goes to lunch.'

As luck would have it, Reverend Billy-Bob Henderson had decided to have lunch catered to a Sunday-school room just down a hall from his office. Unluckily for us, he was not alone. Seated around two long tables pushed end to end were Mayor Adelaide Saunders; her husband and high-school principal Ewell Saunders; his brother Sheriff Ryker Saunders; beautician and now owner of three salons Emmeline Davis; Adam Patel, owner of four motels; Tanya Kitchens, owner of five restaurants or snack bars; tour boat company owner Hoyt Hunter; Reverend Billy-Bob Henderson himself; and my very own great-grandmother, Georgina Legare. Nine people in all.

The hallway was dark, since Mama and I had thought better than to advertise our presence. In fact, the door to the outside had been locked, and we wouldn't have been able to gain entry had it not been for one of Mama's bobby pins. She claimed to have learned the secret of breaking and entering from one of the many crime shows that she watches, she just couldn't remember which one. At any rate, the door to the classroom was slightly ajar, so we stood still as statues, and listened in to what sounded like a business meeting. It began with the mayor, Adelaide Saunders, standing and clapping her hands.

'Well,' she said. 'For the first time that we meet, we are no longer the Big Ten. The Big Nine hardly has the same cachet.'

'I don't get it,' Reverend Billy-Bob said. 'Why is the Big Ten more special sounding than the Big Nine?'

'Because of the Ten Commandments, you idiot,' Gan-Gan growled.

'Anyway,' Mayor Adelaide Saunders said, in a modulated voice befitting a mayor, 'the deed has been done, and one of us has – uh – terminated – our weakest member. I can only surmise that he broke his allegiance to the Big Ten because, as a mere taxidermist, his share of the profits was considerably less than ours. Envy can be a powerful motive – in his case, to spill the beans on us by exposing the secret behind Miss Lucy. But now with him out of the picture, we have total deniability. We only know that he was a liar, and we totally believe that Miss Lucy is real.' Mayor Adelaide Saunders smiled. She also had perfect teeth, befitting a mayor. 'As of yet, I have no idea who terminated Gunner Jones. It certainly wasn't me. The rules we established were that we reach into the bag, and each withdraw a bean in a closed fist, and not examine it until we got home. All the beans were identical in size and shape, and all of them were black, except for one. The odd bean was white, but in all other respects it was identical to the black beans.

'Is the person who terminated our fellow member, Gunner Jones, comfortable with revealing his, or her, identity?' Adelaide Saunders asked.

'I did not terminate him,' Sheriff Ryker Saunders said.

'I did not terminate him,' Principal Ewell Saunders said.

'I did not terminate him,' Mayor Adelaide Saunders said for the second time.

'I did not terminate him,' Captain Hoyt Hunter said.

'I did not terminate him,' Reverend Billy-Bob Henderson said.

'I did not terminate him,' restaurateur Tanya Kitchens said.

'I did not terminate him,' hotelier Adam Patel said.

'I did not terminate him,' beauty salon owner Emmeline Davis said.

'I did not terminate him,' merchandise seller and my great-grandmother said.

'In that case,' Mayor Adelaide Saunders said, 'can we all agree by a show of hands that Gunner Jones was never a part of this group, and that we have absolutely no knowledge of any scheme that he might have been involved in to defraud the public?'

'We all agree,' Gan-Gan grunted a few seconds later. 'So, can you move things along, Addie? I'm fixing to die of old age soon, and I don't want to do it here.'

'Is something ailing you, Georgina?' Mayor Adelaide Saunders asked kindly.

'Nothing that wasn't ailing me twenty years ago, back when this meeting started.'

'Uh-huh,' said the long-suffering mayor. 'However, I would like to mention that I did receive an official complaint from the member who was seated next to the member who was terminated – but who was never a member, of course – that the termination happened while we were in session. She did not appreciate being splattered with blood and can't understand why this necessary action couldn't have happened elsewhere.'

'Oh, my word,' Gan-Gan said. 'Whine, whine, whine. I swear, at this rate, I'll be long dead by the time this meeting wraps up. Lord, take me now!'

Mayor Adelaide Saunders acknowledged my great-grandmother's outburst with the barest tip of her head. 'OK then, Adam, how on track are we with the construction of Mermaid World, the largest amusement park ever built?'

Adam Patel checked his phone. 'Right on schedule. The governor is confident that he can strong-arm the state senate into agreeing to his bill to cut our taxes in half. And as for leasing us the one hundred and fifty acres of Francis Marion National Forest to build it on, he said it's a done deal.'

'How long is the lease for?' Gan-Gan demanded.

'It's in perpetuity, or as long as Governor Harpootlian lives,' Adam said quietly. I could tell that crime didn't come easily to him. 'We will essentially own it, as long as we continue to pay the governor one hundred thousand dollars a year. Even when he's out of office.'

'Heck, if I'd known that so-called termination and a little corruption were so darn lucrative, I'd have never gone into the ministry,' Reverend Billy-Bob Henderson said. 'I don't mind telling y'all that I'm so thankful that I finally know what I'm supposed to do with my life. I'm blessed, I truly am.'

'We all are,' Tanya Kitchens said. Her head bobbled on the end of a long, ropey neck, rather like one of those silly dogs in the rear window of somebody's automobile.

'Amen to that,' Hoyt Hunter said.

TWENTY-SIX

'And how goes it with the Museum of the Mermaid?' Mayor Adelaide Saunders said, addressing Emmeline Davis.

'We're right on schedule with the grand opening next week. Just wait until you see the beautiful new version of Miss Lucy that I had sculpted and cast in latex from a Hollywood design studio. Of course, as we discussed, I had a supporting cast of more than a dozen other merfolk created as well, in various skin tones. But the one thing that we didn't come to a unanimous decision on was what to do with the original Miss Lucy that our dearly departed, and now terminated, former Big Ten member cobbled together.'

Gan-Gan chortled. 'Cobbled? You have quite the vocabulary for a mere beautician. Besides, there never was a group called the Big Ten, remember? We were always the Big Nine.'

Emmeline Davis looked like she'd been slapped in the face. She opened her mouth to speak, but no words came out. Emmeline Davis was a sweet, gentle soul and I felt sorry for the way my great-grandmother had treated her.

Not only was Emmeline Davis a beautician and a salon owner, but she had taken an Introduction to Art class at the College of Charleston, and she had taught herself to draw kittens and puppies in charcoal from a book she found on the net. Puppies, she discovered, were much easier to draw than kittens. It was always their mouths that gave her trouble.

Anyway, Emmeline Davis was the only one of the original Big Ten who had art experience of any kind (if one discounts the earthworms Mayor Adelaide Saunders was forced to draw for her master's degree in biology). Therefore, Emmeline Davis had unanimously been elected director of the museum.

'I have an idea about what to do with that ugly, original Miss Lucy – the one made from ape and fish parts,' Tanya Kitchens said, coming to Emmeline Davis's rescue. 'When is the book burning scheduled? We could dismantle her, chop her up, and sneak her bits in with the books.'

'The book burning isn't scheduled until Saturday after next,' Sherriff Ryker Saunders said.

'Can't it be any sooner?' Hoyt Hunter said. He sounded quite nervous to me.

'I'm afraid not,' Sheriff Ryker Saunders said. 'Governor Harpootlian said it would take at least that long to comb through all the libraries in South Carolina and ferret out any books that mention merfolk in any way. This includes children's books, of course. We can't have any books that reflect negatively on merfolk, suggesting that they are just fictional characters.'

'Well, how about this idea then?' Hoyt Hunter said. 'I could "deep six" her in the deep.' He chuckled, again sounding nervous. 'I think that would be appropriate, don't y'all?'

'What does "deep six" mean?' sweet Emmeline Davis asked.

'I'd tie an anchor to her with chains and drop her overboard. Somewhere way out where the water is proper blue and deep. Nobody will ever see her again but the fish.'

'Yeah, you wiener-brain,' Gan-Gan said. 'Those fish will start in on nibbling at her within five minutes. Mark my words, Hoyt Hunter, by the time you get back to your dock, Miss Lucy will be free from her chains and bobbin along in the Gulf Stream. At that point what's left of her could be spotted by anyone with a decent boat, or she might make it all the way to Cape Hatteras and wash ashore. Then the jig is up, and all because you don't have the brains God gave a rabbit.'

'Really, Miss Legare!' Reverend Billy-Bob Henderson said. 'Do you have to be so harsh?'

'You're one to talk, Billy-Bob,' Gan-Gan snapped. 'You're the one who went all the way to the Supreme Court and got them to rule that merfolk could not compete in swim meets because they possessed an innate physical advantage. Admit it, Billy-Bob, you're a meraphobe.'

'I am not,' the pastor said, stamping a dainty foot. 'You take that back. You should be thanking me, Miss Legare, because I also got the Speaker of the House of the United States Congress to introduce two very important bills. The first would permit merfolk to possess guns, and the second would allow school children, down to age six, to own and openly carry guns into schools. As long as our teachers refuse to pick up the ball and arm themselves on behalf of our kids, then I say, why not let the kids do it themselves? No terrorist in his right mind is going to attack an elementary school knowing that there are five hundred armed shooters inside.'

'In my opinion, the bill doesn't go far enough,' Sheriff Ryker Saunders opined. 'I say it should include pistols for pre-schoolers. Gun-toting, trigger-happy toddlers will keep terrorists away from our nursery schools.'

'You idiot,' Ewell Saunders said quietly. 'The kids will shoot and maim each other. Terrorists can stay home, pop open a beer, and watch it all on TV.'

'Please, everyone,' Mayor Adelaide Saunders said, 'let's not argue. Emmeline, why don't you just wrap Miss Lucy up in an old blanket and put her in a storage closet until book-burning day? Given that she's made us all very prosperous, I vote that we have a Miss Lucy demolishing party the day before – you know, chop her up into unrecognizable pieces for immolation during the book-burning party.

'Now, I hereby call an end to this meeting of the Big Nine. Adam, would you do us the honour of leading us in our group prayer?'

Adam Patel nodded. 'Certainly, Your Honour. But first I'd like to say how grateful I am to be living in America, a Christian country. If my grandfather had not immigrated to America, and converted, then I would surely be in danger of burning in Hell.'

'And writhing in excruciating pain for all eternity,' Reverend Billy-Bob Henderson said.

'With Yankees and liberals,' Gan-Gan put in.

'Not to mention eighth-grade girls who roll their eyes and cuss out their teachers,' Ewell Saunders said.

'Enough!' Mayor Adelaide said. 'Adam, just start the prayer.'

'Yes, ma'am,' Adam Patel said. 'Everyone, please fold your hands and close your eyes, as proper Christians are taught to do everywhere, and then say the words of our official prayer along with me.

'"Now that we are wide awake
We pray the Lord our wealth to make,
We toss our loot into the air,
And ask the Lord to take His share.
With grateful hearts we thank the Lord
That He has put us on this Board
And blessed us with the happy creed
There's nothing wrong with graft and greed."'

'Amen!' Everyone said in unison. It was the first time that they had agreed on anything that day.

I grabbed my mother's arm and tugged so hard that she struggled to maintain her balance.

'What the heck, darling?' Mama said, somewhat miffed.

'Mama,' I whispered urgently. 'We have got to get to Miss Lucy and spirit her away before that fool, Emmeline Davis, returns to the museum.'

'You mean *steal* her?'

'Potato, potahto – although I wonder what they say in Britain. Potahto, potato? Anyway, they're just going to chop her up and burn her, so I'd hardly call liberating evidence as stealing. I'm thinking that we should take her to the Smithsonian Museum of Natural History in Washington, DC. We could do a televised interview there, with her as our evidence that there never was any mermaid.'

'Will it just be you on TV this time, or can I be part of the interview as well?'

'You absolutely can, Mama. I need you to back me up.'

'Then lead the way,' Mama said. Suddenly the legs that had been walking the earth for more than half a century were invigorated by the promise of national exposure, and possibly even fame, or at least infamy.

'Although we might go to jail if we're caught before we get to Washington and have a chance to expose this scam.'

'Ooh, cool,' Mama said. 'That could be fun for a day or two – just as long as we don't have to share a bathroom.'

'Mama, what planet have you been living on? Of course you'd have to share a bathroom, because the toilet would be right there in your cell. Your cellmate will get to watch you do everything.'

'But I have a shy bladder,' Mama wailed.

'Maybe Carla will be kind and turn away – if you ask her nicely.'

'Who's Carla?'

'Your prison wife,' I said. 'In other words, your cellmate.'

'Can't you think of a better name for my prison wife than Carla?' Mama complained. 'I kissed a girl named Carla in middle school, and it did absolutely nothing for me.'

'Then how about Butcher Knife Betty?'

'Now you're talking. What's going to be the name of your prison wife?'

'Three-fingered Thelma. She used to be Betty's cellmate.'

Mama laughed briefly. 'Ugh. But wouldn't that be sort of like incest if we – you know.'

'Mama,' I panted, 'that was a joke, and this is a fantasy. Betty and Thelma don't exist, but prisons do, and trust me, you don't want to see the inside of one. You really do have to take care of your bodily functions out in the open.'

'Even floss your teeth?'

'Even that, Mama.'

'Then run faster,' Mama said urgently. 'Move those short legs of yours, Zoe. If I'd have known you were going to get me into this kind of a pickle, I might have married a taller man. Then you would have longer legs and would be able to run faster.'

'And if I'd have known that you were going to be such a weird mother, I'd have refused to be born to you. Instead, I'd have requested a spot in a large, extremely wealthy Yankee family somewhere up near Boston.'

'Why, I never!' Mama said.

'And I always!' I said.

Given that we were both exceedingly miffed, and neither of us truly desired having a prison wife, we took our frustration out on pumping our arms and legs: mine quite short, Mama's just a wee bit longer. Therefore, we reached the museum much quicker than if we'd strolled there companionably. Given that the museum was closed for the day, there were no cars in the parking lot. *Zilch. Rien. Nada.* If there were any guards on duty, they must have walked to work.

'So how are we going to get in?' Mama asked, quite sensibly.

'We look for a key.'

'What?' Mama said.

I couldn't believe that Mama, who had thirty more years of life experience on me, would ask such a silly question. It's not like she'd hit her head recently. Perhaps all that running had deprived her brain of a skosh too much oxygen.

'How about we start with the most obvious place,' I said gently. 'First we check under the mat, then the flower planters on either side of the entrance, and then above the door, along the top of the header.'

'But, Zoe, darling, these are automatic doors that are opened by punching a code into a keypad. See it over there? You're not going to find a key under the mat, or in either one of these pots of petunias. Even if you did, it is not going to cut the mustard.'

I smacked my forehead. Hard.

'Duh,' I said. But I'm as stubborn as a grass stain on white cotton slacks that have already been laundered. So, what if there was a keypad? I was still going to perform my search. I began by lifting the front-left corner of the rubber mat, and I was immediately successful!

Apparently, Emmeline Davis thought that folks wouldn't search in the most obvious place, on account of it being just that: obvious. Under that front corner she'd placed a slip of paper with the code to the keypad. The paper had been vacuumed-sealed between two pieces of plastic. I can only guess that Emmeline Davis had a poor memory and wished to walk to work some days without a pocketbook, or pockets. Then again, perhaps the code was there for the benefit of workmen, or even volunteers. Whatever the reason, the important thing is that the code worked.

Mama and I tiptoed into the museum with our mouths agape. I'll say this for Emmeline Davis, she certainly had an artistic eye. There were numerous dioramas depicting merfolk beneath the sea in their imagined lives. There were other dioramas of tropical islets, upon which merfolk lay recumbent, sunning themselves. All of them were stunningly realistic and, I sorely hate to confess this, almost made a believer out of me. I mean, who wouldn't want to buy into a belief that there were such beautiful creatures living perfect existences in oceans and seas, places that had once been the abode of monsters and giant serpents? The faces, head shapes, and torsos of the merfolk all conformed to the human ideal of perfection: that is to say that they exhibited symmetry. Their tails were long and tapered, and their flukes, although too large in my opinion, had a beautiful, graceful shape. They too exhibited symmetry.

Compared to the mermaid models on display in the Museum of the Mermaid, the cobbled together Miss Lucy looked like a merfolk's version of a scarecrow – or a scarecrab, or whatever pests they might have under the sea. I found myself feeling embarrassed on behalf of the recently terminated Gunner Jones, until I reminded myself that everything I beheld was all fake. Then I took a couple of quick pictures on my phone and flew into action.

'Mama,' I said, 'run, if you still can, to the back and see if there's a storeroom. I bet Emmeline Davis has a painter's smock or two that we can drape around Miss Lucy. Meanwhile I'll try to unseat her from her fake rock throne.'

'Will do,' Mama said, in a rare moment of cooperation. Then off she went, with more hustle left in her than I could have possibly imagined.

Meanwhile I attempted to gently wrestle Miss Lucy off her fake rock. Her genuine scaly behind had been stuck there with strips of museum putty, which is a tacky substance used to secure fragile items and keep them from falling off shelves. I suppose I could have put my arms around her and given her a good tug. However, not knowing how securely her two parts were attached, I was afraid of ripping her apart, so I sort of wiggled her off her fibreglass perch. She was free at last, but still in my arms, when Mama raced back pushing a wheelchair.

'Look what I found! Back by the first-aid equipment. There is even a heart defibrillator. They've thought of everything.' Mama grabbed a handful of cloth that was draped over the back of the wheelchair. 'You were right, Zoe. I've got two painting smocks here, and a mask. I don't think her mouth looks very natural, do you?'

'I agree. If we cover her nose and mouth that will go a long way to making her look less like an ape. Sunglasses will help too.'

'Which I have,' Mama said, and dug into her valise-size handbag and fished out a pair.

'Headscarf?' I said.

'Don't be silly, darling, I'm a Southern matron.' She produced two scarves. 'Both silk, of course. Which do you want: plain, or patterned?'

'The smock is blue and plain, so let's go with the one with the blue irises, the painting by Vincent van Gogh. Too bad we don't have gloves to disguise her ape hands. The press-on nails Emmeline Davis applied when she did the makeup for Gunner might have done the job to pass her off as a mythical mermaid, but let's face it, how many real women have hands like that?'

'Never fear,' Mama said. She dug deeper into her handbag and pulled out a pair of white cotton gloves. 'Zoe, you don't honestly think I'd go to church every Sunday with bare hands, do you? There is safe sex, but there is also such a thing as safe "shakes." I'm not about to shake someone's bare hand and catch their cold.'

'You go girl, Mama. I don't suppose you have a shawl or cardigan in that bag?' I asked hopefully. While it was a warm summer's day out, Miss Lucy was beginning to resemble a little old lady, and except for the indestructible Gan-Gan, all my other female progenitors of a certain age had always seemed to be cold.

'Will a silk pashmina do?' Mama said. 'It's a darker blue, but still, it's a complementary shade.' She slipped the wrap around Miss Lucy's narrow shoulders, and overlapped the ends, which she then fastened together with a brooch which she also retrieved from her handbag of miracles.

'I don't suppose you have any sandwiches in there?' I said. I was quite serious.

'Actually, I do,' Mama said, 'and a pan of brownies with fudge icing, but don't you think we should put some miles between us and Tidal Shores?'

TWENTY-SEVEN

'Nobody gave us no never mind,' is an expression sometimes heard in these parts. That is to say, not one person gave Mama and me a second look as we wheeled an elderly lady along the sidewalk and to my car. The town was chock-a-block with tourists too, and a good many people exchanged greetings with us – well, except for the little old lady, who was probably too ill to talk. When I lifted Miss Lucy from the chair to put her in the back seat, a nice young couple – Yankees by their accents – offered to help, but Mama politely got in the way.

'No offence, darlings,' she said, 'but my mama can't stand Yankees. She's liable to start screaming if you touch her. She's convinced that the War Between the States is still raging on, that Atlanta is currently burning, and that Sherman and his troops are headed this way. But y'all have a nice day anyway.'

Miss Lucy was shockingly light, and needed to be belted in, lest she fly like a projectile the first time I stopped suddenly. Of course, I stashed the wheelchair back in the trunk, as I was quite positive that we'd be needing it later, because we had one more very important stop. There, we had to sit and wait, as if we were doing a police stake-out which, in many respects, we were. Fortunately, the place where we were doing it was behind an old stately home that was not only surrounded by a wall but had a planting of mature camellias along the inside that offered the lower level of the property complete privacy from the street.

When the party whom we sought to interrogate finally arrived, I let Mama do the apprehending – I mean, negotiating. Then Mama and I got to work modifying poor Miss Lucy so that she would fit into a very large suitcase that Mama had thought to bring down from Charlotte, and which we then crammed back into the trunk of the car. Now, I will not claim that the terms of the negotiation were satisfactory to everyone involved, nor should they have been. I shall only state that if my mother were younger, she might seriously consider a career as a hostage negotiator. I will not go into any more details here, lest I incriminate Mama and myself, except to say that as soon as she'd conducted her business, we buckled our hostage in the back seat, and I drove away from there as fast as possible.

However, given that the town was such a popular destination, driving away from it was slower than walking. It wasn't until we got to Route 17 that the traffic lessened. I had a sudden decision to make. Should I continue up that state route as far as I could go, and then snake over to Interstate 95, or head toward Charleston, and go up from there? The latter would mean backtracking a little, but then I could avoid the stop-and-go traffic of Myrtle Beach.

I hate decisions of all kinds, thanks to Mama. When I was a little girl she would take a piece of red velvet cake, which was my favourite, and cut it into two uneven slices.

'Which serving do you want, Zoe?' she'd ask me.

'The smaller one, please,' I'd answer politely.

'How very kind of you to give your little brother the larger piece.'

The next time I'd be sure to request the larger slice.

'What a selfish little girl you are,' she'd say. 'Just for that I'm giving the larger serving to your little brother.'

It was ever thus, until this slow learner finally figured out that she needed to ask her mama to cut two slices the same size. Somehow my takeaway from the red velvet cake experience was that decisions were to be avoided for as long as possible, because negative consequences could always be lurking around the corner.

All this is to say that after finally reaching State Route 17, spotting the newly opened See Food & More restaurant just a stone's throw to the right, I made a small decision that would give me time to ponder the bigger, more important one. As one might expect, the restaurant's parking lot was full. However, on my third rotation, a family from Ohio lumbered out of the eatery and squeezed into their spacious vehicle. You can bet that I zipped into that empty slot faster than a white lie is uttered at a cocktail party.

'Zoe,' Mama said, 'are you sure you want to eat at a restaurant where the owner can't even spell its name right?'

'It's supposed to be a pun, Mama.'

'And what are we supposed to do with my mother?'

'*Excuse* me?' Mama's mother had been dead for almost thirty years. If Mama was going to start exhibiting signs of dementia, could she not have the decency to wait a week or two? I had a lot on my plate just then.

Mama motioned with her chin. 'Didn't we agree that the so-called "lady" in the back seat was my Yankee-hating mama?'

'Yes, but poor Grandma must be rolling over in her grave. Shouldn't we call *her* that only when necessary?'

'Zoe, darling,' Mama said, 'your grandma had a great sense of humour. If she's moving at all, after thirty years, her bare bones are rattling with laughter.'

I cringed. 'Well, Mama, we can't just leave her in the car, or we could be accused of elder abuse.'

'We won't be,' Mama said, 'if you lock the car, but leave the engine running and the air-conditioning on. Besides, the dear old lady will have fallen asleep while reading her Bible. Nobody's going to mess with a Bible-reader.'

'Where are we going to find a Bible?' I asked quite sensibly.

Mama dove into her ginormous handbag again and retrieved a King James original version of the Holy Bible. 'Just open it to the Book of Proverbs, chapter twenty. It's approximately in the middle of the Bible; that way it should stay open. Besides, the proverbs are fun to read, even though some of them are quite sexist.'

'Mama, you are amazing,' I said.

'I know,' she said, as she proffered her cheek for a kiss.

I gave her a smooch as requested, and then we high-tailed it into the restaurant. There was a hostess on duty, with about a dozen people bunched up near her podium, but nonetheless she greeted us with sweet Southern charm.

'Welcome to See Food & More,' she said, her voice dripping sugar. 'All of my booths are filled, but I do have two spots available at the bar.'

'Bar?' I said.

Just then I noticed that the 'more' in the name referred to a small U-shaped counter, behind which was a continuous bank of television screens. All of the TVs were turned to sports channels. Duh. This was one of those sports-themed restaurants that I tried to avoid, because my interest in sports ranks just below that of sitting in a bathtub full of spiders. I firmly believe that I wouldn't have turned out this way had I not been forced to take gym class first period in the ninth grade, just when my interest in the opposite sex was beginning to intensify. Showering after gym class was mandatory. Not only was I slow to develop (to be sure, I eventually did!), which caused me no end of embarrassment, but on gym days I had to go without makeup, my hair was a mess, and I actually felt less clean than I did before leaving home.

'We'll take the bar,' Mama said, before I could turn around and run.

So we hopped up on the stools, and as much as we both hated to admit it, the food was remarkably good. Shrimp is always on the menu this close to the coast, and that's what we both ordered. While we were eating, two state troopers entered the restaurant and appeared to start scanning the crowded room. Then the younger one, who looked remarkably like Lofton, addressed everyone on a hand-held microphone.

'May I have your attention, folks?'

Cutlery clattered as conversation ceased.

'Who owns the silver Lexus with the license plate that reads: HITMAMA?'

The diners laughed uproariously as Mama's face reddened. She'd actually wanted her vanity plate to read HOTMAMA, but someone else had beat her to it. Even HATMAMA had been taken. She settled for HITMAMA by rationalizing that it implied that she was a 'hit' with children – in other words, a very popular mama. That was at least true on the days that she handed us our weekly allowances.

Reluctantly, and slowly, Mama raised her arm. 'Sir,' she said, 'my vanity plate doesn't mean what you think it means.'

The officer strode up to us. 'Ma'am,' he said, 'are you aware that an old woman has passed out from heat in the back seat of your car?'

'You mean my nana?' I said. 'She's passed out, all right, but not from the heat. We left the car running and air-conditioning on.'

'That's right,' Mama said. 'My mother broke out of Shady Pines up in Myrtle Beach two days ago and has been on a bender ever since. We found her down in Charleston, more pickled than a vat of kosher dills.'

'If she's sleeping off a bender, then why is there a Bible in her lap?'

'The Bible was my idea,' I said. 'It's open to the proverb that reads: "wine is a mocker." I was hoping that Nana would get the hint when she wakes up. This is the third time this year that we've had to drag her out of some bar stinking drunk.' I sighed dramatically. 'But, Mama, maybe you should have turned the fan speed on a bit higher so that cool air gets to the back seat more easily. On the other hand, these old folks are always complaining about cold when you turn up the AC.'

'Ain't that the truth,' a waitress piped up. 'They're always trying to make me turn down the air-conditioning, but then some normal-aged folks come in and complain that it's too hot in here.'

'Boo!' a white-haired couple shouted in unison.

'Well, officer,' I said, 'what would you like us to do? Abandon our lunch now to check on my drunken nana, or may we finish eating first?'

'No, no, go ahead and finish, ma'am,' the trooper said. It was his face that was red now. 'Sorry to have disturbed you.' Then he pressed the speaker button again. 'Folks, may I have your attention again? We are about to issue an all-points bulletin for a very disturbing abduction. Chief, I'm going to pass this one over to you.'

The older man nodded sombrely as he accepted the microphone. 'That's right, folks. My name is Sheriff Benjamin Sawyer, and I'm afraid the news I have to share might come as a big disappointment for any of you who are headed down to Tidal Shores. The mermaid known as Miss Lucy has been stolen – uh, kidnapped – from the Museum of the Mermaid.'

The sighs, groans and murmurs of disappointment reminded me of my old school days when a substitute teacher, filling in for the regular maths teacher, announced a surprise quiz that would be factored into their final grade. Suddenly life had become unfair for the good people dining in the See Food & More restaurant.

Sheriff Benjamin Sawyer tapped twice on the microphone, and that sound got everyone's attention. 'Although we have no other information at this time, we can only assume that Miss Lucy's abductors are armed and dangerous. No doubt most of you already have a good picture in your minds of what the world's most famous mermaid looks like, but nevertheless, my deputy is now going to be passing out photos of her – well, actually they're postcards, but you get the picture – no pun intended. If you believe that you've spotted her in someone's possession, call or text us. Do not, and I repeat, do not, try and take any action yourselves. Do I make myself clear?'

'Yes, sir,' a couple of folks mumbled.

'I didn't hear y'all,' the sheriff said in a voice loud enough to wake the dead three counties over.

'*Yes, sir!*' That time the volume of the diners' response indicated that there was a sizable number of people present who had either served in the military, or who had done time in prison.

'And one more thing,' Sheriff Sawyer said. 'Feel free to make copies of the pictures my deputy will be handing you, and then give those copies to your friends. Are there any questions?'

A hand shot up. 'Is there a reward if we find her?' The speaker was a rotund man in matching red and white checked polo shirt and Bermuda shorts, and sunburned skin. He reminded me of a beach ball that I used to play with at the beach when I was little.

The deputy and the sheriff exchanged looks. The sheriff nodded.

'Yes,' the deputy said. 'Right now, the reward stands at one hundred thousand dollars, but it could go higher. A lot depends on how quickly Miss Lucy is returned, and the state of her condition.'

The restaurant suddenly buzzed with excitement. As the deputy walked by the table with his fist full of postcards, they were snatched from his hand. An untidy queue quickly formed at the cash register, as customers eager to begin their search gave no thought to leaving their uneaten lunches behind. The threat of an eminent tornado could hardly have cleared the See Food & More out any faster. Soon the only two folks remaining, other than employees and the lawmen, were Mama and me.

'Why, I'll be dippity-doodled,' Mama said. 'It's a crying shame to waste all this food when there are starving children in – uh, Zoe, where's a politically correct place to say that about these days?'

'We have hungry children right here in America,' I said.

Mama frowned. 'Maybe so, but not as many as they have overseas. They're called "third world" countries for a reason, dear.'

I rolled my eyes. My mother rolled her eyes back at me and then found a waiter and asked him to box up the remainder of our meals, plus four other meals that had barely been touched. She also asked for two of the jumbo-size disposable drink cups to be filled with ice water, and four extra that were empty.

'Eating strangers' leftovers is just plain tacky,' I said as we got ready to turn on to the highway. I decided to turn right since it was easier, making the route through Myrtle Beach our choice by default.

'Waste not, want not,' Mama said.

'Well, what are the empty drink containers for?'

'There is a petrol station right next door,' Mama said. 'Fill up.

Then we don't need to stop for the next four hundred miles, because we won't be needing to stop for a restroom break.'

'*Come again?*' I said.

'We'll pee in the cups. It's easy-peasy. No pun intended. Your father and I used to do it all the time when we'd drive from Charlotte down to Tidal Shores, on account of your father hated stopping. Of course, that only worked as long as you were in nappies. But once you were potty-trained – well, we tried using the cups a couple of times – no pun intended again – but it was too messy.'

'You can save both your puns and your cups, Mama, because when I feel the urge, I'm *stopping*, and that's that!'

Mama recoiled as if she'd been slapped, which, in a way, she had. Neither of Beatrice Legare Porter's children had ever openly defied her since her husband's death. Of course, since they were quite normal, her children had, on numerous occasions, behaved in ways she would not have approved of – had she been aware of them.

As it happened, we were forced to stop an hour and a half later when we reached Myrtle Beach. This had nothing to do with bladders or roadblocks, but instead with the massive crowd that filled the street for as far as the eye could see.

TWENTY-EIGHT

'Oh Lordy,' Mama said. 'This doesn't look good. You don't suppose the president has been shot, do you?'

'Mama, that's crazy talk,' I said. 'What on earth would make you say a thing like that?'

'Oh, that's right, dear. You weren't alive when President Kennedy was assassinated.'

'Mama, neither were you.' I lowered the window on her side of the car and called out to a young woman who was pushing a stroller down the middle of the street.

'Excuse me, miss,' I said, using my polite voice. 'What's going on?'

The woman deftly turned the stroller, which contained a toddler, and headed toward me, so I shut off the engine.

'Smile, Mama,' I said through gritted teeth.

'You from out of town?' the strange woman said. She had a sweet, pleasant voice, and her accent was decidedly Deep South – either Charleston or Savannah.

'Yes, we are from out of town,' Mama said, 'but our family has lived in this state from before the American Revolution – from back when it was a colony of Great Britain.'

'Well, then you've come here at just the right time,' the young mother said. 'To answer your question, this is a rally for Gloria Moncks-Bracken. She is here in Myrtle Beach, and she has just announced that she is running for president.'

At first I thought I might have misheard. 'Do you mean the United States Senator Gloria Moncks-Bracken?' I dared to ask. 'The whacko who says that our current president and his wife are really reptiles who unzip their so-called "people suits" after dark, and roam around the city of Washington looking for children whose blood they can harvest, in order to keep celebrities looking young?'

'Monkey-Bwacken's a cwazy lady,' the toddler said. She clapped her pudgy little hands. 'Cwazy lady, cwazy lady, Monkey-Bwacken's cwack-ors,' the child sang.

'Hush, Ashley,' her mother said, her face quite red.

'But dat what you said, Mommy.'

'I may have,' the young mother said, 'but if I did, that was *before* Mrs Moncks-Bracken made her big announcement this morning up in Wilmington. From now on we don't call her "monkey" anymore, or say that she is crazy. Is that understood?'

Instead of answering, Ashley squirmed. 'Mommy, I wanna go home. I'm hung-wee.'

'We will, baby, just after we hear who she nominates for her running mate.' The young mother turned to us. 'I don't want y'all to think that I'm crazy, or anything like that, but the reason I changed my mind about backing Mrs Moncks-Bracken is that this morning, up in Wilmington, when she threw her hat into the ring, she vowed to have a mermaid as her selection for vice president! Can you imagine that?

'Just think of what that means for our country. At last, we'll have a female president, and never mind her unorthodox views. We'll just have to learn to live and let live. What really matters is that for the first time in human history, if this ticket wins, then the most powerful country in the world will have a non-human in its number-two position. If something were to happen to President Moncks-Bracken, then we'd have a non-human in the White House! Isn't that thrilling?'

'But Mommy, I'm weally, weally hung-wee,' Ashley whined.

'Hush, dear. Can't you see that Mommy's talking to grown-ups?'

Mama pulled a Styrofoam container from the bag at her feet. 'I have half of a bacon, lettuce and tomato sandwich in here that she can have.'

Ashley's mother shook her head. 'Thanks, but no thanks. We don't accept food from strangers. No offence, because you look normal enough, but one can't be too careful these days.'

'I hear you,' I said. 'Like what if Mrs Moneys-Broken doesn't do a good enough job vetting the mermaid that she chooses as her running mate as vice president. What if at night the mermaid unzips her mermaid suit, and a human emerges to wreak the sort of havoc that requires a being in possession of two legs.'

The young woman's eyes flashed angrily. 'Are you mocking me?'

'No, ma'am,' I said. 'I'm just a cautious person, who would hate to see this country hurting any more than it is. I reckon you've heard about the abduction of Miss Lucy's remains from the Museum of the Mermaid down in Tidal Shores.'

The young woman clapped her hands over her daughter's ears. 'Whoever's done something that awful ought to be shot,' she said.

'Yeah,' I said, 'and you just know that the perps have got to be men. Women wouldn't commit such a heinous crime. So, what I'd do is make them take off their shirts, rub roast beef all over their exposed skin, and then tuck slices of roast beef in their pockets. After that, I'd throw them into a small room with a couple of hungry Rottweilers.'

The young mother howled with laughter. 'Great idea! I'm passing that along.'

Mama snorted. 'You young gals are sissies. Why, I'd take my garden shears, sharpen them really well, then have these horrible men strip all the way and—'

'Mama!' I said. 'Enough! There is a child present, and I bet that she can still hear us, even though her mama has her ears covered.'

'No, she can't,' the girl's mother said, and stepped back from her daughter, removing her hands from the child's ears. 'What were we saying, darling?'

'I dunno,' the tot said, 'but I still hung-wee, and I want woast beef. A woast beef samwich.'

'Listen,' the woman said, 'we must get a move on, or I'm going to miss the big announcement. I just want to say that you're never going to make it through town this way. Not with this crowd. My advice is to turn around and go back until you hit State Route 544. Take that west until you get to State Route 31. It's like a round-about. Just follow it north, and you'll see signs directing you to North Carolina.'

'Thank you, ma'am,' I said. Without waiting for a response, I wheeled away, did a U-turn in the middle of the street, coming within inches of the stroller, and then zoomed back down the road like greased lightning.

Mama kept her mouth shut until we were safely headed north on the round-about. Then she just couldn't keep her motherly trap shut any longer.

'Zoe! You could have killed that young woman and her baby.'

'No, Mama. I knew what I was doing.'

'Well, you could have gotten a speeding ticket. You still can. You're probably driving twice the speed limit right now.'

'At least that,' I said. 'However, all the police are going to be either spectators at the asinine event that's unfolding in town as we speak, or else the police will be there to control the crowd. Correction, there will probably be a few break-ins around town – jewellery and tech stores – so they might draw some heat. But my point is that no one is coming after speeders.'

No sooner had I spoken than a bright-red car barrelled past us doing at least a hundred miles an hour. It passed so close to my side of the car that if I'd been driving with my left arm hanging out the window, my arm would have been sheared off and landed in the road. Partly to irritate Mama, but mostly because I knew that I could get away with it at that moment, I practically stood on the accelerator.

'Zoe!' Mama screamed. 'Slow down! We're going to crash. I'm too young to die.'

'Nonsense, Mama,' I shouted over the sound of the road. 'You're a widow who's borne two children and buried both of her parents; you've lived a full life. What else could you possibly want to do before your ticket gets punched?'

'You're crazy, Zoe, if you think that's a full life. I want to travel. I want to rent a house for a month on the Amalfi coast in Italy. I want to buy a dress six sizes larger than what I wear now and eat until that dress is too tight. Also, and this is very close to my heart, I want to milk a cow. Not just any cow, but a pretty cow, like a Jersey cow.'

'Mama, you're crazy. The first two things I can understand: in my opinion the Amalfi coast is the most beautiful part of Italy, Italian men can be very sexy, and although I don't want to get fat, I would like to eat so much bread, pasta and ice cream that I gained six dress sizes. What I don't understand is why anyone would want to milk a cow.'

'I want to milk a cow,' Mama shouted over the sound of the highway, 'because I read *The Little House on the Prairie* when I was a girl. After that I always wondered if I had what it took to be a pioneer.'

'You mean like stealing land from the indigenous population?' I asked.

'Oh, stop it, Zoe!' Mama said. 'I meant chopping wood, spinning yarn, churning butter – that sort of thing. And yes, you have to milk a cow if you want to churn butter.'

'And of course you'd like to birth your young'uns without an epidural,' I said.

'You're very argumentative, dear,' Mama said. 'When you have children, make sure that they're boys. A son will just eat and grunt, whereas a daughter is like a dog with a bone. Leastways, that's how they are with their mamas. A daughter will gnaw off every last scrap of patience that you possess, just as long as she can get a rise out of you.'

'Nah-unh. I'm not like that,' I said fiercely.

Much to my irritation, Mama said nothing for the next hour. By then we had reached the ferry landing at Cedar Island. At that point, if one had reservations, one could load one's vehicle on to a ferry that takes two hours and fifteen minutes to travel to the Outer Banks Island of Ocracoke. Although it was the height of summer, and thus the tourist season, we were in luck, because there were a number of last-minute cancellations.

'There's something big happening down in Myrtle Beach,' the ferry captain said. 'I think it's a rally of some sort. Anyway, that's how come I have space for you.'

'We are much obliged,' Mama drawled, and favoured the captain with a smile beneath the brim of a tightly secured sun bonnet. Who could blame her? The captain appeared to be around sixty, was tanned and trim, and possessed beautiful white teeth that were just imperfect enough to make Beatrice Legare Porter believe that they might be his own. Best of all, the man was not wearing a wedding ring, and there was no tell-tale pale band of skin at the base of his ring finger.

The captain also seemed smitten with my mama, who was also sixty-ish, trim, not quite as tanned, but possessed even better teeth. Likewise, she did not appear to be married. Based on those criteria, the ferry boat captain invited Mama up on the bridge with him for the duration of the crossing.

Meanwhile, I wandered over to a position along the nearest railing, where I felt assured of some good dolphin watching. I'd made this crossing several times and had never been disappointed. This morning was no different. I had no idea what the dolphins got out of accompanying the ferry, but they sure acted like nothing made them happier than to leap out of the water and entertain the delighted passengers.

I loved wild dolphins, and I was enjoying a much-needed break from months of stress when I became aware that there was a woman standing to my right. The intruder's bare elbow touched mine. I immediately jerked mine away.

'Sorry,' the woman said, sensing my discomfort. 'I got carried away in my excitement.'

'You're British?' I asked.

'English, to be exact. London to be more precise.'

'Well,' I said, 'did you know that there is a little bit of England on Ocracoke Island?'

'Do you mean a tea shop?'

'No, an actual plot of ground that is England.'

'I don't understand; how is that possible?'

'Well, during World War Two, the British Royal Navy sent twenty-four armed trawlers to help us defend our coastline. One of these trawlers, the *HMT Bedfordshire,* was torpedoed by the Germans, killing all thirty-seven members of the British and Canadian Royal Navies aboard.

'Four bodies washed ashore and were buried in a plot donated by an Ocracoke Island family. The little cemetery is now surrounded by a white picket fence, and the flag of the United Kingdom flies over it. This place is remembered as "forever England." The dead here are not buried on foreign soil but are home. Perhaps you'd like to go up to the bridge and see if the captain has brochures. In any case, would you please do me a big favour, and send that garrulous, and overly amorous, old biddy down?'

When the woman touched me again, it was intentional. This time it was with her hand.

'Do you give tours of your island, miss?'

'Uh – I'm not a local. But we have vacationed on the Outer Banks before, and when we were here, we picked up a little booklet describing the cemetery and its origin.'

'Oh. Well, you seem so knowledgeable. My husband Edward is inside – he doesn't care for breezes – but he's quite pleasant, I assure you. At any rate, could you – would you – possibly consider acting as our tour guide for the time we spend on the island? We'd pay you handsomely, I assure you.'

'Thank you, but I'm travelling with my mother. She's a couple of lightbulbs shy of a chandelier, if you get my picture, which hasn't stopped her from climbing up to the bridge to throw herself at the captain. Not that that will get her anywhere, because we're in the middle of a smuggling job, and we must hightail it up north as soon as the ferry comes to a stop.'

The English woman's eyes twinkled merrily. 'What are you smuggling? Maybe Edward and I could help you. We do so enjoy a spot of fun. Frankly, my dear, what's another English cemetery, when we have so many back home, whereas a smuggling caper in America sounds more like our cup of tea.'

'We're smuggling a rather hideous chimera,' I said. 'Getting involved in our caper could be downright dangerous for you. You don't want to end up in an American prison; if you ask for a "cuppa," no one will understand you.'

'Right. But what's a chimera?'

Sometimes my mouth gets ahead of my brain, and I'm forced to acknowledge that fact. This might have been one of those times.

'Well,' I said, 'I'm not sure that this creature even qualifies as a chimera. But in this case, she's half-ape, half-fish, and one hundred percent trouble. I could let you peek at her – for a small fee, of course – but then I'd be forced to feed you to the fishes, to keep you from going to the Feds.'

The English woman took a step well away from the railing as she chuckled nervously. 'And they say that you Americans don't have a sense of humour.'

I stepped in closer to her. '*Please*. I am not an American; I am English. Can't you tell by my nose?'

The English woman scooted further back until her buttocks were pressed against some passenger's car. 'Uh – your nose?'

'Yes,' I said. 'My schnoz. My proboscis.'

The English woman swallowed hard. 'Well, yes, you do have a rather prominent nose, but you don't have an English accent.'

'Which English accent *don't* I have?' I pressed. 'There are many different ones, you know. Yorkshire, Kentish, posh London aristocrat.'

'You don't have *any* of them!' the poor woman wailed. 'You sound American.'

'That's because I gave up my English accent for Lent,' I said.

'You're joking with me. Please tell me that you're joking with me. Then we can both have a good laugh.'

'Oh no, dearie, I'm afraid you're out of luck. I gave up laughing for Lent as well, because I was an extremely wicked woman last year.'

'But it isn't even Lent anymore; it's mid-summer.'

'I'm aware of that. But the asylum that Mum and I escaped from—'

The real English woman skedaddled, leaving me to observe the dolphins in peace for the rest of the crossing.

TWENTY-NINE

I breathed a sigh of relief when I saw that the English woman and her husband Edward disembarked before Mama and I did. I exhaled even louder when the Brits turned on to a side street.

'Tootles,' I said. I waved goodbye to their rental car and continued to follow Route 12 north to the village of Hatteras. We were on a two-lane road now, and we needed to use another ferry, but surely no one would be looking for us way up here. At least no one would be after us for liberating Miss Lucy from that horrible museum, but there was an outside chance that the authorities were after us because we'd been reported as having broken out of an asylum for those suffering from severe mental illness. Under normal circumstances, I would already have consigned my exchange with the English woman to the past, filing it as 'a bit of fun.' Sadly, these were no longer normal times, not when nearly half the country believed in the lie hatched up and perpetuated by the Big Ten. Everything was topsy-turvy now; what was once science, and therefore provable, had been replaced by a fantasy that people somehow found more comforting than facts.

'Why do we have to be in such an all-fired hurry?' Mama whined. 'This is one of my favourite drives.'

I cringed as I turned my head slightly away from Mama. 'It may have come to my knowledge that someone in this car let it be known to an uncharacteristically pushy English woman that we two are a pair of mentally unstable patients, who have escaped the confines of their asylum.'

Mama took a moment to digest this information. 'Was the woman who squealed that old lady in the back seat with the sunglasses and the hat?'

I cringed even further. 'No, ma'am. It was me.'

'Whew! That's a relief,' Mama said, and burst out laughing. She laughed long and hard.

It was an infectious laugh that got me laughing as well. I swear it was not my imagination: even the old lady in the back seat chortled.

The ferry ride had given me a welcome break from driving, but from Ocracoke to our destination of the Smithsonian Museum in Washington, DC involved another eight hours of driving. That did not include stopping, albeit briefly, at a fast-food restaurant to pick up burgers and run in to use the restroom.

I did not trust Mama to drive, and with good reason. Back in Charlotte, Beatrice Legare Porter was known amongst her cronies as the Queen of Fender Benders. This meant that poor me was going to have to quaff copious amounts of coffee to stay awake long enough to reach our destination. But of course, the more coffee I drank, the more often I needed to stop. Then, of course, we had to stop to refuel (something that cruel me made Mama do while I used the facilities).

It was five in the morning when we finally reached the infamous beltway around Washington, DC. There was already a light but steady stream of traffic headed into the city. My interview with the *America Today Show* (the country's second most popular morning show) on the steps of the Smithsonian National Museum of Natural History was scheduled to begin at 7:00, and I was supposed to show up no later than 5:30 a.m. of course!

Well, I could make it on time – just – *if* I could find a parking spot. However, if I didn't turn up by the agreed-upon time, the show would proceed to Plan B, whatever that was. Perhaps the show would profile yet another disgraced senator who'd been caught cheating with his secretary, just after his wife had been diagnosed with cancer. Even if the man asked his wife for a divorce while she was in the recovery room after surgery, his constituents would still vote him back into office. There never seemed to be a shortage of those jerks in power, and voters who seemed to lack a moral compass.

I didn't believe in guardian angels, but Mama did, and hers was named Alice. In a city where parking spaces are rarer than hen's teeth, Alice located an on-street parking spot for us adjacent to the museum. With Alice sitting on Mama's shoulder, protecting us from any mishaps, we unloaded the wheelchair and directed our hostage to sit in it. Then we pulled Mama's large old suitcase out of the trunk, and set off for the white tent.

We Carolina women were greeted warmly by staffers and shown to a makeshift green room, which was really just a white tent that had been erected far to the right of the stage, and next to the walk that ran in front of the building. The tent had been outfitted with several comfortable sofas and well-padded chairs, as well as a small table loaded with pastries and fresh fruit. There was also a large cooler containing various types of yogurts. A not-so-bright-eyed and bushy-tailed hostess stood at the ready, prepared to serve coffee, tea or juice on request.

Upon entering the tent, Mama felt her motherly genes take over. 'Darling,' she said to the girl, 'you look like something the cat dragged in, ate, and then threw up – bless your heart. Now I want you to go fix yourself a cup of coffee and something to eat. I assure you that we can take care of ourselves.'

'Speak for yourself, lady,' growled a shrivelled old crone in a corner of the tent. The woman was all but hidden by the mound of pastries.

'Who the heck are you?' Mama demanded; her gracious Southern manners temporarily overridden by her ire. The one thing Mama cannot stand is rudeness.

'Name is Wilma Scotchman,' the old woman croaked, 'and I'm the Queen of Quilts from Intercourse, Pennsylvania. Every one of my quilts is guaranteed to be hand sewn by one-armed, ambidextrous, non-sectarian, nonagenarian virgins. Youse better not be here trying to usurp my spot on today's show.'

'Y'all must be Plan B,' I said, although I'm afraid it came out sounding a tad uppity. 'But if y'all's virgins are one-armed, then how can they be ambidextrous?'

'And is there really such a place as – you know, that place in Pennsylvania?' Mama asked, as she politely blushed.

'*Intercourse?* Heck, yeah! What a pair of ignoramuses you are,' Wilma Scotchman said. 'My gals stitch with their feet. They are equally adept at stitching with their remaining hand, or either of their feet.'

'At ninety plus years?' Mama asked sceptically.

'Shoot, yes,' Wilma Scotchman rasped. 'Our workplace motto is: *A thousand stitches a day keeps the doctor away*. I just wish there was some magic potion to keep the men away. Last month alone, two of my gals were deflowered and I had to let them go. Janet was ninety-six, and Ronda was ninety-eight. I've heard that it's hard to get back into the job market when one is that old.'

I might have laughed a teensy bit. 'How did you know that they'd been . . . well, what you said?'

Wilma Scotchman's face registered genuine surprise. 'Because I check each gal, like every month, of course. I am, after all, a God-fearing woman. The Lord does not approve of fornicating quilters. Why else do you think I employ only nonagenarians? The fire in one's loins should all be burned out by then – at least it is for me. But apparently for some women, the embers of sin glow on until they've taken their last breath. But enough about me, and my business. Why are you two Southern belles here?'

'Mermaid mania,' I said, and laughed nervously. Who knew what a basket case like the ancient quilter believed about mermaids, or what mischief she was capable of, if we disagreed on the subject? I certainly didn't care to be stabbed in the eye with a needle, or a bunch of needles; I'm not nearly caught up on the TV series that I've been recording, and I really should read a book next year. Of course, it would have to be a work of non-fiction, wouldn't it? I mean, what's the point of reading fiction, when it's all made up?

At first I thought that Wilma Scotchman might have misunderstood me, because she took so long to answer. But when she did, her arms moved in unison like a pair of windshield wipers.

'Talk about sin!' Wilma Scotchman began to rail. 'I don't see any difference between mermaid fixation and idol worship. Well, actually I do. Mermaids appeal to children more than stone or wooden idols would appeal to them, if they had exposure to such things. But the result is the same, isn't it? The young, impressionable minds of our precious kids are being turned away from the Lord by influencers, purveyors of cheaply made, mermaid-themed merchandise from China. What has happened to the God-fearing country that my nonagenarian workforce grew up in? I'm afraid that any day now we will stop calling ourselves a Christian country and start calling ourselves a chimera-loving country. Then we'll all have gone to Hell in one ginormous handbasket, and it won't be lined with comfy quilts, either.'

I felt myself begin to perspire lightly with trepidation (by then I was well past the 'dew' stage). If I began to sweat, then I'd have to turn in my True Daughter of the South card and move up north to live with Yankees. I have nothing against Northerners per se, mind you – I'm sure that there are fine people to be found in any demographic group. It's just that up until then I'd had little first-hand experience with those sorts of people.

At any rate, the show's Plan B, that is Wilma Scotchman, had turned out to be quite a character. I could see how she might easily upstage two more demure Carolina women and grab our number-one spot from us. We had to act fast.

'Mama,' I whispered behind my hand, 'when the program manager returns, I want you to sidle up closer to this quilting phenomenon and give her one of your famous "come hither" looks.'

Mama gasped. '*Whatever* for? You know that I'm as straight as – well, every damned man in the US Senate.'

'I don't expect you to follow through on anything, Mama; I just want you to distract her while I pounce on the manager. I just want to make sure that nothing has changed about the program order. However, if you discover that you and the dame from Intercourse do have this inexplicable chemistry—'

There was no need for me to say another word, because the tent flap opened just wide enough for the very handsome head of Mark Lombardo to poke through. He didn't even have to say a word. A slight nod from him, and I headed straight for the opening with the wheelchair. Of course, Mama followed hard on my heels, even though she was pulling an enormous suitcase that had a stubborn wheel.

But before we were escorted to the stage, hunky Mark Lombardo led us into another small tent. There a makeup and beauty team fluffed and sprayed our hair cement-stiff, and brushed enough powder on our faces to choke a caravan of camels that were used to plodding across the Sahara Desert in dust storms. After that, Mama and I were turned over to a pair of artists who worked us over with lipliners, eyeliners, lipsticks and eyeshadows in various shades, as well as bronzers and blushes. The result was that when, at last, we were declared to be 'camera ready,' Mama and I no longer recognized each other.

When I finally dared to open my eyes and beheld the beautiful woman sitting in the chair next to me, I panicked.

'Excuse me, ma'am,' I said to the young woman who'd completed my transformation, 'did you see where my mother went?'

The beautiful woman's eyes widened. 'Zoe, is that you under there?'

'*Mama?*'

'Zoe, it is you! You're beautiful! You don't look like yourself at all.'

'Thanks, Mama. Same back at you.'

Then we both stared in shock at the occupant of the wheelchair.

'Well, I'll be a monkey's uncle,' Mama said.

THIRTY

As long as I could remember, Marilyn Mitchell had been the host of the *America Today Show*. Over the years the host's wardrobe and hairstyles had changed, reflecting mainstream fashions in the United States, but the woman's face and figure remained virtually unaltered. Well, at least as far as one could tell from watching her on television. If I'd been an astute, or at least regular, viewer then I would have noticed that, for the past decade or so, Marilyn Mitchell spent the better part of each show with her hands in her lap.

Just as eyes are the window to a person's soul, a woman's hands are the betrayer of her age. All the Botox in the world is not going to straighten fingers that have gotten gnarled by arthritis or disguise the elevated fan of tendons that connect them to the wrist. Age spots can be bleached, but nothing can be done to treat the ropes of raised veins that criss-cross the hands in higgledy-piggledy fashion.

The instant that the *America Today Show* host extended her hand to greet me, I believed the rumours that I'd read about her over the years in the supermarket tabloids. I could easily believe that Marilyn Mitchell was well into her eighties, and that her bio was bogus – to put it politely. However, her co-host, Jonas Clyburn, might well have been in his thirties – he just wasn't the straight arrow that he tried to project on the tube. That too had been the subject of rumours for several years. I had always thought it was unfair for me to form an opinion without even meeting the man, but that's all it took: one face-to-face meeting, and the handshake that accompanied it. It was just a handshake, but it was a handshake utterly devoid of even the tiniest sexual spark. I might as well have been shaking hands with my brother.

Nonetheless, both the host and co-host of the *America Today Show* were gracious and made Mama and me feel welcome, rather than put on the spot. On the stage four chairs had been placed, with the wheelchair dead centre. Mama and I sat on either side of the wheelchair, with Marilyn Mitchell on my right, and Jonas Clyburn on Mama's left. After a rather long and flowery introduction, Marilyn Mitchell addressed me.

'You, Miss Porter, have promised that today, live, on national television, in front of millions of people across America, and indeed the world, you will prove conclusively that Miss Lucy, the first mermaid to make contact with us humans – is in fact a fake.'

Gasps could be heard from an impromptu crowd that had gathered in front of the museum to see what the hullabaloo was all about. When folks saw that a television show was being taped, they stuck around like gum on a hot sidewalk. Marilyn Mitchell was a seasoned pro, and she waited just the right amount of time before picking up her line of questioning again.

She flashed her famous smile at the closest camera. 'Miss Porter, it's your contention that the Town Council of Tidal Shores, a group that includes merchants, a beautician, a high-school principal, a minister – and even a police chief, for goodness' sake – that calls themselves the Big Ten, conspired to create a fake mermaid from the body parts of two very different kinds of animals. They then named this *thing* Miss Lucy, and intentionally proceeded to lie to, and even defraud, the general public.'

The TV hosts exchanged glances and smiled while the crowd, which was rapidly growing, booed. Then a bizarre thing happened. The occupant of the wheelchair, which many observers, as well as the hosts, had taken to be Miss Lucy, rose slowly to her feet. At that point the crowd gasped again, and the hosts shrank back in their seats.

The erstwhile Miss Lucy's lap blanket had slipped to the stage, and before raising her head to reveal her face, she removed her large hat and flung it into the crowd. Several women shrieked in terror as the sunbonnet sailed directly at them, and I'm almost positive that I also heard a man yelp with fear.

'What the frigging frock!' Marilyn Mitchell exclaimed. As a consummate professional, she knew innately what 'F' words she could use, and not have a second of her popular morning show censored. (Even as a live show, it was on an eight-second delay.)

'Language, dear,' Mrs Georgina Legare said stiffly. 'In my day – well, by the looks of you up close, we probably share the same proverbial day – a lady did not swear. But judging by your anonymous TV accent, you may not have been born and raised in God's country – that is to say, the Deep South. On the other hand, many good Southern girls go to the North for their so-called "higher education," and when they get there, they quickly learn that they

The Mermaid Mystery

have to shed the dulcet sounds of our Southern speech, lest they be perceived as ignorant.'

'Well, boo-hoo, hoo,' Marilyn Mitchell said. 'I was born and raised in Brooklyn, New York, and I had to take elocution lessons in order to erase my accent. And for your information, toots, I was *not* swearing. You'll know it when I am.'

I was shocked. The *America Today Show* host was renowned for the gracious way in which she treated all of her guests. It was Marilyn Mitchell's pleasant demeanour, no matter how odious her interviewee, that made celebrities and dictators alike vie to be on her show.

My great-grandmother was unruffled. 'I am the president of the town council of Tidal Shores, darling, and I am willing to swear on my great-granddaughter's life that everything she says is the gospel truth. We, the town council, also known as the Big Ten, did indeed create a simulated mermaid. However, our intention was not to defraud the public, but to revitalize our little village with increased tourism.

'We never dreamed that the American public could be so gullible as to take the dang ploy literally. We figured that after a while someone with brains would come along and figure out what was what, and that the public might get in on the joke. Like with Bigfoot. At any rate, we have brought with us proof—'

'Bigfoot is real!' a man in the crowd yelled.

Someone else hurled a bagel at my gan-gan. It missed the top of her head by less than an inch, a fact which made the dear old lady very cross. My great-grandmother was ravenous, having not eaten anything since we'd spirited her away from Tidal Shores the day before. Had the pastry hit her, it would then have fallen at her feet, for her to pick up and consume. After all, back when Mrs Georgina Legare was a girl, there was no such thing as a 'five-second rule,' because manna literally fell from Heaven and covered the ground every morning for six days a week.

As one might expect, co-host Jonas Clyburn had a different take on Gan-Gan being belted with bread-stuffs. He ordered two security agents, who had been on standby, to clear the crowd from the space immediately in front of the stage. Unfortunately for the show, even though *America Today* had made prior arrangements with the National Park Service for its use, the sidewalk was a public space. But, as they say in the business, 'the show must go on.' So, after a very brief pause for an unscheduled commercial, while the co-hosts huddled with their staff, Mrs Georgina Legare was given the green light to resume speaking. Now, however, one of the security guards stood directly between her and the crowd, and a mobile camera had been repositioned to view her from this new perspective.

'As I was saying, before I was so rudely interrupted by a clearly uneducated person,' Mrs Georgina Legare said in her silky Southern drawl, 'we have proof with us this morning that the famous Miss Lucy is nothing more than the top half of a monkey, and the bottom half of a fish.'

'Heresy!' a woman cried.

Several people laughed, but not enough to let me know if the majority of the people even knew what the word 'heresy' meant. Also, there was no time like the present to clear up another bit of misused nomenclature.

'The top half is actually that of an ape,' I said loudly.

My great-grandmother was not amused at being corrected. 'Apes, monkeys – what's the difference? They both swing from trees and eat bananas, don't they?'

'Perhaps,' I conceded, 'but Miss Lucy's top half was once a bonobo, the most human-looking of all the great apes. Her species is renowned for settling their squabbles through sex, not fighting. They even participate in same-sex gratification, as a way of relieving stress.'

'Sinners!' a woman yelled. She sounded like the same person who'd shouted 'heresy.' This time a good many people laughed, me included. I mean, how ridiculous is that, to believe that animals are capable of sinning?

'Influencer!' a burly man hollered at me through cupped hands.

That did it. 'Listen, mister,' I hollered back. 'How is stating facts influencing anyone? Or have I tempted you to engage in same-sex gratification now to relieve your stress?'

A fair number of people roared with laughter. I also heard some loud boos. The man who'd dared to call me an influencer now gave me the finger and pushed his way to the rear of the crowd.

Mrs Georgina Legare stole a precious few seconds to glare at her favourite descendant. 'Well, anyway,' she said in her gravelly voice, 'one of the Big Ten was a taxidermist who cobbled together these two very disparate – uh, Zoe, darling, what's the correct word?'

'Species,' I said. 'But actually, in this case it's more than one word. Fish and apes belong to two different classes in the *phylum chordata*.'

'Don't be a show-off, darling,' Gan-Gan said. 'It doesn't become you.'

A smattering of people applauded.

'Now y'all don't be mean, either,' Gan-Gan said and, stepping around the security guard, shook her finger at the crowd. 'My great-granddaughter might be getting a little long in the tooth, but she is still of breeding age. She has firm, round breasts, child-bearing hips, and comes with a dowry of half a million dollars that I will supply to the first man, or woman, who can pass my rather rigorous requirements for a great great-grandson via the sacred bonds of marriage.'

Although my eyes were tightly closed, I felt myself flush a deep pink, from my scalp, down through my firm, round breasts, past my child-bearing hips, and all the way to my toes. I was also acutely aware of the crowd's reaction. I heard only a couple of laughs – they seemed to come from children – but these were followed by what seemed to be offers. Proposals for my hand in marriage. Damn that old lady; if time wasn't of the essence, I would have given that ancient bag of bones tit for tat – forget Southern manners, never mind that Mrs Georgina Legare was not only my oldest living relative, but she was also the key to proving Miss Lucy's inauthenticity.

I opened my eyes wide, and walked as gracefully as I could to the front of the stage. The cameras followed me.

'The bottom half of Miss Lucy,' I said, 'is a giant freshwater fish from the Congo River and its tributaries in central Africa. The common name for it is the goliath tigerfish. On Miss Lucy's head is a human-hair wig, and she's wearing false eyelashes. I'm going to show y'all this right now, if I can have a stagehand bring out the suitcase that I left in the makeup tent up here to the front of the stage – and also a chair.'

'Do what she says,' Marilyn Mitchell barked, and her orders were followed immediately.

'Thank you, ma'am,' I said. 'Mama, I could use your help now.'

'What about me?' Gan-Gan said. 'You drugged me, and then dragged me all the way up here to Washington, DC, which has the highest concentration of braindead politicians in the world.'

'Granny,' Mama said, 'you shouldn't speak so disparagingly of your own political party.'

That remark elicited a great deal of laughter, probably because no one in the crowd knew which party was being referenced. I, of course, knew Gan-Gan's politics, which were diametrically opposed to mine. I was also keenly cognizant of the fact that to accomplish my mission, I needed the old woman's cooperation.

'Of course I can use your help, Gan-Gan,' I said. I pointed to the chair, which a stagehand had just delivered and positioned near the front of the stage, next to the steps. 'Sit next to the chair, please. Mama, push her up here, please.'

'I can wheel myself up there,' Gan-Gan snapped. Nonetheless, she allowed a handsome stagehand to wheel her up next to the straight-back chair.

I turned to face the primary host of *America Today*, Marilyn Mitchell. 'Ma'am, while my mother and I set up a physical proof on this chair next to my great-grandmother, could you please instruct your technicians to run that short clip that I sent you earlier. It shows a member of the Big Ten, an expert taxidermist named Gunner Jones, assembling Miss Lucy from two different preserved animal specimens that his grandparents had brought back with them from the Belgian Congo. They were missionaries there in the 1930s, and Gunner inherited these pieces from his mama, who inherited them from her parents. The provenance of the bonobo – the ape, in the film – as well as the goliath fish – are impeccably documented.'

Marilyn Mitchell nodded *her* well-preserved head to someone off stage. 'Go ahead, roll the tape.'

THIRTY-ONE

I can only guess why Gunner Jones, may he rest in peace, taped his work. One guess is that he was proud of what he knew he could accomplish and was hoping to share his skills later. Another guess is that Gunner Jones did not fully endorse the Big Ten's objectives, and he was making a record of his work to use as possible leverage at a future date, should things get out of hand in his estimation. Which, of course, they did. Whatever his reason for taping his work, Gunner Jones had supplied an audio, and since he was able to edit the footage down to a salient four minutes, he did the narration himself. His words haunted me.

As the tape played, Mama and I worked furiously to unpack the contents of the large suitcase and position it in the chair. Before leaving her house in Charlotte for the coast, Mama had managed to locate her largest suitcase in the nether reaches of her attic under piles of discarded and useless clothes and dump out its contents of old photographs that she would never get around to sticking in albums. Half the people in those photos were from her parents' generation, or before, and Mama hadn't a clue as to who they were. At any rate, the suitcase was so large and heavy, that just lugging it empty downstairs was no picnic. At least the dang thing had wheels.

But even with a suitcase that large, back at Gan-Gan's, Mama and I had found it impossible to stuff Miss Lucy inside without compromising some of Gunner Jones's exquisite workmanship. One of Miss Lucy's extended arms had to be broken at the elbow, and it now dangled in its leathery skin envelope like a five-fingered pendulum. Her mermaid tail was also too long to fit inside the valise without modification, so luckily Mama was able to locate her grandmother's tool collection in her garage. She also found a small hand saw, and several rolls of duct tape in various colours. In a matter of minutes, the resourceful widow had managed to separate approximately the last eighteen inches of goliath tigerfish's tail. Of course, she added this last bit back into the suitcase with Miss Lucy's remains, along with a roll of duct tape, because one never knows what one will need these days to stay out of trouble. As for the duct tape – it can't mend a broken heart, but it can fix virtually everything else.

But by the time Mama and I had finished putting Miss Lucy on display next to Gan-Gan, both her tail and her broken arm had been mended. Also, by then, the gobsmacked hosts and the gathering crowd had seen the entire film clip that I had given the technicians.

'This is going to win us an Emmy for sure,' Marilyn Mitchell said gleefully. Her comment was directed to her co-host, Jonas Clyburn, but she forgot to whisper, so that in fact millions of people across the nation, and even the world, heard her.

'Doesn't anybody care that I was abducted, sedated, and driven here against my will?' my great-grandmother whined.

'Oh, give it a rest, Granny,' Mama said. 'You're a lush, and a drunk. We found you passed out on the floor, behind the front seats when we were halfway here. What were we supposed to do? Stuff your hungover butt in a box, and mail you home?'

'Why, you lying bitch!' Gan-Gan shouted. I'm sure she still felt a tad woozy from the sleeping pills she'd been administered in a drink that she'd eagerly drunk of her own volition, when we confronted her at her home after we'd spied on the Big Nine, and taken Miss Lucy. Also, she probably would have stood up then to better confront me, except for one thing: it had been many, many hours since she'd been to the toilet. The grand dame needed to keep her knees pressed tightly together and move as little as possible. The adult diaper we'd put on her could hold only so much liquid.

'So anyway,' I said, 'as you have all seen, the famous Miss Lucy is half ape, and half river fish. And if I rip off her wig, like so' – I did just that – 'you can see that it still has a label here in the back. Can I get a camera close-up on this?'

'Camera Three, zoom in,' the stage manager barked.

'Excellent,' I said. 'See? Here it says: "Made in China," and below that: "One hundred percent human hair." So, even if there was such a thing as a bald mermaid, which there isn't, she wouldn't be wearing a human-hair wig. It would have to be one made from mermaid hair, right?'

'Not necessarily,' Jonas Clyburn said. 'That wig could have come from a drowning victim. Who's to say that mermaids don't shop at an underwater store that stocks wigs, false teeth, fake eyelashes –

you name it – beauty aids that have been collected from recently sunken ships.'

'You're a first-class idiot, Jonas,' Marilyn Mitchell said. 'Last night I ate a turnip that had a bigger brain than you have.'

'Ha, that's impossible,' Jonas Clyburn said. 'Turnips don't have brains.'

'My point exactly. Jonas, you're fired.'

'*What?* You can't fire me on national television!'

'It's in my contract, and so I just did. Get off my set.'

Jonas Clyburn reacted by squaring his shoulders and jutting out his rather handsome jaw. He certainly made no move to vacate his seat.

'Until I see your contract, I'm not going anywhere,' he said.

'Security!' Marilyn Mitchell screamed angrily.

Before four rather doughy, but heavily armed, security agents could clamber on to the stage, two members of the audience, both wearing white hoods over their heads, with eye and mouth holes crudely cut away, leapt into action. They made it up the steps in a flash, and on to the stage in a single bound. Without a second's pause, one of them snatched Miss Lucy, and the other grabbed the suitcase, and then off they went, back through the assembled throng which was now milling about in confusion. Apparently one of mermaid-nappers had left behind a boom-box which was blaring out the tune to *My Country, Tis of Thee*. Incidentally, it also happens to be the identical tune for 'God Save the King.' However, the words to this song were original.

My country tis of thee,
Sweet land of Miss Lucy,
Of thee I sing.
Shores where free mermaids swim,
For them we sing this hymn,
Amongst the breaking waves
It's mermaid love that saves!

In spite of my deep research into mermaid mania, I'd never heard that song. And even though I'd been raised a lukewarm Episcopalian, I was nonetheless shocked by the last stanza. Wasn't Jesus supposed to be the only one who could save us from our sins?

As for Marilyn Mitchell, she might have been almost as well

preserved as Miss Lucy, but she was certainly no heathen. She was also a lot spryer than one might have concluded, judging by her frozen face. Although she was wearing six-inch heels on feet that were at least eight decades old, the TV star was able to hoof it to the edge of the stage in seconds.

'Stop it,' she shrieked into a handheld microphone. 'That's blaspheme, it's unpatriotic, and most of all, it's ridiculous. You have just seen with your own eyes, and heard with your own ears, evidence that there was no mermaid named Miss Lucy. She – I mean, *it* – was an ape-fish, a *thing* created by a taxidermist. You saw how he did it, step by step! Why can't you believe it? What is wrong with all of you? Are you ignorant, or just plain stupid?'

'Fake news,' a woman said, who was standing up front. She had a toddler on her hip and was trying to quiet a fussing infant by rocking it in her arms. They looked so darn normal.

'But it's *not* fake news,' I said. I pointed at my great-grandmother. 'Here's the woman who started it all. She'll tell you. She'll even confess to writing a prayer that her town council says before each meeting, thanking God for their greedy natures.'

'It's a sin to lie, young lady,' a middle-aged man said. I was taken aback to see that he was wearing a clerical collar.

'Greed is good,' an elderly man said. 'That's what sets us apart from them socialist countries like Britain and Western Europe, where they tax everyone to death, and where they all have to live in houses with bedrooms so small that you can't fit a king-size bed in them. I know this for a *fact*, because I watch *House Hunters International*. It doesn't pay to be greedy over in them foreign places. America, however, is the land of unequal opportunity, where some of us, if we work hard, get to live in McMansions.'

'Or if you inherit your money,' Mama said, her voice dripping with sarcasm.

'Of course,' said the same elderly man. 'But that's because one's ancestors were greedy. God bless greed, and God bless America.'

'And God bless mermaids!' This began as a chant by a pair of busty blonde twins who were wearing tank tops that exposed more mammary gland than could be seen on any small dairy farm. Their inane and sacrilegious chant was quickly taken up by the majority of the crowd.

Unfortunately, the land of greed was also the land of free speech, so there wasn't much Marilyn Mitchell could do to stop them. After all, it was she who had received permission from the National Park Service to televise her show on the steps of the museum, and since she knew full well that it would draw a crowd, she'd requested, and received, a permit that allowed for a gathering of up to three hundred people. The current group was probably just under capacity.

'We're screwed,' she said, again into her open microphone.

I grabbed the mic from her. 'Not necessarily,' I said into Marilyn Mitchell's ear. 'Just give me a second to think, while you pretend to talk to me. Don't worry, the mic is off now.'

Marilyn Mitchell nodded and then faked a warm smile for the crowd. 'You're a freaking bitch,' she whispered into my ear. 'If my show survives this – or especially if it doesn't – I'm going to sue that cheap department store dress off your back, and then strangle you with it. But since I'm a woman of a certain age, I probably won't be strong enough to kill you, so while you're still passed out, but very much alive, I'll have my hired goons feed you to a wood-chipper.'

I turned the mic on. 'That's wonderful news! Folks, you're not going to believe this, but there's been a mermaid sighting in the Potomac River near the Lincoln Memorial. In fact, word just came in that it's a mother with an infant. If confirmed, this will be the first ever baby mermaid sighting on record. Someone needs to be there to film—'

I didn't even get to say the best part. I was going to add that the baby appeared to have been born with two rudimentary human legs and a fishlike tail. Instead, I watched as the crowd turned in unison, like a murmuration of starlings, and made a beeline in the direction of the Lincoln Memorial, and the Potomac River beyond. In an even more shocking move, Jonas Clyburn, the fired co-host who had proved to be a twit with fewer brain cells than a turnip, unhooked the microphone attached to his shirt collar, and with a running leap, jumped off the stage and cleared the steps leading up to it. It occurred to me that the nincompoop must have competed in track or gymnastics in school, because he struck a perfect landing and, after a second or two to regain his equilibrium, he too was off in the general direction of the Potomac River.

THIRTY-TWO

'What a dingus that Jonas Clyburn is,' Marilyn Mitchell said. 'I take back what I said about him having less brains than a turnip. He doesn't have *any* brains inside that gorgeous head. I only agreed to have him on as my co-host because he's so damn pretty and comes from the *right* sort of background – if you know what I mean.'

I was dumbfounded by what I'd just heard. Surely the political-correctness pendulum had not swung this far back already – at least not in public. Or was the old broad so rich and so senile that she either didn't care, or was impervious to, what studio executives thought? Popularity, coupled with indifference, can be a powerful combination.

Clearly Marilyn Mitchell was fully aware that her show was still being televised, because as she spoke, she beckoned two of the three cameras to follow her back to her seat. No sooner had her designer-clad bottom settled back into the plush kidskin leather, than something even more unexpected happened. Two brawny men wearing walrus masks seemed to appear out of nowhere. These masks were not cheap Halloween ones either, but massive, highly detailed, hooded creations that enveloped their shoulders as well. The tusks seemed to be created from solid material – possibly resin. They certainly looked dangerous to me.

Without saying a word, the heavily muscled men grabbed the wheelchair, still containing my gan-gan, hoisted it up to their shoulders, walked around to an official off-ramp for the stage and gently carried my great-grandmother off with them. *America Today*'s security team did nothing to stop them, but then again Marilyn Mitchell remained silent during the abduction – if indeed that's what it was: an *abduction*. After all, my gan-gan had not appeared to be in the least surprised when she saw two giant men with walrus heads, and she certainly made no objection to being carried off by them, practically airborne as it were. She almost had to know who these freaks of nature were; otherwise the old biddy would be screaming her head off in terror, given that she can't ride a department store escalator without taking a beta-blocker.

'My gan-gan is in on it,' I said.

'I beg your pardon?' Marilyn Mitchell said.

'She means her great-grandmother,' Mama said. 'The old crone that those two beefcakes just carted off on their broad shoulders was my granny.'

'Mother!' I said. 'How could you, at a time like this?'

'Don't be silly, dear,' Marilyn Mitchell said. 'There is never a wrong time to sexualize men. They do it about us all the time. A little tit for tat is good for the whole.'

'*Excuse* me? Did you just say that on national TV?'

'Indeed, dear, I did. The *whole* of one's being benefits, *if* one can maintain an active and imaginative sex life for as long as one lives.'

'Does this apply even to centenarians?' Mama said.

I knew that Mama was not only fishing for our host's age, but she was probably wondering about what Mrs Georgina Legare and Grusha also did behind closed doors.

Marilyn Mitchell smiled wide into Camera Three, which was apparently her favourite. 'Why yes, dear, it can apply to centenarians. But herein lies the rub – so to speak.' She laughed heartily at her little joke, but there was no response except for the crew to laugh along with her. After a moment of silence, she continued. 'Sex does not have to be restricted to bodies thrashing about like two dogs under a duvet fighting over a bone. Huddles and cuddles can lead to puddles just as well, you know.'

'Ooh, gross,' I exclaimed. 'I can't believe you said that stuff on national TV.'

'Grow up, young lady,' Marilyn Mitchell said with a wicked smile. 'I didn't say anything untoward; you simply inferred things with your dirty mind.'

There were few things I hated more than to be told to 'grow up.' This, however, was not the time to argue about my status as a mature adult. I was pretty sure that I still loved my gan-gan, despite the old woman's manifold flaws, and I would miss her terribly if I never saw her again. At the very least, I felt responsible for the greedy old crone's disappearance, since it was my idea to 'Granny-nap' her, and drive her up to Washington, DC in the first place.

No, to be brutally honest, I didn't want to get in trouble if my self-centred, super-wealthy forbear, who was possibly guilty of murdering Gunner Jones, went permanently missing, or turned up dead. I had plans for my life that did not include a prison wife, and sharing a metal toilet that offered no privacy. The trip up to our nation's capital had not gone according to plan.

It had been my intention to educate the ignorant masses, but they hadn't been interested in learning. Perhaps it was because the world was going to hell in a handbasket, but a dismaying number of people were willing to abandon critical thinking when something new came along that was powerful enough to distract them from their everyday troubles.

'Oh, shoot,' I said, hitting my forehead with my palm. 'I think I failed. I think I might have just contributed to the problem.'

'Camera Three on the kid,' Marilyn Mitchell whispered. 'How so?' she asked into the microphone pinned to her lapel. 'Which problem did you just contribute to?'

'Well,' I said, 'my intention was to show everyone in America – or anywhere – that Miss Lucy was a fake mermaid, and that she had been the brainchild of my great-grandmother, who was the president of the town council of Tidal Shores, a group known as the Big Ten. Their intention in creating her was to make money in order to save the town, which they did, but they apparently also killed one of their own, the taxidermist who created Miss Lucy, because he regretted what he'd done.'

'You have no proof,' Marilyn Mitchell said impatiently. 'But we do know that they more than exceeded in saving the town. In fact, they got super rich, because they got mega-greedy. They even wrote a prayer thanking God for their greed. It was all there in the film that we watched. But why on this dying earth do you think that you failed?'

'Because not only did I not convince anyone of the truth, when I told them that mermaids had been discovered in the Potomac River, they believed me. You saw how fast they cleared out. Anyway, by saying that there were mermaids in the Potomac, I undermined everything I'd said earlier. Geez, what a stupid *schmuck* I was.' Huge tears fell unbidden from my makeup enhanced eyes.

Marilyn Mitchell clamped a liver-spotted hand over the mic that was pinned to her sweater. 'You're not Jewish, are you?' she whispered.

'No. Why?' I whispered back.

'You said *schmuck*. That's a Jewish word, you know.'

'I picked it up in college,' I said.

'Just checking. I don't normally have *their kind* on this show.'

I was stunned. As a reporter I'd long been aware that anti-Semitism was on the rise in the United States. My two best friends were Jewish, both from pre-school on up. Sure, they had been the victims of hate speech, and Linda Zimmerman's car had had red paint thrown on it during Passover, but it was my Jewish friends who had been the victims of anti-Semitism, not me. Having it suddenly revealed to me that I wouldn't have been invited on *America Today* had I'd been a member of *their kind*, by virtue of my birth, infuriated me. My first cogent thought when I recovered from shock was to call Marilyn Mitchell out for what she was – a bigot – and then to storm off the set in a rage.

But before I could even open my mouth, Marilyn Mitchell acted first. She took her hand off her microphone, got up, walked over to me, and laid an arm gently around my shoulder.

'Oh, honey, you'll be all right,' she said loudly, as she smiled widely for the camera. 'I'm sure this mermaid mania is just a passing fad. Anyone who was watching the show would have to be crazy to think that you, of all people, believe in such nonsense.' Marilyn Mitchell kissed me on the forehead with collagen-enhanced lips. 'Well, I'm afraid the time has come to say goodbye to you and your beautiful mama. Thank you for being my first guests this morning.'

'Thank *you*,' I said, as I pecked her Botox-smoothed cheek in return. 'Being your first guests allows us time to go to synagogue for morning prayers. Given that we're strangers here, we were wondering if you could tell us the name of *your* synagogue.'

Marilyn Mitchell recoiled in shock. 'I – uh – I'm *not* Jewish! I don't go to synagogue! How dare you?'

'Oh, my bad,' I said as casually as I could. 'I thought I read somewhere that your maiden name was Schwartz, or Schneider, or one of *those* names, if you know what I mean. Anyway, we Jews can always pick each other out, by looking into each other's eyes, no matter how much work we've had done. Hope I didn't spill the beans.'

Marilyn Mitchell's many years of Botox all came to naught in one tremendous tug of war in which time, plus anger, triumphed over chemistry. It was like watching a colossal building collapse, but when it was over, instead of dust-covered rubble, fifty years of skin layers had given her face a new topography that was, in its own way, rather beautiful. Of course, Marilyn Mitchell was not holding a mirror then, so she could not appreciate her newfound beauty.

'I'm going to sue you within an inch of your life,' she shrieked.

'What an interesting expression,' I said. 'Nonetheless, what are you going to sue me for? I didn't defame you. I merely made an assumption that may, or may not, have turned out to be false. Was your mother's maiden name Schwartz?'

'My mother's maiden name is none of your damn business,' Marilyn Mitchell spit. 'Besides, there are lots of people named Schwartz who aren't Jewish.'

'In any case,' I said, 'you did tell me, in so many words, that you refuse to have anyone on your show who might be distantly related to Jesus. And you have many listeners who would be happy to remind you that America is a Christian country. How do you reconcile those two things?'

'No comment,' Marilyn Mitchell roared. 'Stop the show. Security, get these two Carolina crackers off my stage! Now!'

THIRTY-THREE

'Now what?' Mama demanded. 'Mrs Georgina Legare – "Granny" to me and "Gan-Gan" to you – is on the loose in our nation's capital; we were kicked off one of the most popular TV shows in the country by a raging anti-Semite, and we're not even Jewish; and you just announced to the world that mermaids can have babies.'

We hadn't even reached the car yet. I had a vague idea of what we needed to do next, but I was so tired and hungry, I could barely function. I'd driven all night, and nerves had kept me from eating anything from the pastry piles in the green room. Now, all I wanted to do was eat a doughnut – or three – and curl up on the back seat while Mama drove me home. There was one caveat, however, and that was with Gan-Gan presumably away from Tidal Shores, there would only be eight members of the original Big Ten to deal with, were I to stick my investigating reporter's nose back into the matter of Gunner Jones' murder. Since I'd heard with my own ears, all nine of the remaining Big Ten claim that they had not killed Gunner, even though they had drawn lots to do so, obviously one of them was lying. It was even possible that my beloved Gan-Gan was the killer. *Or*, maybe they'd all been telling the truth. Maybe Gunner had been shot by accident – by someone else. Maybe their intended target was Gan-Gan, who had been seated beside Gunner Jones. Pistol shots are notoriously inaccurate. A pistol shot by the shaking hand of an enraged person from across a room – well, what were the odds?

'Mama, how well did you sleep on the long drive up here?'

'Zoe, what kind of a question is that? I don't think I like where this is headed.'

'Mama, dearest, you know that someday I will change your adult diapers for you – if that's what you need me to do.'

'Is that so, Zoe, dearest? Would you still change them for me, knowing that I'd cut you out of my will?'

'My answer is whatever you need to hear. In the meantime, I need you to drive, because I'm just too sleep-deprived to drive back safely.'

'Roger that. Where's the hotel?'

'No hotel, Mama. We're headed straight back down to Tidal Shores. As long as Gan-Gan's out gallivanting with her beefcakes, we're going to wreak havoc on her stomping grounds. Watch out, Big Eight, Hurricane Porter is packing a double whammy, and she's headed your way!'

Mama giggled briefly, then her face grew tensely sober. 'But I hate to drive,' she said.

'Nonsense, you drive me crazy all the time.'

'I mean that I hate driving cars. And that I hate driving on the freeway. I get too nervous. And I make you too nervous as well. Your face scrunches up so tightly that your eyes disappear, you keep stomping on an imaginary brake pedal, and every now and then you yelp like my dear departed dog did, when I accidentally stepped on his tail.'

'Let's pretend that's all true, Mama,' I said. 'This time, however, none of that will happen because I'll be fast asleep. I'm plum wore out – or as the Brits would say, I'm "knackered." So, unless you want to die screaming while I steer us off the highway, and into a tree going seventy miles an hour, I suggest you – no, I implore you – do your motherly duties, and come to your baby daughter's rescue one more time.'

Mama laughed. 'Baby daughter, my eye! You started walking at nine months, talked a blue streak at one year, and could already read by the time you were two. When you were ten you threatened to sue me for emancipation because you still had a bedtime. I can't think of a prior time that you needed rescuing.'

'Well, now I need rescuing. *Please.* If we want any justice for Gunner Jones, then we need to drive as fast as we can back to Tidal Shores – while the cat's away. So to speak.'

Mama chuckled sardonically. 'Oh, Zoe, honey, that cat has very sharp claws. I've known her a sight longer than you have, and she invariably catches her prey, and then rips them to shreds.'

'Well, maybe this time her boy toys will keep her away long enough for us to do our detective work. By the way, Mama, do you have even the slightest clue who those two stud muffins might be?'

Then Mama cackled gleefully. '*Stud muffins?* Why, I declare! Zoe, those were your cousins, the famous Johns twins.'

'John John?' My cousins were identical twins, sons of Mama's sister, Aunt Dottie, and her husband, Uncle Norman Johns.

Unfortunately for everyone who ever met both boys, their parents included, my aunt and uncle could not agree on names. When the infants were christened at the age of three months, John John Johns was the default name for each boy.

'That's them,' Mama said, 'unless you know of any other identical twins with those same names in this family.'

'I still can't believe their parents got away with that.'

Mama shrugged. 'I wanted to name you Cleopatra, but your daddy was dead set against it.'

'You did not!'

'I did so. Then again, I was very young, and I had just seen the movie *Cleopatra* starring Elizabeth Taylor.'

'Ugh,' I said. 'Kids would have called me Cleo. I would have hated that. But back to the Johns twins. What are they doing in our nation's capital?'

'Oh that,' Mama said, and then mumbled a string of words that might have been Mongolian, or perhaps Basque, or even Swedish – no, I probably would have recognized Swedish, since I dated a Swede in college.

'What did you say?' I said.

Mama mumbled a wee bit louder, but her words were no more distinct.

'Articulate, please, Mama. Or else I will have to conclude that you're speaking Yankee.'

'The John John Johns are male escorts,' she said, her face turning salmon pink.

'Say *what*?'

'Oh, Zoe, do I have to explain?' Mama wailed.

'Relax, Mama, I know what a male escort is. I'm just surprised that people to whom I'm related would be in that biz, and that Gan-Gan—'

'Oh, look,' Mama interjected happily, 'there's a Krispy Creme factory with the red light on. That means they have freshly made doughnuts, still warm even.'

I needed no convincing. We bought a dozen traditional glazed doughnuts, and a quart of milk, and when all that was left was the grease on our fingers, we felt revived enough to talk strategy. At that point, who gave a rat's ass about cousins who worked as male escorts.

'Mama, you grew up in Tidal Shores. I realize that you're not the same age as those greedy folks on the town council, but you might have had some dealings with them, or their parents, when you lived there. Maybe you have some clue about their character. Or something scandalous that we can use to blackmail one of them with.' I laughed sinisterly, like an amateur actor performing in a community theatre's production of a murder mystery.

Mama carefully wiped her fingers and patted her mouth daintily on a paper napkin. 'Actually, I do. And this concerns Adelaide Saunders, the la-dee-dah mayor of my hometown. Do you remember when she used to babysit you?'

'Mama, how could I? You said I was a baby when we moved to Charlotte.'

'Silly me. Of course. But when you were about six months old, when we were still living there, Adam Patel's parents threw one of their legendary, to-die-for, New Year's Eve parties. Anyway, we needed a babysitter, and someone suggested Adelaide Parsons, who was a senior in high school then, and supposedly a very religious girl with high moral standards. Long story short, when we came straggling back from the party, we found prim and proper Miss Adelaide Parsons in bed – *our* bed – with a boy.'

'Well,' I said, 'that's both interesting, and disgusting, but hardly useable information in this case.'

'Oh, ye of little faith,' Mama said. 'If only you would let me finish talking.'

I wished for another doughnut. Stuffed as I was, swallowing it would have been far more pleasant than swallowing my irritation.

'Please continue, Mommy dearest,' I said.

THIRTY-FOUR

Mama flashed me the evil eye. 'The boy that prissy Miss Adelaide Parsons was doing the hoochy-coochie with was Ryker Saunders.'

'*Our* Ryker Saunders? I mean, Sheriff Ryker Saunders of Tidal Shores? Adelaide's brother-in-law?'

Mama nodded happily. 'And that was *after* Ewell Saunders had gotten involved with her. The entire town knew that Ewell and Adelaide were high-school sweethearts, and that they were "saving themselves" for marriage, which wasn't going to be until they'd graduated from college in another four and a half years.'

I was dumbfounded – but just briefly, of course. Nothing can leave me speechless for long.

'So why the heck was she making the beast with two heads in your bed?' I asked. 'And especially with the other brother?'

Mama shuddered. Even though she was recalling something that had happened decades ago, clearly the mental image repulsed her. Then she shook herself vigorously, as if she could shed the memory like dogs rid themselves of excess water by shaking themselves.

'I've thought about that a lot over the years. The only plausible thing I can come up with is that in Adelaide's teenage mind, even though she was having sex with Ryker, she was *still* saving herself for marriage with Ewell. Plus, given Ryker's somewhat dark complexion, there were a number of people in town who firmly believed that Virginia Saunders, who was separated from her husband at the time, spent the night of the twins' conception with more than one stranger down in Charleston.'

'Mama, are you trying to say that these bigots think that Ryker Saunders is black? And if so, what does this have to do with why Adelaide slept with him?'

The dear, sweet woman who bore me, reached over and patted me with a hand that was still just a tad greasy. 'Darling, you have the naiveté of a new-born Yankee. It's like this: perhaps Adelaide merely had a strong libido, or perhaps she was unsure of her sexuality, but in any case, having sex with a black boy didn't really count toward breaking the vow that she made with a white boy. Just as long as they didn't get caught.'

Then I was truly dumbfounded. The cat got my tongue and ran away with it. I think that rascally feline might even have buried my tongue somewhere in its litterbox, because try as I might, I was only able to stammer a few nonsense syllables whilst waving my arms in frustration.

'Vermillion mutton and drip squash in a pan?'

'Precisely,' Mama said. She always could read my mind. 'The last thing that Adelaide Saunders, her Honour the Mayor, needs is to have her marriage fall apart because of the revelation that she slept with her husband's brother. And it has nothing to do with Ryker's supposed parentage, but everything to do with Adelaide's husband, Ewell Saunders. He and Ryker have been competitors their entire lives. Their mama used to tell the story that Ryker pushed Ewell out of their shared crib when they were infants. Imagine his reaction if, or when, he learns that his brother deflowered his wife.'

'Mama, I'm shocked!'

'Well, it's true! Ask your gan-gan next time you see her.'

'I meant that I'm shocked your vocabulary includes the word "deflowered."'

'Zoe, this might surprise you,' Mama said, 'but I've been around the block more than a few times. Heck, I'll go so far as to say that I wasn't even a virgin when I married your daddy.'

'Mama, stop! This time I really am shocked, and I refuse to listen to another word on the subject – unless I have a daddy different than the one I thought that I had, and that this new man is somebody rich and famous, or preferably both.'

Mama kept her lips tightly sealed. This could only mean that I'd been born into the same upper-middle-class family that I'd always known to be mine. If I wanted to be rich I would either have to marry for money, or else do a better job of sucking up to Gan-Gan. The plan of seeking justice for Gunner Jones that was forming in my head was not going to endear me further to our family matriarch. In any case, regardless of which path I chose to go down, I would still do my level best to set the world straight on the existence of mermaids. No matter how much money my gan-gan had already accrued during the past year, I knew down in my gut that another public outburst from me would be the last straw.

To prepare me for the stress that invariably lay ahead, I turned the driving over to Mama, and lay down in the back seat of the car. I told her not to wake me until we got to the last gas station before the turnoff to Tidal Shores. Heaven forfend that I confront Mayor Adelaide Saunders on a bladder fixing to burst.

Somehow my dear little mother managed to keep herself from going to sleep, and us on the road, and in our lane. We arrived at the gas station in what I thought must have been record time. After using the facilities, we met up back at the car with cola drinks in one hand, and moon pies in the other hand. The way I see it, if one is facing an extremely stressful situation, one should treat oneself kindly, and fortify oneself with a sweet of some sort. That is the essence of the Golden Rule, isn't it? What I mean to say is that I asked Mama if she wanted a moon pie before I entered the little store connected to the gas station, and she said yes. Therefore, I was biblically obligated to treat myself in the same manner as I had treated her.

From that point on I drove, which was a good thing, because I have more patience than she did when it came to driving in heavy traffic. We arrived in Tidal Shores at the dinner hour, so the town's administration offices were closed. That meant that we needed to pay Mayor Adelaide Saunders a visit at her home. Although some of the town's *nouveau riche* had torn down their former digs and replaced them with 'McMansions,' this family had not. Adelaide Saunders, née Parsons, was the sole heir of Tidal Shores' only banker, and the family home was quite the showplace at one time. The two-hundred-year-old plantation style Parsons family home was plenty big; all it needed was a fresh coat of paint, new kitchen appliances, and some updated bathroom fixtures. Even the landscaping remained the same, because no amount of money could replace the character that such old and established shrubs and trees gave the mansion.

Even if Mama had not been with me, I could have driven myself straight to Mayor Adelaide Saunders' house, because she was Gan-Gan's next-door neighbour. We wanted to hang on to our element of surprise as long as possible, so we parked in my great-grandmother's driveway. Then, pretending that we were really on a secret mission, we searched the dense row of camellias that divided the two properties for the pavement stones that formed a curved path that led to the mayor's kitchen door. Once we found it, we tiptoed along it, giggling like grade-school girls – until a motion-detecting light popped on when we were still only halfway to our goal.

'Oh, crap,' I said.

'Now you've done it,' Mama whined. 'Now we're going to jail for sure. Promise me that if we share a cell, you're going to look away when I use the toilet.'

'OK, Mama, *I* promise, but what everyone else does is up to them.'

'What do you mean by everyone else?' Mama's voice rose several octaves. Had she been holding a champagne flute, it would have shattered.

'I doubt if our cell will have curtains, Mama. So, we best hustle our bustles over to the back door, and put the screws to the mayor before she has a chance to call the cops.'

Mama flat-out ran. Although I'd seen her scurry on a couple of occasions, this was the first time I'd seen her run. At last, I could believe the tales she used to spin about being a track star back in high school. She'd also claimed that the many medals that she'd won, along with the school yearbook documenting her achievements, had sadly been destroyed in a fire that consumed the family home during her freshman year of college.

I know that I've digressed, but I did so to explain why it was that when Mama arrived on the side porch of the mayor's house, she wasn't even breathing hard, whereas I could hardly catch my breath. More's the pity, because I pride myself on being reasonably in shape. Mayor Adelaide Saunders herself answered the door, and when she saw the pair of us standing on the kitchen porch, her face registered perhaps only a flicker of surprise, if any. Now *there* was a woman who could keep her cool.

'Well, if it isn't Miss Georgina Legare, and a handsome young man, showing up just when we're sitting down to dinner. Come on in, y'all, and join us. I know we have enough pork chops – if the men don't help themselves to a second one – but the two of you will have to share a baked potato.'

'You watch your tongue, Adelaide,' Mama said angrily. 'I am not Miss Georgina Legare. I am her *granddaughter*, and a good fifty years younger than she is.'

'And I am *not* a man,' I said. 'I am Miss Georgina Legare's *great*-granddaughter.'

The mayor was wearing a pair of bifocals that hung on a pearl chain from her neck. She put the glasses on and peered at us closely.

'Why, I'll be dippity-doodled. You,' she said to Mama, 'are Beatrice Legare Porter. I remember you.'

'As well you should,' Mama said. 'I caught you *in flagrante delicto* with your future brother-in-law, Ryker Saunders. Yes, I know that you were just kids then – well, in your late teens – but still, I don't think that either of your spouses would be pleased to picture the two of you doing the mattress mambo together.'

'The *what*?' Tidal Shores' classy, well-bred, impeccably groomed mayor was trembling, and I actually felt sorry for her.

'The mattress mambo is a silly term for the two-sheet tango – they both mean sexual intercourse. My mama gets these euphemisms from the Pennsylvania Dutch mysteries with recipes that she reads,' I said. 'And why did you think that I was a man?'

'Oh that,' Her Honour said. 'You were bent over gasping, so I couldn't see your considerable womanly attributes. Plus you have short hair.'

'Well, it's not that short,' I protested.

'Yes, it is,' Mama snapped. 'Zoe, stay on point, here. Madam Mayor, either you help us find Gunner Jones' killer, or my daughter is going to tell your husband all about your tryst with the sheriff.'

'Me?' I gasped. 'Why me?'

Mama's eyes flashed. 'Because Gunner Jones was your lover man, not mine. Have you forgotten that this is essentially your murder investigation? It wouldn't be fair of you to make me carry the ball from here on out.'

Mama was so right. So far I had been a self-centred, lily-livered lumpkin. Well, no more!

'Listen, toots,' I said, 'we heard y'all talking about drawing beans for which one of y'all had to rub poor Gunner Jones out. And then nary a one of you confessed to doing the deed, when clearly one of y'all had to have done it. But now, I ain't standing for that kind of BS. Either you spill, sister, or it's curtains for you.'

Mama grabbed my arm and yanked me aside. 'What's up with the dialogue from a gangster movie from the Roaring Twenties? Are you supposed to be Al Capone?'

'I was trying to put the fear of God in her,' I said.

'You put any more fear in her, and she's going to have to change her britches before we can talk further,' Mama said.

I jerked my arm loose. 'All right.'

'Is everything OK?' the mayor asked. She sounded sincere.

'Everything is fine and dandy,' I growled. 'Or it will be – if you tell me who shot and killed Gunner Jones.'

Mayor Adelaide Saunders patted her tasteful single strand of pearls and swallowed hard before answering. 'We weren't lying that day that you overheard us. None of us on the city council killed Gunner Jones. In fact, the bullet that ended poor Gunner Jones' life wasn't even meant for him; it was meant for the person sitting beside him. Unfortunately, the shooter, who was hiding behind a pair of dusty drapes, got some dust in her eyes. As a consequence, her aim was off quite a bit, and although she hit Gunner bad enough to kill him, the person sitting next to him, who was her real target, was merely winged.'

Mama and I exchanged horrified glances. 'Who was this winged person?' Mama demanded.

'Your granny, Mrs Georgina Legare.'

'But why?' I cried. 'Who would want my gan-gan dead? Besides maybe a hundred people. Yes, she's a miserable old crone, who's mean to everyone around her, but she has a nice side too. One just has to spin her around a dozen times to find it.'

'We're all pretty sure that it was her wife, Mrs Grusha Legare, who wanted her dead,' Her Honour said sombrely. 'She was visible behind the drapes.'

'Grusha?' Mama said. 'I don't understand.'

'As you can imagine,' the mayor said, 'I'm kept pretty busy at the office, but when I am home, Grusha Legare prefers to hang out over here with me. Or I go over there, because we've gotten to be friends over the last year. You see, Mrs Georgina Legare is always at work, filling those coffers of hers with the almighty dollar. Anyway, little by little Grusha Legare began to share with me how angry and betrayed she felt when she learned that Miss Georgina had kept her isolated and ignorant for purely selfish reasons, and not for her protection. I could feel her resentment start to boil over. Then when Mrs Georgina told me, in confidence mind you, that she had given her black bean to Grusha, because Grusha would do anything for her – well, I just couldn't believe her hubris!'

'Did you warn my granny of Grusha's state of mind?' Mama said.

From a distance, one might have observed Mayor Adelaide Saunders casually remove a speck of lint from her sleeve. Close up, one could see that her hand was trembling.

'Listen, ladies, just tell me what it is that you want me to do.' She glanced over her shoulder. 'Ewell will be coming out here looking for me any second. As it is, I don't know what story to concoct for the others when I head back inside.'

'Tell them anything that you please,' I said. 'As for what we want: we want you to get Sheriff Ryker Saunders to arrest Mrs Grusha Legare for the murder of Mr Gunner Jones. Tell him that if he doesn't, I will run a feature story in *The Observer Today*, titled *Sex, Lies, & Murder Amongst Tidal Shores' Self-styled Elite*.'

'What's this about murder?' a man's voice said.

I looked up and past the mayor's head. There, standing behind her in the doorway, was her husband, the straight-laced Ewell Saunders.

I grabbed my mother's hand. 'Come on, Mama,' I said. 'Show me again just how fast you can run.'

THIRTY-FIVE

Although Mama could really shake a leg when she needed to, neither of us could outrun the vitriol directed at us that was spreading across the internet. We weren't even halfway back home to Charlotte when Mama's phone alerted her to an image taken by her door cam.

'What the hell?' Mama said.

Since Mama never swears, I grabbed her phone from her. On it was the unmistakable image of her next-door neighbour, Pennelope Williams, dumping a large bag of rubbish on Mama's front steps. Since Mama had Pennelope's number on her list of 'favourites,' I immediately called her, even though I was driving and that I am one hundred percent against folks who drive while on their phones. Sometimes rules are meant to be broken.

Pennelope stared at her phone for the first two rings, but she answered on the third. 'Killer,' she said.

'*Excuse* me?' I said as I put the phone on speaker.

'You heard me. I saw you on TV. You and your mother are murderers.'

'That wasn't even a real mermaid.'

'You're a lying unbeliever.'

'But how can I be both things? If the remains were real, then I would have to believe, right?'

'You and your mama need to watch your backs,' Pennelope said, and hung up.

'I've known that woman for twenty years,' Mama said incredulously. 'When her husband George died, I sat with her until the EMTs arrived. She was so broken up over his death that I had to help her notify her family and friends, and we visited the funeral home together to choose the casket and plan the service. She called me her "rock" then, and now I get her garbage?'

Before I could put together some comforting words for Mama, my phone pinged. Just call me Pavlov's dog. When my phone pings, I am compelled to look, and the message is potentially my reward. I am, after all, a newspaper columnist. Who knows when

The Mermaid Mystery

the Pulitzer Prize committee will try to get in touch with me – at least one can always hope.

This time my reward was rather unpleasant. 'Die, bitch,' a man's gravelly voice said. 'You and your mother are both toast.' He hung up.

I was angry enough to call him back, but I kept getting a busy signal. Meanwhile Mama got a text that read: 'We'll wait until you're sleeping, and then we'll strike.'

'Mama, turn off your phone,' I said.

'OK,' she said, 'but whoever sent that took care with their punctuation and spelling.'

'Oh goody, Mama, we can look forward to death at the hand of an English major.'

'Don't be silly, Zoe, we're not going home; we're going to stay with your brother in his penthouse. He has a doorman.'

'Well, we need to get our clothes and things first. So, we're driving directly to Charlotte's police headquarters. I know Chief Winterhouse from when I did a profile on him when he got his promotion two years ago. I'm sure that I can get him to assign us some protection while we pay a quick visit home.'

'Take nothing for granted,' Mama said.

Her comment irritated me because not only had Chief Winterhouse and I gotten along exceptionally well, but the chief also had a reputation for being fair-minded. My irritation morphed into paranoia when, upon arrival at headquarters, the chief, who was indeed in at the time, declined to speak to me.

'Tell him it's a matter of life and death,' I told the desk sergeant. 'Show him my phone.'

'And mine,' Mama said.

After reaching the police headquarters, Mama and I had turned our phones back on, only to discover a total of thirteen death threats between us – some of them in gruesome detail. That number didn't include the promises to merely maim us, should the senders learn of our whereabouts.

Sergeant Chloe Snodgrass grabbed our phones, disappeared down a long hallway, but returned just a minute or two later. She tossed the phones on the counter that separated us.

'I know who you are now. You're those ladies that like to kill people's dreams. Well, I ain't saying that the chief said this, but you can quote *me* if you want for your damn Commie liberal paper:

there are consequences for everything. Maybe y'all should have thought of that.'

'We're tax-paying citizens,' I said angrily. 'It is y'all's duty to protect us!'

But Sergeant Chloe Snodgrass studiously ignored us from that point on. Even when Mama burst into tears and trotted out her 'I'm just a helpless old widow woman' act, the sergeant paid us no never mind. When we finally got it into our little pumpkin heads that we were really on our own, we hightailed it to Lofton's well-feathered nest in the sky. Fortunately, Mama knew both the doorman and the code to my brother's expansive penthouse.

Lofton was, of course, delighted to have his mama with him, so that she could cook and do his laundry (as well as clip his toenails after long baths). Since he knew that Mama and I were a package deal, Lofton was cordial to me, just as long as I dusted and vacuumed, thereby saving him the cost of maid service (trust me, some of the richest men are also the stingiest).

Three weeks and two days later, Lofton handed me his phone, telling me that the call was for me.

'Who is this?' I asked with a good deal of trepidation.

'You are dead to me!' Gan-Gan rasped and hung up.

I called back. She immediately picked up again.

'This is a ghost,' I said, 'who wants to speak to her gan-gan.'

'Her Gan-Gan doesn't believe in ghosts and wishes not to be disturbed. Ever.' Mrs Georgina Legare promptly hung up a second time.

When I called a third time, she waited until the second ring before responding. '*What?*' she snapped.

'If you really don't want to be disturbed, Gan-Gan, then why do you keep answering? Besides, don't you want to chew my head off for what I did – whatever it was *exactly*?'

'You know what you did!'

'Is it that Mayor Adelaide Saunders paid a quick visit to Sheriff Ryker Saunders, who arrested your dear wife, post-haste, for the murder of Gunner Jones? With any luck, this all happened while you were still up in Washington cavorting with your rather handsome twin nephews, and as such weren't home to interfere. Of course, I imagine that someone had to fill you in on this dreadful turn of events, and who better informed than the town's top purveyor of gossip, Emmeline Davis? After all, she owns Turning Heads, the town's premier beauty salon. Am I right?'

'Why, you horrid little thing,' Gan-Gan gushed. 'After all that I've done for you. For your information, Grusha was the love of my life, but now she's gone. Gone! No one knows where, and all because of you!'

'No, Gan-Gan, she left because of you. You treated her as an enslaved person with benefits for fifty years.'

'Ha! That shows how much you know; it was seventy years in November, not fifty. That ungrateful Russian took everything that I gave her and left me just a note with five words on it.'

'Oh, really?' I said. 'What were the five words?'

'*I was aiming for you.* Imagine that! My own wife was trying to kill me!'

'You should be happy that she missed.'

'Yeah? Well, I took her to target practice every week, but she never applied herself. One would think that Russians would be more trigger-happy. What a waste of money!'

'Money, money, money. Is that all you ever think of?'

'Look, Baby Child, you're going to wish that you had thought a great deal more about money before you forced Sheriff Ryker Saunders over to my house to put the fear of God into my little Babushka. As of this moment I'm cutting both you and your mama out of my will, which, by the way—'

'That's fine and dandy,' I said.

'You didn't let me finish,' Gan-Gan said. 'You both stood to inherit millions.'

'So?'

'Don't you care?'

'I care about you, Gan-Gan, because I love you, but I don't give a damn about your money. Right now, I care about staying alive. Countless people have threatened to kill Mama and me. That's why we're staying with Lofton. He supposedly has a secure building.'

Gan-Gan gasped. 'What about the police, Baby Child?'

'They've washed their hands of us. We've made our beds, and now we have to lie in them. My words, not theirs, but it amounts to the same. They won't even give us safe passage back to our house so that we can collect our clothes. All our windows are smashed in – not that it matters, because the front door has been busted open. And the words *mermaid killer* have been sprayed in black paint across the front of the house.'

'Oh, Baby Child, oh, Baby Child,' Gan-Gan said. 'I take back what I said before about the money. That was just angry me speaking. Can you ever forgive me?'

'I will always forgive you, Gan-Gan, no matter how rude and mean you get.'

'Such music to my ears, little one. Give me five minutes to think and I will call you back.'

Gan-Gan took more like ten minutes, but then she is old. 'Look, Baby Child, text me your savings and checking account numbers, plus the routing numbers. Same thing for your mama.'

'Why?'

'Just do it,' Gan-Gan said, and hung up.

I didn't speak to Gan-Gan again until the following day when I called her. 'Gan-Gan, what the heck? Mama and I each have two million dollars in our savings, and another two million in our checking accounts! Where did all that money come from? Is that – uh – dirty money?'

'Don't look a gift horse in the mouth,' Gan-Gan growled. 'Besides, it isn't your so-called dirty money. It comes from various properties your great-grandfather and I sold back in the day. His philosophy was to buy up as much land as we could back in them early days, on account of "God ain't making any more of it." We must have owned half of Tidal Shores at one point. Anyway, we invested that income wisely, putting most of it into bonds, and only a small portion into stocks. At any rate, I've done very well with those accounts.

'Now, Zoe, listen to me very carefully. I have a team of lawyers working on a solution for you and your mother. But it is going to require sacrifice from the two of you, as well as your complete cooperation. Beginning now, you may never use your phones again. Smash them, and then trash them.'

'But I need to call the paper, Gan-Gan. I want to write a column about what happened at the Smithsonian.'

'No, Baby Child. For your protection, you have suddenly gone off-grid. This is the sacrifice that you must make.'

'But Gan-Gan—'

'Listen, Baby Child, and listen good. I have the resources to protect you and your mother. But you have an ego that can stop me. What will it be?'

'We're in your hands, Gan-Gan.'

'Good. Now tell me about Lofton. Can you get him to keep a secret?'

'Hmm. Let's just say that Lofton will do *anything* for his precious mama.'

'Fair enough. That's all I needed to hear. So just hang tight where you are, until you hear from me. Stay in Lofton's penthouse, do you hear?'

'Yes, ma'am, Gan-Gan.'

So that's what we did for almost two months and, surprisingly, it was rather pleasant. Since Lofton dotes on his mama and had all our meals delivered to the door, there was very little for us to do but vacuum occasionally and make our beds. There were large-screen televisions in both Mama and my bedrooms, so I was able to stay reasonably entertained, as well as informed.

However, what I learned from the news was that during the weeks since I'd dismantled that fake mermaid on national television, the number of Americans who believed that mermaids were real had climbed by five percent. Even more distressing was the fact that only seventeen percent of those surveyed were willing to state flat out that they believed that mermaids were fictitious creatures.

Then two months to the day after we took refuge in my brother's penthouse, a certified package arrived for him from a law office in Columbia, the state capital of South Carolina. When Lofton opened it, his expression changed from curious to one of resignation. Gan-Gan and her money had managed to procure two new birth certificates, as well as two passports, along with two one-way, first-class tickets to a new life for the two women that she now loved the most.

We will always miss the Carolinas, and we will always be loyal Americans. However, the English-speaking island where we now live is, hands down, the most beautiful place I have ever been, and I have travelled all over my beloved United States. Yesterday Mama and I went on a quest to find the grove of the world's second tallest trees (California Redwood trees are the tallest). We got a picture of one tree that was so tall that no matter where we stood to take the photo, we couldn't fit the tree in the frame. We had to use the phone's video function to scan the tree from bottom to top. On our way back to our island's capital city (it is a state, not a country) we drove along a river, upon which a flock of around one hundred black swans were feeding. *Black* swans! Who knew such things existed.

The people here are super friendly and helpful. They also seem very happy. Perhaps it's their relative isolation, or maybe it's due to the practical outlook that often comes with being an islander, but mermaid fever never caught on here. The folks that I've talked to about it have all told me that mermaids belong in fairy-tale books.

Lofton calls us regularly from burner phones. He says that because Mama's house sits empty, and I never contacted work, the police have finally conceded that Mama and I were the victims of foul play. The chief gave an interview to *my* paper, in which he stated that he suspects that we were involved with a Mexican drug cartel, and that we are lying beheaded somewhere in the Mexican state of Chihuahua. Lofton thinks that Chief Winterhouse could have a second career as a crime writer.

As for my dear Gan-Gan. She may have played with God as a child, but Lofton said she's going to have to do some fast talking if she expects to get into Heaven. Anyway, Mrs Georgina Legare finally departed her well-worn, much-wrinkled mortal shell a year and three days after we arrived on our island refuge.

At the funeral, which we could not attend, of course, Lofton learned that Gan-Gan had lived to the ripe old age of 109. She was a complicated woman, with her share of faults, but in the end, she loved her family. She will be missed.